Between Two Loves

Shelter Somerset

Published by
Dreamspinner Press
5032 Capital Circle SW
Ste 2, PMB# 279
Tallahassee, FL 32305-7886
USA
http://www.dreamspinnerpress.com/

Between Two Loves

Cover Art

ISBN: 978-1-62798-183-5
Digital ISBN: 978-1-62798-184-2

Printed in the United States of America
First Edition
September 2013

To Guido, the best little boy in the world.

Your spirit, bravery, and perseverance will always inspire those who knew and loved you.

Made by little angels—and taken away to rejoin them—you will forever be my sweet nugget.

Chapter ONE

INTERRUPTING his late afternoon coffee break, Aiden's cell phone chimed on the dining table beside him with the generic ringtone. The caller was a stranger, or someone he hadn't spoken with in quite some time. He knew this because each of his friends and Daniel had his or her unique tone, and his business contacts were recognizable by a "calling all cars" old police-radio dispatch.

The word "private" showed on the display. Whoever was calling wanted anonymity, as if he or she feared Aiden might disregard the call if he recognized the number. He was about to do just that, but his reporter's inquisitiveness refused to let him reject the call so easily.

"Hello," he said into the phone with a tentative voice.

"Aiden?"

"Yes, this is Aiden Cermak…." Hearing the name of the caller, Aiden stiffened. "How—how have you been, Conrad?"

"Okay, I guess." Conrad hesitated and asked with an artificially light voice, "What's new with you?"

"Where do I begin?" Aiden stared out the window into the milky whiteness of the Montana sky. "I have to be honest, I'm surprised to hear from you."

"I wanted to talk. It's been about two years. I contacted your parents down in Maryland and they gave me your cell number. Was that okay? Your dad said you moved again. Where're you this time? Back in Chicago?"

"We're living in Montana now."

"We?"

"My partner Daniel and I. It's a long story. So what makes you call after all this time?"

Aiden's hand shook, and he wanted to click off the phone as he listened to Conrad's simple yet incongruous reason. He wished he had ignored the call like his instincts had first told him. Yet he listened to each syllable, his mouth losing more and more elasticity.

"I'm sorry to hear that," he said once he had a chance. "How are you doing otherwise?"

Conrad continued to express his issues, and Aiden stifled his shaking arm by bringing his elbow down onto the table. What Conrad said next left him befuddled, and he barely knew how to respond.

"Well, I—I don't know," Aiden said, trying to work spit into his mouth. "Are you sure about that?"

"If it's too much to ask, I understand. I didn't mean to put you into an awkward position."

"No, Conrad, it's just that I'll have to ask Daniel, of course. Is it okay if I call you back later? Maybe tomorrow?"

"Sure."

"You'd better give me your number. It came up private on my phone, and I no longer have my old address list." Aiden switched the phone into his right hand and reached for a notepad and stumpy pencil lying beside his laptop and scribbled the number. "Okay. I got it."

"You'll let me know? Promise?"

"Of course. Promise."

"Great. Bye for now, Aiden. Nice talking to you again."

"Nice talking to you too. Bye."

Aiden snapped the phone shut and let his hand fall limp. Bewildered and shocked, he stared out the window. Lofty spruce and hemlocks framed the Salish Mountains barely visible in the western horizon. Winter still clung to the mountains, as new snow on the craggy peaks indicated, but the Flathead Valley temperature was expected to rise to seventy by midafternoon, setting a record high for late March. Snow runoff had begun to fill the slim creek next door. He could hear the faint gurgling whenever he walked outside.

The view was the main reason why he chose the fifteen-hundred-square-foot rancher west of Kalispell. It was a compromise once Daniel insisted they move to meet the needs of Daniel's expanding carpentry business, which had outgrown their old red cedar cabin, no larger than a one-car garage. Aiden enjoyed their crumbling cabin in the shadow of the Swan Range. But he grew to love their new home perhaps more.

The first consideration to pass through his mind while he gazed outside was that he should have informed his parents not to give out his phone number to anyone unless he okayed it. He never imagined his old boyfriend Conrad Barringer might want to contact him after their last meeting. They ended their unexpected reunion on bad terms.

At that time Conrad was belligerent, even cunning. A moment ago, his voice came across the phone soft, near pleading. Never in a million years had Aiden imagined Conrad posing such a crazy request.

Conrad picked an awful time too, when spring burgeoned like a bison hoisting its robust snout from the snow, and Aiden and Daniel were settling into their new home together after so many hardships.

Aiden noticed his reflection in the windowpane. Lines pulled down the sides of his mouth, and his eyes, yellow from the glow of the overhead light, appeared wild with disbelief. He looked ill, frightened. Not the contented man he was a few minutes before.

With the phone still in his hand, Aiden traced with his eyes the snowy ribbons winding through the distant crags that would soon turn to massive waterfalls, which appeared to barely move from miles away. Life flowed like that, he thought. Slow and quiet. Until the final crashing.

Leaving the phone on the table, Aiden shoved Conrad's number inside his pants pocket and moved to the kitchen. He washed his coffee mug and started fishing for something to make for dinner when their dog of four months scratched at the kitchen door. At the Flathead County Animal Shelter, they'd picked out the thirty-six-pound mixed breed, which Daniel aptly suggested naming Ranger, from among dozens of dogs. That was another one of Aiden's conditions for caving to Daniel's insistence they relocate to a home with more modern conveniences and closer to his new woodshop—a dog to love and care for.

Aiden wiped his hands on a dish towel and opened the door for Ranger. He squatted to greet him and graciously received his sloppy kisses.

"Did you go potty like a good boy?" Aiden picked grass and pine needles from Ranger's thick yellow fur. "You're a sweet fellow, aren't you? Give Daddy kisses. That's a good boy. What a sweetie you are."

Aiden stood and Ranger circled him, wagging his tail, which threatened to knock over anything below table height. Aiden fetched a doggy treat from Ranger's special cupboard, crammed with items to spoil their three-year-old, and tossed him a pig ear. Ranger absconded with it to his favorite spot by the fireplace and soon the sounds of gnawing filled the house.

Their energetic hound complemented their home. Aiden had everything he could imagine. And at only twenty-eight, who could ask for more?

He remembered the roast in the freezer. He filled the sink with cold water, allowed the wrapped roast to bob up and down like a football, and sat on the sofa. With his mind stuck on one issue, he took out Conrad's phone number and analyzed the shaky scratch.

Should he make good his promise or flush the number down the toilet?

Ranger tired of his pig ear and jumped up beside Aiden. Almost by instinct now, Aiden rubbed Ranger's head and patted his back with his mind on more weighty concerns. The dog's insistent kisses and friskiness eventually drew Aiden away from his sober thoughts. He smiled and brought Ranger nearer to his chest.

"You're a good boy, aren't you? Poppy and I love you."

Ranger responded with more rigorous licking. He leapt on and off the sofa. Aiden winced from his tail whacking him in the face, but he laughed and pulled him even closer. Aiden's hands paused over Ranger's fur, and Aiden fell inside himself again, imagining what life might be like for him and Daniel—and Ranger—if he agreed to Conrad's desperate appeal.

INTERMITTENT puddles sloshed under the tires of Daniel's sturdy Chevy Suburban. The atypical warm weather had melted much of the snow, and the spruce boughs that seemed to hold on to it like a catcher's mitt held a baseball, dripped with heavy slush. Hemmed in by cottonwoods and hemlocks, he turned on his windshield wipers to clear the sporadic splashes.

He appreciated the lush canyon-like drive from his woodshop in the village of Rose Crossing, where he worked crafting furniture for people around the world. The shop had been the main draw for him and Aiden to move. He needed the space, and liked the idea of working within a few miles from home. When he had come across the shop and rancher for sale, he knew God drew him to them.

Nice to once again put a "Schrock Furniture" sign above a shop he owned. He'd closed the one in Illinois he ran with his family before the economy bottomed out. Rent in Rose Crossing was a minor pinch to their pockets since he liked having a shop to commute to where he could focus on his work away from home.

The radio was switched to its usual "off" position. Despite having fallen in love with his two-year old Suburban, the Amish in him still insisted he forego too many fancy things, like loud music. The frenzied whistling from the wind blowing through the partially open window played as his musical backdrop and buoyed his already high spirits.

He cleared the canyon and came into the familiar high ranch country. Under the canopy of the darkening sky, the Salish Mountains glowed in the distance. Silhouettes jetting into a sky as wide and encompassing as anything Daniel had ever known from his boyhood home of central Illinois. Montana was a place he saw as a spiritual retreat, long before meeting Aiden Cermak.

The mountains inspired him, brought him closer—literally and figuratively—to God. When he sat atop the world, answers seemed to fall into his mind, like cottonwood snow fell upon the earth in summer. Seedlings, white and tickling, sprouted fresh ideas. Indecision burgeoned into concrete action. What loomed as agony would suddenly appear clear and expectant.

He and Aiden survived their first winter in their new home. Luxury compared with what he experienced growing up in an austere ultraorthodox household. And certainly nicer than the tiny cabin he and Aiden once rented on the other side of Kalispell.

Daniel brought in more and more money for his furniture and cabinetry. He was perhaps wealthier than ever. Money only meant as much as it should—providing independence, security, and a sense of accomplishment. Handsome recompense was never frowned upon by the Amish for a job well done.

Riches revealed themselves in more ways than financial, he speculated, detecting a grin creeping above his moustacheless beard. He valued his time with Aiden. But a healthy relationship required time apart, when a man could work hard and return home satisfied, filled with self-worth. In Amish Country, he might have spent his days out in the oat field, or at the family shop, but without the need to toil the land, Daniel sought his sowing elsewhere. In a small, suitable shop, and a life partner who, when not helping in the store, waited for him at home.

Now that spring showed the first signs of emerging, he went through the mental checklist of chores needing done on the house. Next to their porch, a cottonwood branch that had been poised to collapse on their heads throughout the winter needed sawed down. There was also the garage wanting a good cleaning. And he must remember to ask their good friend and neighbor Nick Pfeifer to borrow his ride-on mower. But that could wait until the snows stopped for good. His farm-honed nose predicted a few more inches before the end of April.

He turned the last bend and smiled at the pillar of gray smoke rising from their stone chimney, along with the rustic scent of the smoldering pinewood. Aiden must have felt the need to light a fire despite the unusually warm weather. Perhaps he had done it out of habit. Daniel liked to keep power heat low, and Aiden loved the cozy fires and couldn't wait to light one at the first sign of cold weather, even if it came on a July evening.

But the moment he stepped inside the house, Daniel's good feelings sunk deep into his gut, and a sensation of foreboding enveloped him. Aiden peered at him through the kitchen's pass-through. In an instant, he detected something in his expression that threatened their peaceful home, and he knew a major change was heading their way.

Chapter TWO

DANIEL held tight to his chest the fifteen-pound bag of dog kibble Aiden asked him to pick up before he left for work. It was easy to get since the pet store was in the same shopping center as the woodshop. The door opening and shutting pulled Ranger's attention from his hearthside bed. He shook and trotted to Daniel.

At first hesitant to get a pet, Daniel came to expect the loving greeting by their loyal hound. It was Aiden's idea to train Ranger to recognize Daniel as Poppy to distinguish him from Aiden. Daniel thought it silly, but he'd grown used to the name. He patted Ranger's head and brushed him away when his loving became too frisky. Sidetracked by the chicken kibble, Ranger pawed at the bag. Daniel nudged him off farther so he could set the bag down and remove his boots.

Aiden came from the kitchen. "Good, you remembered Ranger's food." He carried the bag away from Ranger's snout and sat it on the pass-through. "We were almost out."

"No trouble," Daniel said, unlacing his boots. He noticed the aroma of roast beef and boiled potatoes and carrots—one of his favorite meals. Nonetheless, the nagging chill continued to travel along his nape.

After Daniel stowed his boots by the front door and stood, Aiden gave him a burly hug. "I missed you."

Daniel, a foot taller than Aiden, kissed his curly head the way Aiden liked despite Daniel's still being unused to showy forms of affection, even in private. Aiden tightened his arms around him, and Daniel rubbed his back. He reveled in the loving, but knew something was up.

Daniel stepped back and Aiden gazed up at him. For sure, worries percolated behind those honey-brown irises that still could sap Daniel of his breath. Pulling on his beard, he asked, “Why do you look at me that way?”

“What way?” Aiden said, shrugging. “I’m glad you’re home, that’s all. I want to take you in with my eyes. I didn’t see you all day.”

Daniel hung his jacket on one of the hooks by the door and lifted the day’s mail from the console. “I’m sure that’s it.”

“You got a letter from your sister,” Aiden said.

Ranger dropped a stuffed toy by Daniel’s feet. Daniel tossed it as far down the hallway as he could. “I’ll read it later.” He sorted through the rest of the mail. Same old things. Bills. Junk.

“Did you have a good day?” Aiden asked, his voice higher in pitch than normal.

Daniel eyed him. “As good as usual. How did your day go? Anything newsworthy?”

Aiden made an exaggerated sad face, one that masked the inkling of burdensome truth. “Newsworthy?” He scratched behind his ear and shrugged. “Mostly Ranger and I have been home alone.”

“Haven’t you got started on your new writing assignment, the one you told me about the other day, to keep you busy?”

“About strip mining in Glacier National Park? I started to, but got preoccupied with spring cleaning.”

Daniel expected Aiden to say more. He noticed the extra creases in Aiden’s forehead and the wavering smile. Years studying people who seldom expressed emotions but couldn’t help but reveal them on their faces had taught Daniel when someone harbored a secret.

Rather than worry about it right away, he chose to move past Aiden and wait for him to broach his troubles when he was ready. Down the hallway, he took the stuffed toy from Ranger’s mouth and chucked it into the living area. Tail wagging, Ranger raced after it.

In the bedroom he sat on their queen-sized log bed, the one he made special for Aiden, and tore open Elisabeth’s letter. Choosing to defy the ministers, she was the only one of his family members who remained in regular contact with him since the shunning. He also stayed in touch with his brother Mark, who wrote once or twice a year, and on a few occasions sent him a text message from work asking for advice on money or his young marriage. Lately, since Mark and his wife had a baby, those texts seemed to lessen.

Elisabeth's letter expressed her usual thoughts, highlighting family news. Everyone was healthy. Their baby sister, Gretchen, whom Daniel had only met on two separate occasions, was growing faster each day and had begun walking and making words. David and Moriah were starting to show an interest in the opposite sex. Grace, at eighteen, found herself in the throes of love more often than when the moon rose. Mark and his wife Heidi were trying for a second baby, but so far God chose to withhold any more blessings. Elisabeth, as usual, refrained from mentioning much about herself. She merely wrote that her students at the one-room schoolhouse where she taught first through eighth grades were becoming smarter than she. She also had her funny way of asking about Aiden. Although Elisabeth was aware of Daniel and Aiden's relationship, she never stated that she knew. "Hope Aiden is well and continues to help in your endeavors," would be the most she'd say.

And their parents, Elisabeth wrote, continued to toil into their middle ages. Dad complained about his aches and pains and the harshness of waking in the dark during winter months. Mom, her arms full with the bobli Gretchen, wore a worn expression common to most women with squirming babies. Elisabeth's subtle language maintained an optimistic air, but Daniel read enough between the lines that she wanted him to understand how much Dad and Mom missed their eldest son.

"There's nothing that can be done about it," he mumbled to himself, scanning Elisabeth's letter one last time. He wanted to stay in touch with each family member, but he could not force them to refuse the ministers' ruling. He missed his family, yet understood his parents' desire to maintain the customs of their Amish denomination even if it did pain them to avoid him. They needed to live by their creed. Daniel also needed to exist by his.

He slipped the letter in the envelope and tucked it inside his dresser drawer for later correspondence. He addressed Elisabeth's letters to her school so that their austere father would not intercept them. Meanwhile, a hot shower and change of clothes seemed more appealing than writing a letter.

Fifteen minutes later, dressed in fresh clothes and with a damp head of hair, he returned to the dining table, where Aiden had set out the steaming roast and potatoes and carrots. Ranger sat expectantly under the table. The hound was still learning discipline, and Daniel would put up with no dog hankering by his feet while he ate. Daniel called for him in a low voice, and Ranger slinked to the fireplace and waited on his belly. The embarrassing, yet delightful, sensation of warmth and power swelled Daniel's breast each time Ranger obeyed his commands. The symbiotic relationship of man and beast. He appreciated the loyalty and obedience from growing up on a farm, where animals were a way of life. A way of life he often missed.

Wondering when Aiden would crack, he sat down to the table and led grace. Afterward, they ate mostly in silence. Ranger's tail thumped against his bedding with anticipation for the meal to finish when Poppy or Daddy would reward him with a treat.

"What did Elisabeth write?" Aiden said.

Daniel glanced up over his plate. "The usual. Everyone is healthy and well. She mentioned you again. Grace has a new boyfriend this month, from Kansas."

"Maybe she'll marry him and move there, and we'll be a little closer."

What difference would it make, Daniel wanted to say. "Most likely she'll find another boy. You know how girls are at her age, Amish or otherwise."

Aiden asked about the shop, and if any new orders came in. Daniel told him no, and that he heard the door chimes ringing maybe four times. Phedra, the shop girl he hired last month when Aiden became bogged down with new writing assignments, said she sold a few knickknacks and consignment items. He asked why Aiden lit a fire on such a warm day.

"Guess it gives me and Ranger extra company without a TV."

"How would TV give you company?"

Aiden puckered his mouth. "I guess you wouldn't know about that. Just a dumb reference. Never mind."

"Are you wanting a TV?"

Aiden shook his head. "I prefer not. I'm the one who wants to live as rustic as we can, remember?"

Daniel ate more of his roast beef and mentioned needing to prune the cottonwood tree out front. The more he rambled, the more he anticipated Aiden would cut him off and disclose the troubles concealed behind his blinking eyes. Daniel was surprised when Aiden cleared their dessert dishes and yet no word.

Perhaps Daniel had misread the ominous signs, and Aiden merely was experiencing the first pangs of spring fever. He'd grown accustomed to Aiden's restlessness during the early spring, when the snowmelt called out the birds and animals and Aiden yearned to join them in the surrounding forests.

Aiden tinkered on the computer while Daniel sat in his favorite easy chair by the fire, sketching a new design for a bureau a wealthy young couple in La Salle contracted him to build. Working from drawings was new to him. Since he was a boy, he and his uncle cut straight from the wood, harnessing generations of instruction on where to cut without needing calculations or figures. The Amish had an intuition for measurement and mathematics that did not require blueprints or book learning. Nevertheless, one day when Daniel became overwhelmed with the increasing workload, Aiden suggested he make rough sketches to keep track of the projects. A few days later, exacerbated yet happy with the work, he reluctantly tried it, and he found it to be a good way to settle his mind, although he never admitted this to Aiden.

Within eyesight of Aiden, he sketched for at least a half hour. Finally, Aiden cleared his throat. "Daniel, there's something I have to tell you."

"What is it?" Daniel kept the pencil point to the paper, though he'd stopped drawing.

"You were right. Something newsworthy did happen today." Silent a moment, Aiden continued. "I've received an unusual call today. I'm unsure what it means, but it involves you."

"Who called?"

Aiden stood from the computer and sat on the sofa catty-corner to Daniel. He fixed his eyes on the fireplace, where the orange flames had shrunk to thimble size.

He licked his lips and swallowed. "Conrad called me."

Daniel recognized the name and understood he had been an important figure in Aiden's past, but could not place a face. "Who is he again?"

"My ex-boyfriend."

The pencil went limp between Daniel's fingers. He tapped the eraser end against the paper. "And what made him call you after all these years?"

Aiden shuffled to the fireplace and seemed to strike a pose by the mantel, which Daniel made for Aiden as a surprise housewarming gift a month after they moved into their old red cedar log cabin.

Daniel repeated his question. "What made him call?"

"He wants to come here," Aiden said.

Daniel gripped the pencil. "Is it so bad for someone to visit?"

"We haven't had any visitors to our new place yet," he said with a shaky smile. "Odd he'd be the first. Wouldn't you say?"

"Not so odd." Daniel lifted one eyebrow. "Unless it causes you much worry? Is there something else that bothers you about him coming?"

Aiden sighed and paced before the fireplace. "All afternoon I've been tinkering around the house, barely thinking about anything but Conrad's phone call. I wanted to drive up to the shop and see you, but I decided to wait. I was afraid I might plow into a tree with my mind so full of everything."

Daniel's curiosity piqued. He watched Aiden walk back and forth, until Aiden stopped and stared at him. Daniel read the doubts in his golden-brown eyes. "I figured something was up when I first stepped inside the house. Tell me, Aiden, what does he want from us?"

Aiden turned to face their portrait on the mantel taken during one of their backpacking trips into Glacier National Park. The frame replicated a log cabin, much like the one they lived in before settling in their rancher home. They looked happy together. Grins stretched their suntanned faces, and a brilliant twinkle shone in their eyes.

Seeing himself in photographs still unsettled Daniel. He harbored the ancient Amish belief that photographs snatched one's soul. Theirs wasn't the only religion to believe in such superstition. He learned in school that Muslims also discouraged picture taking. On some level, he knew cameras could not steal away souls. Yet the sight of his own image seemed arrogant and haughty, and he turned away with heated cheeks.

Toward the photograph's shiny glazing, Aiden said, "I don't know how to phrase this exactly." He turned fully and accepted Daniel's hard ogling. "He wants to stay here longer than a visit. He's sick, Daniel. He's very sick and needs people to care for him. He wants *us* to care for him."

THE fireplace sighed after Aiden spoke the words that had stewed in his mind since Conrad telephoned. To hear them suddenly seemed surreal. He widened his eyes and stretched his mouth, limbering his lips before revealing more.

"He told me he has cancer and no one to help him," he continued without averting his eyes from Daniel. "Out of the blue, he asked that I—that we—be his caregivers while he receives radiation treatments." He swallowed hard and, waiting for Daniel's reaction, turned back toward the fireplace and tinkered with the mantel.

Even without looking at him, Aiden could picture Daniel pulling on his moustacheless beard, which he kept neatly trimmed now that he was no longer in the Amish order. Aiden knew Daniel wanted to form his phrases in his mind before speaking. It was that Amish patience that sometimes irked Aiden.

He would do whatever Daniel wanted, regardless of Conrad's needs. Yet Aiden uttered his news with such acute tones he gave Daniel little room for dispute. He clutched the mantel and slowly looked over his shoulder. "What do you think of that?"

Daniel licked his lips. "What did you tell him?"

"I told him I'd have to speak with you first, of course. I'm still shocked he asked such a thing."

"Why can't he stay with friends or family?"

But as far back as Aiden could recall Conrad had few friends, and his family, living in Michigan, maintained limited contact with him. He held back from saying too much about the Barringers, realizing that Daniel, too, had such a family. “He doesn’t have many friends and his family isn’t very supportive. Plus he was laid off a few months ago from his computer job, second time in two years.”

What Aiden took for sympathy passed over Daniel’s ebony eyes. Daniel’s gaze fell to the carpet. “Where is he now?”

“Virginia, near DC.”

“Isn’t he getting treatment there? Surely he can find the best medicine in the world around the nation’s capital. Why would he want to come here?”

“He says the doctors insist he have someone to help him, or his prognosis will be less positive. Studies prove it. I checked on the Internet. I think he thought I was still living in Maryland with my parents. There’s a state-of-the-art cancer clinic right here in Kalispell. I’ve driven past it a few times.”

Daniel peered at his slapdash sketching. “I’ve driven past it too.” The hiss of fire filled the pause. Daniel said, “You say he was laid off. How will he pay for these treatments? He didn’t ask that we do?”

Aiden shook his head. “He won’t ask us to foot the bill, I’m sure. At least I think I am. I’m guessing he has COBRA or he’s using his savings. Conrad always was frugal, more than you in some ways.”

Daniel’s shoulders rose higher and a shudder seemed to grip him tighter than the pencil he squeezed in his large, calloused hand. Aiden hadn’t meant to judge Daniel against his former lover, even if he had delivered his words as a compliment. He never compared the two of them in any way, not intentionally.

For Daniel, Aiden was his first—and only—male lover. That Aiden knew for certain. He had no other man with which to compare Aiden. When they first met while Aiden was working on his freelance article in Henry, the heart of Illinois Amish Country, to report on Amish customs for *Midwestern Life* magazine, Daniel had no need to admit his naivety for Aiden to understand.

Those clumsy days trailed behind them. Their future was theirs to grasp and make into whatever they wished. Now, another obstacle sought to disrupt their world.

After a thoughtful pause, Aiden said, "Look, Daniel, I don't like this any better than you. We just moved here. We have a life to build together."

Daniel's expression was full of the agony of being forced to decide between two horrible choices. Bring a man who was a stranger to Daniel into their home, or leave him to face cancer alone. He drew in his lips. "What kind of cancer does he have?"

"I didn't think it was proper at the moment to ask for details."

"There're all types of cancer." Daniel's words traveled to Aiden's ears in fragments. "Some cancers in the United States are as easily treated as simple maladies. Others hold death sentences."

"I guess when I call him back I can ask, but I'd like to be able to give him an answer one way or the other."

Daniel exhaled for what seemed the first time since Aiden revealed his news. His breath came out so heavy, the pages in his lap quivered above the sound of the dying fire. Aiden paced before the hearth again, savoring a moment of vital life while trying to shirk the burden of disease that poised over their heads.

A bitter taste lingered on his tongue. He hankered to speak more, despite realizing he must wait for Daniel to find his proper words first.

Daniel lifted his eyes to meet Aiden's. Aiden stopped pacing and edged closer to Daniel on the easy chair. Daniel appeared to want to leap across the pine coffee table and shake him. But Aiden faced back toward the fireplace, providing him the courtesy to speak without restraint.

"It's all strange," Daniel mumbled. "So very strange."

Aiden pivoted his shoulders and gave Daniel a hopeless, pleading look. "What should we do, Daniel? How are we to handle this? I know the answer, but please, speak it for me."

Daniel stroked his beard. "You should call him back," he said under his breath. "Tell him he can come. How do you tell a sick man who asks for help you cannot give it?"

All along, Aiden knew, those were the words Daniel would speak.

Chapter THREE

AT HIS laptop, Aiden checked Conrad's flight from Dulles Airport in Virginia and his connecting flight in Seattle while Daniel was likely getting ready to close the woodshop. Each flight had taken off on time. He texted Daniel asking if he wanted him to wait, so Daniel could go with him to pick up Conrad. Daniel replied, "No."

Alone, he headed to the airport, wondering if he and Daniel had made the right decision. If only he had asked Conrad for more time to mull over things.

Aiden expected at least two weeks' preparation before having to accommodate Conrad. Everything happened so quickly. Conrad became ecstatic when Aiden telephoned to say they agreed to take him in. Aiden was surprised when Conrad called back two hours later with his travel itinerary. He scheduled a flight into Kalispell's airport for Monday—a mere five days away.

Daniel remained quiet on the topic most of the week while Aiden stocked up on toilet paper, soap, and groceries, including many of what he remembered were Conrad's favorites: nachos and salsa and strawberry Pop-Tarts. Through the weekend, he dusted and vacuumed and prepped one of the two spare bedrooms and made sure fresh sheets lined the bed. He lost his thoughts in the sweat of his toil, hoping that concentrating on his work would force him to forget the reason for it.

On the way to Kalispell's regional airport, he passed the sprawling ranchers and larger homes with numerous annexes built onto them. These were the homes of the Hutterites, where families with as many as fifteen children resided.

From what Daniel told him, they were too communal even for him. The Amish had more of an independent sense in their tight communities. Hutterites, although more modern, expected everything to go into one big collective pot, like Israeli kibbutzim without the mud walls. The small colony with the cluster of close-knit homes survived on the fringe of society, yet many members attended public schools and worked in regular jobs, including Daniel's shop girl, Phedra.

Lights from the Flathead River Valley sprawl came into view over the last of the major hills. Streets widened, buildings popped up and became more common than trees. It was a healthy growth, Aiden surmised. He could understand the allure of the area. The beauty was unmatched and the cost of living remained low compared with most regions of the nation.

With the swelling population came the increased issue of "light pollution," and the surrounding area attempted to limit the spread of glare into the mountains and Glacier National Park by pointing lighting downward. Above in the darkest part of the eastern sky, a small aircraft with white and red flashing lights was making a descent into Glacier International Airport. Aiden's heart backflipped in his chest. Could that be Conrad's plane?

An increasing and nagging desire to turn back home and leave Conrad stranded provided Aiden temporary relief. Despite Conrad's having abandoned Aiden in much the same way years before when they had lived in Chicago, Aiden could never do anything so cruel.

During a moment of weakness, Aiden had researched public guardian options in Washington, DC, and Virginia. Why bother to have Conrad travel two thousand miles if he could find care closer to where he lived? But he couldn't drop him off at a stranger's doorstep, even from clear across the country. Not after he requested Aiden's help.

Gripping the steering wheel, he forced himself to inhale pride for himself and Daniel being the sole ones capable of caring for Conrad. Yes, they would nurse him to health. They would take him into their home, provide him comfort, and see that he took his medications and recovered from his radiation treatments.

Aiden followed the signs on Route 2 for the airport and watched as the plane he noticed minutes before touched down on the lighted runway. Before Aiden had time to turn into the surface lot, Aiden's text chimed. It was Conrad. He landed and they were taxiing to the gate.

He left his used GMC pickup truck they bought before the winter in the parking lot and crossed Glacier Airport Road for the baggage claim. A small group of people began to gather by the conveyor. Two other flights arrived within ten minutes of each other, and the crowd grew with the usual excited energy. Aiden was unsure he'd recognize Conrad after two years, especially with the effects of cancer. Suddenly, a man broke through the crowd, waved, and hollered Aiden's name.

DANIEL sat in his easy chair, sketching a bureau design when headlights flashed through the window of the dining area and fanned above his head.

Thirty minutes ago Aiden texted him that he and that man named Conrad were heading home. He forced his mind away from their new lodger. Strange to have to meet a boyfriend from Aiden's past. He did not like it, but what else could they do?

He thought often of his sister little Leah, who died from metachromatic leukodystrophy, and how his parents labored to care for her, from when she had first begun to wobble and her speech faltered, to when she became wheelchair bound, and to her final demise at age eight. He tried to garner strength from both Leah and his parents. He reminded himself he and Aiden had ample room in their three-bedroom, two-bath rancher. He figured they had enough room in their hearts too.

He and Aiden lived by the code of individual ruggedness, separated from the sentimental and helpless public. Encased in that philosophy was the respect of their fellow man. To do for themselves also must mean to do for others without relegating responsibility to a coldhearted bureaucracy. *Each man should give what he has decided in his heart to give, not reluctantly or under compulsion, for God loves a cheerful giver,* says II Corinthians 9:7.

Daniel was the recipient of his people's goodwill during his stint in the hospital what seemed ages ago, and Leah too benefited from their generosity. He acknowledged that Aiden's kindness was all the more impressive considering what Conrad did to him in Chicago. Aiden had more of the Amish spirit of generosity than him, Daniel realized.

Daniel mustn't think so harshly about a man who faced possible death. His last days on earth might be spent in their company, inside their home, which was meant to rise as an emblem of Daniel and Aiden's life together, an eternal love that blazed above formidable obstacles and heartache.

A man requested their help—or at least Aiden's—for an untold amount of time, and Daniel understood Aiden would never turn away a sick man and Daniel could never expect him to.

Laying aside his sketches, he glanced at the clock. Good thing Conrad was coming later in the evening. That meant less time to spend with him during those initial awkward hours upon their first meeting.

He wondered suddenly if he should have gone with Aiden to the airport like Aiden had asked. Reflecting, he realized Aiden would be the first to greet Conrad, thus cementing a special bond between them from the start. A bond Daniel worried existed before Conrad stepped off the plane.

The echoing slap of Aiden's truck door, followed by a second, cut through the night. Compelled to watch, Daniel moved to the dining area and stared out the darkened window as Aiden and the man retrieved from the bed what looked like luggage for a party of four. The man Aiden had once loved with all his heart stood beside Aiden. The lampposts revealed a man of medium height, wavy strawberry-blond hair, and sparkling white piano keys for teeth noticeable even from a distance. He didn't look too sickly. Perhaps a little thin. Other than that, not bad.

Ranger placed his paws on the windowsill beside Daniel and let loose a low excited growl.

"Calm down, Ranger," Daniel whispered toward the glass. "He's like you in a way. Picked up from the pound and brought into our home for safekeeping."

FOR Aiden, the walk up the cement footpath, lit with the two lampposts that cast emerald orbs over the green lawn, seemed to take longer than the drive to and from the airport. His cheeks burned against the evening chill blowing off the mountains. He knew full well that

Daniel was peeping at them through the dining window. What might he be thinking after seeing the four large pieces of luggage they lugged up to the door, as if Conrad planned to move in with them indefinitely?

They gave one another no deadline. Simply, Conrad needed care while he received lifesaving cancer treatment. How long would it take to cure what Conrad told Aiden was stage three non-Hodgkin lymphoma?

From the literature Aiden read on the Internet, lymphoma came in many types, but he understood Conrad's evasive answers when he hinted for additional details. Who wants to rehash what they'd heard from doctors over and over? Aiden was relieved, however, to discover non-Hodgkin lymphoma had an 85 percent survival rate in the United States. But stage three? Aiden understood that degree of cancer was rather advanced.

Yet when Conrad rushed to him by the baggage claim, he looked much like Aiden pictured him after their last meeting years ago: same sharp eyes, delicate nose, square jaw, and a youthful blond radiance.

Aiden's shoulders relaxed once Daniel opened the door and helped haul the luggage inside. Daniel would not retreat into a shell the way Aiden feared. He extended his hand to Conrad and they shook. Officious and distant, yet respectful. Daniel kept his eyes pinned on Conrad enough to show he was not afraid of him.

"Nice to know you." A typical overconfident smile outlined Conrad's lips. "I'm grateful for you letting me stay here. I hope I'm not putting you out."

Ranger sniffed Conrad's legs and backed off when Conrad reached to pet him. His tail remained mostly still, only the tip vibrating like a rattlesnake's. His ears pulled far back against his oval head and he kept his snout low. They received few visitors, other than their neighbor Nick and one of Daniel's clients who once picked up a cabinet from the house. Perhaps Ranger, uncomfortable with strangers, had as many reservations about Conrad's staying as he and Daniel.

Aiden requested that Conrad take off his shoes. Strange to see his shoes next to Aiden and Daniel's in an intimate row. With the stink of stocking feet filling the space, Conrad stepped into the living area. "So this is where you live?"

"This is it," Aiden said.

"Nice place," Conrad said, wriggling his toes through his socks. "It's one big great room, like the *Brady Bunch* house, only a lot smaller."

Aiden chuckled, but he noticed Daniel gaping at them with a creased brow.

"It's more than we need, to be honest," Aiden said. "For the price we couldn't say no. Plus it's so near Daniel's shop." He glanced at Daniel, puckering his lips and flexing his hands into loose fists.

Eager to get Conrad settled, Aiden led him to the spare bedroom closest to the hallway bathroom. The room was medium sized with negligible sunlight since it faced north, but adequate. Daniel dropped off the largest of the four suitcases and retreated back to the main part of the house. Aiden hadn't been alone with Conrad in such an intimate space since they'd lived in their crummy one-bedroom in Chicago. He stepped back toward the threshold, tried to force a smile for Conrad's sake.

"We put our old bedroom furniture in here when we moved," Aiden said with as pleasant a voice as he could conjure. "Daniel made our new bedroom furniture from pine logs. This isn't half as nice, but sufficient."

Still looking around as if dazed, Conrad said, "It's fine with me." His gaze stopped hard and penetrating on Aiden. "It's almost surreal that I'm here."

"I guess it is kind of weird," Aiden said, turning away from Conrad's blue eyes, "since you've mentioned it."

"I'm asking a lot from you."

Aiden shrugged and stared at the dark-gray carpet, left behind from the previous owners. "People help each other out, right?"

Conrad resumed gazing about. "Not always," he snorted. "I knew I could count on you, though."

Conrad's words failed to pacify or impress. A sharp stab pierced Aiden's gut. He tried to push aside the irritable memories of Conrad's mistreating him during their short one-year relationship—a lifetime in gay terms—and replace it with empathy. Suddenly he wanted to leave. He stepped backward into the hall. "I'll let you settle in. Dinner will be ready soon. Bathroom is directly across the hall. It's all yours, so you won't have to worry about being disturbed."

Aiden found Daniel in the kitchen. Since moving into their new home he'd become more helpful, although most of the housework had been relegated to Aiden. This arrangement made sense considering Aiden worked on his writing from home most of the time. Aiden suspected Daniel withdrew to the kitchen to avoid Conrad. Who could blame him?

"Thank you again for being so open to this, Daniel," he whispered to him as he began grabbing for pots and pans and setting them atop the stove. Daniel kept quiet, and Aiden went on. "I realize his being my ex makes things extra awkward."

"Too late to worry about that now," Daniel said in a low voice. "I'll help with supper."

Aiden smiled. "I'm going to sauté some chicken breasts and make a cream sauce. You can slice the mushrooms. I bought some when I went to the market Saturday. They're in the bin."

"I invited Nick," Daniel said under his breath as he reached into the refrigerator.

"You did?"

"Was I wrong to?"

"No, that was a good idea. I look forward to seeing him."

Daniel moved around the kitchen like a man worried he might wake the dead. Aiden lightened the mood by making wisecracks about his drive into Kalispell and not being used to traffic. Daniel's shoulders finally relaxed and he nodded with a smile. Aiden leaned in and kissed him on his firm lips. He still enjoyed the tickle of his beard.

"You guys are so sweet."

Aiden turned to see Conrad smiling at them through the pass-through with wide eyes and his signature white teeth.

Daniel turned to the stove and pretended to fiddle with the pots. Aiden leaned into the counter. "We're a happy home here," he said with a prideful inflection. "Did you get settled in your room okay?"

"I love it, but I guess I'll be spending most my time out here with you guys, right?"

"Of course," Aiden said, his arms locked. "Make this your home. We don't expect you to spend all your time in the bedroom. Unless, of course you'll feel—"

Conrad turned his back to Aiden and spoke before Aiden could finish. "You'll be home, won't you?" he said, peering around the great room. "You said you're in between jobs."

"I do freelance," Aiden replied while Daniel fumbled with dinner. "I've been very busy lately. I have a new assignment I'm starting. It'll take me on a few day trips. Other than that, I'll be here most of the time. Daniel has his shop in Rose Crossing's village center, which I sometimes help out in. You can come see it, and maybe help out too, whenever you're feeling up to it."

Aiden turned in time to see the blood vessels in Daniel's neck pulse, and Aiden went about showing Conrad the kitchen. He swung open the cupboard by the stove. "Look. I've bought all your favorites. I remembered you like nachos and strawberry Pop-Tarts. Still your favorites, right?"

"You kidding? I live off them. Tarts especially. Eat at least four a day. My staple."

"Daniel made that awesome soda fountain machine over there that releases carbon into bottles." Aiden had enlightened Conrad about Daniel being raised Amish during the drive from the airport, and Conrad didn't look surprised that he was handy. "You still like Dr Pepper?"

"I do," Conrad said with a light nod.

"I can make you one. It's not the real thing, but we buy generic flavored syrups."

Aiden made two quick sodas and with the chicken breasts sautéing under Daniel's watch, Aiden and Conrad carried their drinks into the living area. Conrad sat in the plush armchair, molded from many months of use by Daniel's strong body.

"Would you like me to start a fire?" Aiden asked.

"Whatever you normally would do. Don't do anything special on my account."

"We don't have TV, so we have a lot of fires. They make good substitutes."

"No TV?"

"Are you disappointed?"

Conrad gazed around. "I'll just use my laptop. Now that I think about it, I watch more TV shows and movies from the computer these days anyway."

"Daniel and I do too, when there's something we really want to see."

The fireplace was prepped with logs, and Aiden needed only to strike a match to the newspapers balled underneath the iron grate. With the flames reaching higher, he sat on the sofa. "We're having a neighbor for dinner with us tonight, is that okay?" Aiden said.

"Sure. Invite anyone you'd like. Don't be afraid to have people over with me around."

Ranger stayed by the hearth, sprawled on his side. He glanced at Conrad a few times, his tail thumping the sides of his bedding, then falling flaccid against his hind legs. A knock at the door brought him to attention.

"That must be Nick now," Aiden said.

Ranger jumped up first, but Daniel started for the door so Aiden stayed seated. Their tall, stalwart neighbor wiped his cowboy boots on the welcome mat as he usually did before stepping inside and flashed everyone a stout smile.

"Howdy, you all," he said. "Am I too late for supper?"

Chapter FOUR

"SUPPER'S cooking on the stove, Nick," Daniel said. "Come the house in."

Nick shook Daniel's hand and kicked off his boots. His salt and pepper hair and wide, friendly gray eyes, offset by a rounded jaw, shimmered in the lighting above the door entrance. Aiden thought he moved his tall frame as gracefully as one of his horses galloping across his clover-strewn field. Ranger rushed to his side. Nick rubbed behind his floppy ears.

"Nick, this is an old friend of mine, Conrad Barringer," Aiden said, standing to present Conrad. "Conrad, this is our neighbor who lives on the big horse ranch across the street, Nicholas Pfeifer."

"Actually, my full name is Nick," Nick said, reaching for Conrad's outstretched hand. "My parents gave me a nickname straight off from birth. Get it? Nick name?"

They laughed, and Aiden appreciated Nick's occasional lapses into silliness, which seemed odd for such a sophisticated man as he. His entire lifestyle seemed to clash with his personality. He was a horse farmer with a degree from Stanford. A cowboy with the vocabulary of an English professor. The consummate country gentleman.

"You fellows look comfy with drinks in hand and sitting by the fireplace," he said, standing in his socks.

"Your usual, Nick?" Daniel said.

"If it's no trouble." Nick widened his smile and sat beside Aiden, who scooted over to provide him room. Grinning at Conrad, he said, "Daniel tells me you flew in from the nation's capital?"

Conrad's eyes seemed duller even with the flickering firelight. He squirmed to sit taller. "I just got in tonight. Used the last of my frequent flyer points to get here. Had to fly from Dulles Airport all the way to Seattle. Then some dinky plane to here. Considering all that, it wasn't so bad."

"That's usually the way it's done," Nick said, nodding. "Sometimes in summer during the tourist season you can get nonstops on larger jets from the major hub cities like Chicago and Atlanta. What part of DC are you from?"

"I'm from Michigan originally, but live in northern Virginia. I was a computer engineer before having to leave."

"I have a few friends in the Washington region. One in Howard County and the other in DuPont Circle. You familiar with those areas?"

Conrad and Aiden swapped grins. "We've been to those places," Conrad said. "Especially DuPont Circle."

"Nice as far as urban areas go," Nick went on, sitting back against the sofa, "but I couldn't live there. Too expensive. And the traffic! Last time I was there we sat for what seemed hours trying to get onto the expressway from the airport."

"I don't have to worry about that anymore," Conrad stated. "I'm through with it."

"So after spending a few hours in our wonderful state, you've already decided to ditch home and move out here for good like the rest of us?" Nick snickered. "It happens to the best of us. Even met a couple from Australia a few years back who couldn't resist wanting to retire here after a ski trip."

Conrad faced the fireplace, but he appeared to see past the flames and find little humor in Nick's playful conversation. "You could probably say that, in a sense," Conrad said.

Unsure how to take Conrad's comments, Aiden inhaled a deep breath, full of the scent of smoldering pinewood and sautéing chicken. From the kitchen Daniel rattled the drinking glasses. Did he hear Conrad's cryptic words? Smells from their dinner pushed Aiden to think fast, for he feared Daniel and Conrad might become enemies before the night's end if Daniel believed Conrad intended to stay too long.

Wanting to erase the unease, Aiden turned to Nick and said, "Daniel thinks we're going to have a few more snow showers before

May. What do you think about that? You know how smart he is about the weather."

Nick laughed. "If Daniel's farm-honed nose tells him snow, I believe it. He's sharper than my horses when it comes to predicting a turn in the weather."

Conrad turned back to the company, his Dr Pepper-flavored drink held at ear level and his elbow pushing into the armrest. "What kind of horses do you raise, Nick?"

"Mostly mustangs." Nick scratched his crossed leg. "About ten years ago I bought a pair from a wild herd the state put up for adoption."

"There're still wild horses in the west?"

"One of the largest herds in North America is less than two hours south of here, Conrad. That's where I got my first two."

"They have wild horses in Maryland too," Aiden declared, relieved the conversation made a pleasanter turn, away from Conrad's visit. Or had Conrad meant something else when he'd hinted he might never return to Washington? Was his lymphoma more advanced than he had indicated?

"That's right." Nick nodded. "Many of the East Coast barrier islands have feral horses dating back hundreds of years. They got there from storm-ravaged Spanish ships, they believe."

"The ones in Virginia are privately owned and are auctioned off, but not the Maryland herd," Aiden said with a haughty lilt to his voice. "The forest service manages them and occasionally sterilizes the females with dart guns to control overpopulation."

"When I bought my first two mustangs," Nick said, "I didn't know Montana sterilizes them from time to time too. I wondered why my couple wouldn't breed." He snickered. "I worried they weren't smitten enough with each other."

Conrad rubbed his chin with his free hand. "Maybe they were gay."

Nick chuckled uncomfortably and Aiden noticed a deep flush bloom over his cheeks. "Luckily the sterilization wore off after a few months," he said.

"You have an interesting accent," Conrad said with knitted eyebrows. "Is it from around here?"

"Tulsa, Oklahoma, born and raised." Nick lowered his chin and his shoulders fell forward. "I came out to Montana for… well, the same reason why Aiden and Daniel and many others do, I reckon. To get into the mountains, away from everything I was used to." He cast his eyes downward and chewed his bottom lip. Under his breath he said, "After leaving Oklahoma, I realized Montana was a good place to forget your troubles and start fresh."

Beside him, Aiden said, "Nick attended the most prestigious prep school in the Midwest. He roomed with the prince of a Middle Eastern country."

Nick jerked with a hearty laugh and waved off Aiden's fawning. "He was a descendant of the Qajar Dynasty. His great-great-great-grandfather was the Shah of Iran at age eleven. Farzad might have become crown prince himself if the family hadn't been forced into exile. He was raised by wealthy friends in Iran, in the lap of luxury behind high garden walls. And then when the Ayatollah Khomeini came into power, the family shipped him off to private school in Tulsa. Many in Iran still considered him Head of the House of Qajar."

The ice inside Conrad's drink settled and cracked. "Sounds interesting," he said. He spread his legs and arms wider over the chair. "I haven't met many Iranians before."

"You probably have and didn't realize," Nick said. "Especially if you live in the DC area."

Daniel came into the living area holding two drinks, one for Nick and the other for himself. Nick settled back with his scotch and soda and Daniel sat on the rocker chair by Ranger, taking large swallows from his homemade root beer.

"We used to rib him pretty good," Nick carried on after taking a sip. "Only in America could a person face teasing for being royalty. Apparently, young Farzad loved it. The boy grew up with everything he ever wanted. Servants catered to his every need and women, for who even wearing the chaderi couldn't hide their feminine figures, surrounded him. And yet all he really wanted was to be one of the guys." Nick chuckled and shook his head. "We still keep in touch after all these years. He lives in a gated community in New Jersey with his wife, not much different from what he had in Tehran. I keep trying to persuade him to come out and visit me, but the bastard always has something going on."

Nick never mentioned much about his private life back home in Tulsa or at the esteemed Albany Ridge School where he once roomed with the would-be prince. He lived alone, no children, not even a dog, on a ranch twenty times larger than Daniel and Aiden's property. Other than a housekeeper who came once a week and a part-time ranch hand, he spent most of his days and nights alone.

Aiden often pondered how their gregarious friend managed to circumvent speaking intimately about himself. Had he ever been married? Did he have any children? And the one question that Aiden had once or twice voiced to Daniel—was Nick Pfeifer gay?

Daniel, a private man also, rarely speculated about their neighbor in the open. Aiden kept most of his musings to himself. He watched him now, his curiosity growing.

When the conversation lulled, Nick, still grinning, peered at Conrad and said, "No one from Tulsa has graced me with a visit since I've moved to Montana over ten years ago. And here Daniel and Aiden have been in the neighborhood less than a year already hosting a good friend from back East."

"Unfortunately," Conrad mumbled, "I didn't come for fun."

Nick crinkled his forehead. "Oh?"

"Didn't Aiden or Daniel tell you?" Conrad sipped his soda and licked his lips. Looking straight into Nick's eyes, he said, "I'm getting cancer treatments at the local clinic. Aiden and Daniel are going to see me through it. I have lymphoma."

Aiden was at first surprised by Conrad's forwardness and thought it impertinent. But the more he considered it, he realized Nick would appreciate Conrad's honesty. He spoke the truth. What was wrong with that? Or, he thought after a moment, still flushing from Conrad's frankness, perhaps he was scouting for sympathy.

Nick's eyes widened. Otherwise he appeared undaunted. He cleared his throat and asked Conrad if he started the radiation treatments in Washington, and Conrad explained that his doctors didn't wish for him to begin unless he had homecare. "Aiden was the only person I could think of," he added.

"I'm sorry to hear about your illness, but it's wonderful you have good friends like Daniel and Aiden to rely on. Are you going to the Flathead Valley Cancer Center?"

Conrad gave a limp nod. "That's the only one in town, isn't it?"

"I've played golf with one of the doctors there. Can I give him a word and make sure they'll pay extra good attention to you?" Nick asked without flinching.

Conrad slumped further into his chair and yanked on his collar. "I'm sure he's a good oncologist, but I wouldn't want any more special treatment than anyone else would get. Besides, my doctors back in Virginia helped with the setting up of everything and I wouldn't want to confuse anybody at the clinic."

"Nonetheless, if you run into a Dr. Lyndon Vintos, tell him you're a good friend of mine. Never hurts to have a few connections. And let me know if I can help you out in any other way during your stay."

"That's nice of you, Nick, but I'm afraid I'm putting Aiden and Daniel out enough as it is. I feel awful burdening them."

"I'm sure they don't see you as trouble," Nick said with his chin to his chest and his voice deep. "I've only known Daniel and Aiden for a handful of months, but they are already better friends than the last family that lived here. I don't think I ever once had dinner at their home. Then again I never invited them to mine."

"Do you live alone?" Conrad asked.

"If you don't include my horses and the stray cat that likes to play with mice rather than eat them, yes, I live alone."

"We've kind of adopted Nick," Aiden said, patting his shoulder. "He's our big kid."

"And no better parents could they be." Nick nodded with a slight pinking of his cheeks. "You'll discover that for yourself, Conrad. No two better people."

The stove timer buzzed. Aiden jumped to his feet. He checked on dinner and shouted for everyone to come to the table. Conrad looked uneasy when Daniel led the prayer. Being raised Amish, Daniel insisted on grace before each meal. Aiden had learned to expect it and appreciated the opportunity to show gratitude for their abundance. Nick bowed his head lower than the rest and crossed himself with sincere and unabashed movements, as if he'd briefly slipped into his own world, where no one existed but he and perhaps God.

Nick's robust personality kept the rectangular table alive with chatter while they passed the serving platters and bowls. Conrad propped his arms on the table, ate slowly, one eye on Nick beside him and one eye on his food. Aiden hardly believed he and Conrad were once again within a mere arm's length of each other.

Once they finished dessert, Nick stated how tired they must be and he made his departure with his characteristic warm farewell. Conrad yawned several times while helping scrub the larger pots and pans. Aiden ushered him off toward his bedroom and told him to get some sleep after his long trip. Surely his health issues complicated the difficulty of travel.

With Conrad in bed, he and Daniel finished cleaning the kitchen. Afterward Daniel relaxed on the sofa with Aiden at his feet, their faces warming before the smoldering fire. Aiden leaned closer into Daniel's legs and said, "What made you think to invite Nick to dinner?"

"Thought it would be nice, for everyone."

Aiden stared at the waning flames. "I guess it was. Nick's a natural icebreaker."

"I figured we could use the buffer."

"What did you think of him tonight?"

"Conrad?"

"Actually, I was thinking of Nick. It was nice of him to take an interest in Conrad. Did you see the way he blushed when Conrad joked about his horses being gay?"

"Aiden, you're toying with that notion of yours again. If a man keeps his private life private, we should provide him that respect. I don't like to gossip. Besides, don't you think Nick is a bit old for Conrad? He's probably near sixty."

"Some of the longest lasting relationships are May-December romances." Aiden glanced up at Daniel. "You know, Nick doesn't wear a wedding ring, which means he's probably never been married, unless he's widowed and he removed it."

"I never wore a wedding ring."

Aiden refaced the fire. "No Amish wear wedding rings, married or widowed."

Hot breath parted the curls atop Aiden's head from Daniel's snickering. "One way or the other, you never figured me for gay."

It was odd hearing Daniel use the term "gay," especially in reference to himself. He rarely acknowledged that side of himself verbally. Rather, he showed his interest in a manner more pleasing to Aiden. "I had an inkling," Aiden said.

Daniel patted Aiden's shoulder. "You had no clue. I had you pegged, though."

Aiden twisted to look up at Daniel. "You did not."

"I did too. I started to suspect anyway."

For several minutes they sat quietly, staring into the flames, until Daniel stood. They spread out the blackened logs, sealed the glass screen in place, said good night to Ranger, and tiptoed to bed. Snuggled under the covers of their queen bed that Daniel had made for Aiden's twenty-eighth birthday last February, Aiden hunkered closer to Daniel, but Daniel flinched.

"What's wrong?" Aiden asked.

"He's down the hall."

"He must be asleep by now."

"We might wake him."

"Are you saying you don't want to make love the entire duration of his stay?"

"No need to get sarcastic," Daniel said. "Give me time to get used to him being around. It's only the first night."

The first of how many, Aiden wondered. "I'll give you five seconds." Grinning into the dark, he reached under the covers and grabbed Daniel.

Daniel grew rigid and Aiden chuckled at flirting with a man who still had difficulty expressing his emotions. He came from a strict upbringing, but once Aiden pushed him over the edge, he was as generous a lover as any Aiden ever had. Or ever wanted.

Better than Conrad, for certain. Yet he never compared the two in bed, at least not consciously. His stint with Conrad seemed blurred, like a window covered in grime.

Daniel slipped farther under the covers and took Aiden into his burly arms. His chest was hard against Aiden. Daniel glanced up a few times, stopped, and whispered he'd heard someone skulking in the hallway. Aiden reassured him it was Ranger shifting positions, and Daniel fell into motion. He did not let up. Instead of dithering, he'd become more forceful. Aiden wondered if Conrad's being down the hall hadn't spurred Daniel to go harder, filling him with a daring illicit desire to stake his territory. The physicality of their sex, with a weak sickly man nearby, emphasized the drive for closeness and completion.

Breathing heavy and drained of wakefulness, they rolled to their separate sides and Aiden tried for sleep. But he kept picturing Conrad in bed down the hallway. How might the ensuing days and nights pass with him there?

Chapter FIVE

EARLY next morning Aiden walked with Ranger out back to let him relieve himself and chase a squirrel or two up a tree. The air was crisp and the pine scent seemed extra heavy. Golden rays of sunlight flickered through the lower branches of the hemlocks and spruce trees and left bright slashes on the greening lawn. Aiden tossed a tennis ball, and Ranger, wagging his tail and kicking up pine needles, raced after it. Ranger dropped the ball by Aiden's feet, panted, and barked. Aiden warned Ranger to keep hushed so he wouldn't wake their guest and chucked the ball again.

"Nice toss."

Aiden turned to see Conrad standing on the back stoop. He looked refreshed, dressed in beige corduroys and a navy-blue sweater. Ranger, noticing the stranger, gave him a quick sniff along the way to Aiden's side.

"Good morning," Aiden said, tossing the tennis ball, sticky with Ranger's saliva. "Did you sleep okay?"

Hands in pockets, Conrad edged into the yard. "Not bad." He kicked at the grass, as if testing the ground before walking farther. "I woke up forgetting where I was, then it all came back to me."

"It's always like that in a new place," Aiden said, his voice swallowed by the towering trees. "Daniel's already gone for the shop and we've eaten. I didn't want to wake you and thought you could use the rest. You ready for something?"

Conrad shook his head. "I'm okay for now. Not much of an appetite."

Aiden's smile waned. "Whenever you're hungry. Let me show you the grounds since you're up and out."

Ranger trailed after them while Aiden led Conrad over the yard. Conrad turned his nose up, sniffed. "Smells like cows."

"That's Nick's horse farm. When the wind shifts you can sometimes smell it. Does it bother you?"

"Reminds me of central Michigan." Under the light of day, Conrad's pale blues lit like gems and he seemed more curious. Scanning a red cedar, he said, "I haven't seen trees this tall in all my life."

"I was amazed by them too when I first came out here. Imagine, they're in my own backyard."

Conrad gazed at Aiden under his brow. "So you just up and left Maryland for good, huh?"

Aiden nodded. "Why not? Life's too short." He cringed realizing the insensitivity of his choice of words. To discard any discomfort, he added, "I wanted to dare myself to do something I've never done."

Conrad remained still, peering about the yard, his lips taut. "Like that time you moved to Chicago with me?"

Aiden had a premonition Conrad would wish to discuss that period of their lives together. He was not ready. Without a doubt his tailing Conrad to Chicago was a bad idea. But a mistake that ultimately led him to Daniel. And now Conrad had come back to him, almost full circle.

Inhaling a deep, cool breath through his nose, Aiden said, "That was long ago, Conrad."

"Seems so, but it really wasn't. The older you get, four years seems like four months. We are getting older, aren't we? I'm on the verge of thirty."

The tone to Conrad's voice surprised Aiden. Conrad was never one to reflect, since he seemed lacking in depth. Aiden supposed facing possible death would soften even the most insensitive man and bring him to a quick penetrable understanding of life's shocking succinctness.

Aiden wondered why Conrad hadn't used this new profound view of life to make amends with his estranged family in Michigan and to ameliorate old sores. Aiden had never met any of Conrad's family, but he could gather from how Conrad evaded discussing them that the issue still weighed on him.

They explored deeper into the yard by the thin grove of cottonwoods and blue spruce on the north side of the property, stopping before encroaching on the neighbors' land. A sour man and his bashful wife lived next door with their two yappy Scottish terriers. Daniel and Aiden met them a few times since moving, but the new neighbors never spoke. Whenever Aiden caught either of them looking at him, they gave an obligatory nod and mediocre wave, but seemed put out by it. Fortunately, their land had so many trees they couldn't see much of each other unless they happened to be retrieving mail at the same time at the bottom of their driveways.

Conrad kept his eyes on the little details that Aiden showed him. Foraging animals. The soft hemlock leaves. Striations of the red cedar bark. The delicate, pink spruce tips. He remembered Conrad being disinterested in details. In the past, if Aiden showed curiosity in something, Conrad seemed to take it upon himself to dislike it. That trait set off the first of the warning bells when they started to date in college.

Now Conrad peered along with Aiden, touched what he touched, their hands brushing against each other's as they squatted to examine nature's wonder. He spoke little. The deepening lines across his rosy face indicated a man pondering life, and perhaps death.

Conrad placed his hand on Aiden's shoulder. Aiden supposed he needed to steady himself when he squatted, and he allowed him to rest it there in case he needed the extra support. After a while they stood, and with Conrad's hand still on his shoulder, Aiden pointed past the detached garage.

"This side of the street and higher up into the hills are mostly suburban-style housing they built in the 1980s. Part of the growing Kalispell sprawl. Funny thing, the ranchers on the other side of the road seem the friendliest toward us, especially Nick."

"You were always easy to get along with."

Aiden's face heated and he nodded toward the garage. "Let's go look at Daniel's workspace." He took a step forward that allowed Conrad's hand to slide off his shoulder.

They entered through the side door into the workshop. Daniel had walled off the garage section and a second door led to where Daniel sometimes parked the Chevy. The narrow shop was roomy enough for him to work on smaller crafts at home in the evenings or on Sundays, since he kept to a lifetime of Amish custom and never opened the Rose Crossing shop on "the Lord's Day."

"Daniel made most of the furniture in our house," Aiden said. "He's very handy."

"It's weird how he still looks Amish with the beard," Conrad said. "I have to admit, I was taken aback a moment by his accent and appearance."

Aiden snickered. "He'll always be Amish."

"Doesn't that bother you?"

Aiden waited a moment before responding. "Why should it?" he said. "Part of the reason why I fell in love with him was because of his being Amish."

Conrad peered around, silent. His mouth puckered, as if he were chewing on his words. He wandered to the jigsaw table and swiped his fingertip across the sawdust, then rubbed his hand on his pants leg.

Conrad bent over to examine the underside of a small night table Daniel had completed, which would be shipped once the client's payment came through. Next he squatted, stretching the corduroy of his pants over his thighs, and ran his fingers over the ornate legs. He seemed so alive and healthy that Aiden needed to turn away, thinking that beneath what appeared to be a sturdy exterior an ugly cancer battled against his life.

"Did he carve this too?" Conrad said.

Aiden looked back at the wooden truck that Conrad, now standing, held raised in his hand. "Daniel does all his work himself, even the toys. He likes to make the little things, I think because it relaxes him. We sometimes give them away to needy children during Christmas."

Conrad set the toy aside, stood straighter. "How's the business doing?"

"With the website I help keep up, he's got clients from all over, even a few from Germany. They sometimes think it's cool that there are Americans whose first language is German, so they buy things from them."

"Must be nice to have a strong man around the house, huh?" he said after a moment.

Aiden was unsure of Conrad's tone. "He's the best."

"And soon I'll be a weak, frail man?"

"Of course you won't."

Conrad gave Aiden one of his infamous wry smiles that had at one time sent quivers up Aiden's spine. The same sensation tickled his limbs, but for a different reason, he suspected.

"I heard you two last night," Conrad said unexpectedly.

Although Aiden understood Conrad's connotation, he looked away with burning cheeks. "What do you mean?"

"You two are still honeymooners, huh?"

Aiden thought they'd been extra quiet while making love. He lowered his eyes to where he formed a small circle on the sawdust coating the cement floor with the toe of his sneaker. "I hope we didn't keep you awake," he mumbled.

"I didn't mind. Remember how it was with us when we first got together?"

Aiden did remember, but he fought back the images from creeping into his consciousness. For what purpose would he want them?

"Are you two monogamous?" Conrad asked, his solicitous smile still stretched across his face.

The question seemed ridiculous to Aiden. Did heterosexual people ask each other such things? He was monogamous by nature, as much as he was gay. "Of course we are. I was with you too. That's the kind of guy I am."

"You always were different like that." Conrad shuffled around the small shop, his feet sweeping over the sawdust. "Like wanting to live in a cabin in the woods."

Conrad often scoffed at Aiden's dreams of living a more rustic lifestyle. At their last meeting, Conrad's words had been something like *You're living in a dream world.... It's not the 1800s.*

Conrad had a way of making Aiden feel smaller than a weasel for what he was and wished for. He even mocked his profession. Between jobs, Conrad mentioned a few times since his arrival to Montana. Yes, Aiden agreed, he probably was realistically *between jobs*. And he probably would be for the rest of his life. Did Conrad have to remind him?

While he disliked Conrad's occasional sneering attitude, he could see a new man fighting to break through. He snickered, shook his head. Wanting to shake off the unpleasant past, he said, "I guess I always was a bit of a romantic."

"That's what attracted me to you," Conrad said. "You were about the only guy I ever considered being faithful to."

Aiden fixed his gaze out the window. Ranger lay in a patch of sun. When Aiden said nothing, Conrad went on.

"Moving to Chicago and the new job, I was so stressed out. I wasn't sure you and I would last there. Guess I was right." Aiden sensed Conrad had turned to look at him with his sparkling blue eyes. "Isn't it funny that here I am with you now in Montana? Wasn't that your dream to move out here with me all along?"

Rather than draw out the dramatics, Aiden emphasized the reason for Conrad's reaching out to him. Perhaps it was Aiden's way to seek a small revenge, or maybe he wanted to simply change the subject. "I can drive you into town for your treatments whenever you have them. Do you know when they'll be?"

Conrad shrugged. "Tomorrow is my first one, I think."

"They're expecting you, right?"

"My doctors in Virginia coordinated everything. All I have to do is give them twenty-four hours' notice. I'll call once we get back inside." Conrad touched a few objects, scuffled around the jigsaw table until he sidled beside Aiden. "I can take a bus, if you like."

"Don't be ridiculous. It's not too far. Fifteen miles."

Stiff silence passed between them. Conrad sighed and startled Aiden when he reached for his hand, but quickly brought it back to his side. Turning toward the window, Conrad stared into the morning light that highlighted his strawberry-blond hair. "Maybe I shouldn't have come here after everything. Who knows what a burden I'll be?"

Aiden understood that in Conrad's own way he was apologizing for the hurt he had caused him while they had dated, and especially for the fiasco that took place in Chicago. His actions were cruel, but Aiden surpassed it, and was happy to hear his gentle words of regret.

"You're here and you're welcome," Aiden said. "The only thing you need to worry about is getting well." He found an excuse to move farther from Conrad and opened the door to the backyard. Once outside, he secured the door latch and led Conrad across the grass to the far side of the yard closer to the creek. They stopped and listened to the crisp water gurgling through a grove of spruce. Aiden pointed due west. "Right between those big trees there. See?"

Conrad put his cheek close to Aiden's. His sour breath was warm against the morning chill. "You mean that mountain peak?"

"Isn't it awesome?" Aiden chuckled from the pride rising in his voice. "I discovered the view last summer while I was on the ride-on mower. I almost fell off. I couldn't believe I was seeing it, and from my own property. You can't really see all the taller peaks from the house, but this is a perfect window for that one."

Framed by trees, a sole mountain peak, capped with white snow, jetted toward the blue sky, overshadowing the other more distant crags. The tree line broke near the top, and the white point stood stark and dramatic.

"Pretty as a postcard," Conrad uttered.

"I already took a million pictures of it and sent them back home."

Conrad turned away and kicked at the pine needles layering the grass. The sun shifted higher. Ranger trotted to them, and Aiden used Ranger's nearness as a perfect excuse to rub his back rather than place his hand on Conrad's shoulder like he found himself wanting.

Conrad peered toward the visible mountain. "I had a boyfriend until a few months ago." He cast his eyes downward and massaged behind his right ear. "After I told him about my lymphoma, he left me."

"Conrad, I had no idea. I'm sorry."

He smiled at Aiden. "I guess I had it coming to me, right? Karma. Isn't that what people call it? Maybe that's why I got cancer."

"Don't say things like that, Conrad."

There was much Aiden wanted to add, in both defense and condemnation of Conrad. Empathy for his loneliness and the sickness that left him shaken overtook him. Before realizing it, he squeezed Conrad's shoulder. "We better get back inside," he said using his softest voice. "It's still a bit chilly out. You don't want to catch a cold while you're in treatment. They say it suppresses your immune system. You have to be careful about that."

Conrad chuckled and Aiden asked him what was so funny. "You were always so nurturing. I guess I never really appreciated that side of you." His laugh muscles weakened and he gazed solemnly at the ground. "That is, until now."

"Hey," Aiden said, lightening the mood. "Let's get you something to eat. How about some strawberry Pop-Tarts? Still not into toasting them?"

Conrad's face brightened. "That's right. You remembered I like them raw."

"Of course."

Conrad's lips curled into a soft smile. He rested his hand on top of Aiden's, still heavy on Conrad's shoulder. "Thanks, Aiden. I really don't deserve a guy like you."

Flushing, Aiden walked with Conrad back to the house while Ranger danced circles around them.

Chapter SIX

DANIEL'S lone employee, Phedra Ayers, greeted Daniel when he stepped inside the shop. She was a Hutterite and, having retained the bashful disposition of a girl generations removed from her peasant origins, simpered at him under her soft brow. Peppered with an American improvisational style when the going got tough and Old World attention to detail when uneventful days trudged ahead, Daniel appreciated her more and more.

He hired Phedra in large part because she reminded him of his three sisters, Elisabeth, Grace, and Moriah. Three hardy girls who had never shied from difficult chores. Moriah especially, who demonstrated the legendary Amish reserve commingled with a cunning rebelliousness that had led her more out of trouble than into it. In other words, Phedra, like Moriah, was crafty as a crow.

Although they traced their roots to German-speaking people—Daniel's ancestors came from Switzerland and Phedra's from Austria—and maintained an unconventional communal lifestyle, the Hutterites yielded to modernization more than the Amish. Phedra's father was a Flathead County paramedic and her mother worked as a dental hygienist in the nearby village of Somers. Phedra grasped the modern America that Daniel still struggled to comprehend.

A Brady Bunch house?

What did Conrad mean when he uttered those words after entering their home? Aiden, of course, understood fully.

Daniel was glad Conrad slept in and he hadn't had to face him at breakfast. The evening with Nick went smoothly enough. Still, his resentment toward Conrad's presence hadn't diminished like he hoped.

He disliked being burdened with nursing a near stranger who saddled him and Aiden with uncertainty. Perhaps if Daniel hadn't been so rash to move from their old tiny cabin, they could have refused Conrad on grounds they had no room.

That Conrad was Aiden's old boyfriend made coping more difficult. He had tried the entire evening to set aside his selfishness, but found himself chewing his lips and averting his eyes more than he intended.

Daniel never liked intruders. He also at one time saw Aiden as an outsider, interrupting his family's simple oat farm in Illinois. And look where that had led!

The couple had been through much since. Throughout their courtship, mountains of self-doubt, anger, disbelief, and terror stood before them. Until they found each other by chance at Glacier National Park, and all the misery seemed to have wavered behind.

"Did you have a pleasant Sunday?" Phedra said. As usual, she spoke to him in broken German. She was always eager to please, and used her German regularly around him. But hers was as spotty as Aiden's. Still, far from his hometown in Illinois, he appreciated the chance to speak his first language.

She wore a long jean skirt and a long-sleeved blouse, the same outfit even in summer. Her Hutterite order permitted the women to go without head coverings. Daniel was glad because he did not want his shop to become a caricature of an Amish tourist attraction like the one he had run with his family.

He studied her for a second, long enough to dig deeper into her brown eyes, which reminded him of a horse's. She never appeared to guess about his sexuality. Aiden was around often, and she seemed, if anything, to have a crush on him. He figured she knew they lived together. The Hutterites were so close-knit, collective living was a religious way of life, and perhaps she might have assumed he and Aiden cohabitated for the same reasons.

He considered telling her about Conrad's staying at his home while he underwent cancer treatments, but decided against it. "My Sunday was nice and quiet," he replied in Pennsylvania German. "And yours?"

"We worked on the books for our medical center," she said in English, probably since she didn't know the correct German words. "We're thinking of building one of our own with community funds." She added in German, "I think it is for the best of our people that we become more independent."

And Daniel thought it likewise best that he and Aiden should too. "That's a good plan," he mumbled toward the wood floor.

Phedra slipped into English when he turned for his workshop in the back. "Should I dust today?"

Daniel stopped and looked at her over his shoulder. "No need to overdo yourself. It's Monday. Watch the register. But if you want, later you can drag a rag around the shelves and sweep."

He stepped inside his spacious workshop, already flooded with sunlight pouring through the southeast-facing windows on the garage that he used to remove larger furniture. In warmer weather, he could open the rolling doors and allow the outdoors to come inside.

He placed his lunch inside the small refrigerator where he and Phedra stowed their lunches and snacks, poured a glass of whole milk, swigged from it, and focused on finishing the console for the lobby of a high-end lodge in Columbia Falls just outside of Glacier National Park. Sometime that day he also needed to add finishing touches to the small dining table he was making for a family in Spokane. He had four more large items on his to-do list for clients from Houston to Los Angeles. And more orders came each week.

Don't use choring as an excuse to hide, his aging father would say. It had always been Daniel's way, whether God or his father approved. Daniel shrugged off his father's sagacity and his people's ultraorthodox dictums, and allowed work to bury his worries.

He'd already cut the legs and side frames for the console, but he needed to smooth the wood before attaching the legs. He pushed sandpaper into the hard pine. The scratching sound sung to him like warblers on a sunny summer morning. Noticing two or three discrepancies in the legs' widths, he leveled them with his plane. Shavings curled from the blade and tickled his exposed wrists. He worked another fifteen minutes, and once satisfied with his efforts, he used holding glue to attach the legs and secured them with wood clamps. In another hour, he might add the slats.

He gazed out the garage windows. The blue sky, emerald trees, and rolling hills left him forlorn and empty for the first time since his coming to Montana, a place that had stood as a spiritual retreat for him.

He escaped to northwestern Montana before his first marriage to Esther, and then again days before he was to exchange wedding vows with Tara Hostetler. Two times venturing to Montana, both for the same reasons. His last journey led him into Aiden Cermak's arms. The empty sensation deep in his gut convinced him their journey together faced yet one more mountain to climb.

Balls of nimbus clouds eased eastward across his view. Rain would come later in the day, perhaps sleet, and for sure more snow in the higher elevations. Winter clung fast, but warmer weather would soon sit upon them like a bear guarding its cache.

He returned to work, and spent the remaining morning sanding, assembling, and using his Swiss-made tools to fashion intricate designs on the feet of the table for the Spokane family. The wife insisted on rosettes.

The electronic door chimes rang several times throughout the morning, but neither time did Phedra come for him, which meant patrons had either bought items on display or were fantasy shopping. Before long his hand cramped and he set aside the gouge to shake blood back into his fingers.

Phedra stepped inside the workshop and said in English, "Okay if I break for lunch? I didn't bring one today. I'm going to Beadsman's."

"Did we have many customers this morning?"

"You sold a toy box and a foot stool. One lady might return later to place an order for a pie chest." In German, she repeated, "May I go to lunch?"

"*Ya, du consht gese.*"

After he heard the door chime behind Phedra, Daniel took a break himself. Often Aiden would come to the shop at lunchtime if he wasn't there helping and bring him something fresh from a deli or leftovers from home. Daniel enjoyed their lunches together. But he figured Conrad would be filling his days for a while.

He warmed the leftover chicken and mushrooms in the microwave and spread his lunch on a desk that a customer never retrieved. He at least paid the down payment. Eating alone, he tried to find solace in the solitude. Outside, the south mountains, farther beyond the valley, stood clearer in the noontime sun. He and Aiden shared a love for such views, but what mattered now in their world was the ugly reality of heavy burdens.

The door chimed in the midst of his crumbling the lunch wrappers to toss them into the waste can. The sound met his ears with a different resonance than usual. Next came muted voices. He realized at that moment who had arrived.

"Surprise," Aiden said, poking his head inside the workshop. "I wanted to show Conrad where you work."

Conrad moved from behind Aiden and was the first to fully enter his workspace. "Nice place," he said. "You make what you sell right here?"

Daniel nodded. "Here and sometimes at my workshop at home."

"I showed him that too," Aiden said, grinning. "He's really impressed with your talent."

Daniel's face heated. When he was a boy, his parents and the elders warned him that *hochmut*, or haughtiness, would gain disfavor with God. Yet he could never stop himself from grinning with warmed cheeks whenever anyone complimented his craftsmanship. "I make it all," he said. "Keeps me off the streets, as they say."

Aiden escorted Conrad back into the main part of the shop. They looked quite a pair, Daniel thought, while he stayed planted by his worktable and stared at them through the open door. Nearly carbon copies of each other. One fair and blue eyed, the other darker with shocking bright-brown eyes. They walked shoulder to shoulder, mirroring each other's casual strides as they made their way down the aisles.

Daniel considered joining them and explaining to Conrad some of his most prized creations like he had once with Aiden back in Henry, but he waited until they finished wandering the shop and Aiden returned to his work area.

"We're heading out to get something to eat," Aiden said. "Want to tag along?"

"Tag along? I had my lunch." Daniel lowered his head to the console. "And I have a lot of work here."

Aiden blew a kiss. Seconds later, the electronic door chimes echoed in Daniel's head. He wandered up front and watched them climb into Aiden's pickup. The patient must be pampered, Daniel thought, shaking his head.

Chapter SEVEN

DURING lunch Conrad asked Aiden to see more of the area, and Aiden was eager to please. “We’ll drive into the Salish Range when we’re done,” he said. “You’ll love it there.”

They finished their deli sandwiches in the same shopping center as Daniel’s shop, where earlier they met Phedra leaving Beadsman’s Deli. Aiden had introduced her and Conrad before placing their orders. She seemed extra coy around Conrad.

With the shopping center behind them, Aiden steered deeper into the high country. The road swept them upward and the first bend provided an unhindered vista of Snowshoe Peak, forty miles west.

“I can never get enough of the way the sun strikes the snow-covered peaks,” Aiden said. “They sparkle like caramel-dipped ice cream cones.”

“You sound like a poet,” Conrad said with a snicker.

“I was an English major, remember? You used to tell me I was wasting my time.”

Conrad shrugged. “And here I am, the great computer whiz with no job and failing health.” He pointed toward a horse and buggy passing them from the opposite direction. “It’s one of those Amish buggies.”

“We live in a community with Montana’s second largest Amish population. It’s not huge, but we see their buggies now and then. That’s the first one I’ve seen in a while.”

“Daniel must feel at home, then.”

“We didn’t plan on moving so close to them. It’s a bit awkward for him, to be honest. I like it. But he feels ashamed sometimes.”

Many Amish in Rose Crossing were recent transplants from the Midwest, and Daniel often voiced concern one of them might recognize him. The Amish community in Illinois was large and distant relatives and acquaintances popped up in strange places. One time during a day hike through Glacier National Park, they came across Daniel's second cousin and his young family. They exchanged pleasantries, shook hands, and moved on.

Aiden, allured by the idea of living like nineteenth-century pioneers, loved the idyllic lifestyle of the Amish and often wished there were ways for a same-sex couple to fit among them. But he realized that was as likely as a mountain lion and a mule deer sharing the same lair. He glanced in his rearview window at the shrinking buggy with the required orange triangle on the back and swallowed a lump in his throat.

"Certainly is a crazy country," Conrad said. "Amish, Hutterites, Cowboys."

"Don't forget the gays," Aiden said, steering along.

Conrad laughed toward the truck's ceiling. "Them too."

The first genuine good feelings of camaraderie passed between them. Aiden's hands relaxed on the steering wheel, and he noticed how Conrad's square jaw seemed to flinch with each new sight.

"Do you remember those weekend backpacking trips we used to take?" Conrad said, watching the scenery pass. "I used to live for those trips."

Aiden recalled how his first experience connecting with nature came via Conrad, who grew up in central Michigan, near pristine pine forests. Conrad showed Aiden parts of Maryland he never knew existed, including the rustic western panhandle where the Appalachian Trail crossed along South Mountain. Leery at first, the moment his borrowed boots hit the rugged trail, he was hooked. From that moment he looked farther west, ultimately to Montana, as a dream, a dream that Conrad never shared.

"Those were some good times," Aiden said, fixing his eyes on the ribbon of gray road. "Remember that time we went backpacking in the Shenandoah Valley?"

Conrad chuckled. “Once we got to the campsite, we stripped naked and leaped into the creek.”

“And suddenly all those people showed up out of nowhere, like a party of fifteen.”

“We were trapped.”

“Those ladies didn’t seem to mind.”

Their laughter faded, and Aiden, with Conrad a few feet beside him, pondered life lived to the fullest brought to a skidding halt with the suddenness of illness. Conrad, a man overflowing with memories of a youthful, robust, promising life, now wrestled with mortality.

But didn’t everyone?

They rode the gentle high plateau, passing lumberyards and trucking companies, until they came to the deep rock ridges that abutted the road and concealed the high country ranches. Through the gaps in the outcroppings, cows lay in the green clover fields. Aiden learned from Daniel that meant rain was nearing. He gazed at the western sky. Still blue with an occasional fluffy gray cloud. They had at least a few hours before the rains would come.

“Are you feeling all right?” He noticed Conrad’s face slackened and he was grasping his knees.

Conrad sighed. “A little hot all of the sudden, but they said to expect fevers from the chemo.”

“You’re already taking pills?”

“For the past month.” Conrad eyed him with an eerie frankness. “They weren’t doing enough, that’s why I’m starting radiation therapy.”

“Want me to crank on the air conditioning for a minute?”

“I’m okay for now. If I get too hot I can crack the window.”

Aiden turned right onto Pleasant Valley Road toward Little Bitterroot Lake. They passed through the tiny village of Marion, where “Main Street” was an undivided road. Outside of the village, pines and spruce leaned into the narrow road that shone from the snowmelt like a pristine sheet of tar paper. Snow berms lined the eastern side under the long shadows of the trees. A stained log fence bordered the property of someone's luxurious log cabin home, partially hidden by towering blue spruce.

At Bitterroot Lake, he parked alongside two other trucks. Most likely they belonged to retirees fishing or hiking the trails. He led Conrad closer to the lake, near the aspens covered with furry green buds. He motioned for them to sit at a picnic table. Aiden sat on the top and Conrad on the bench.

In the distance a hawk squealed. An avian hunter announcing its victory. Against the sky the hawk appeared, flying toward the higher summits. Something dangled limp from its talons.

Conrad wiped sweat from his forehead. "It's chilly but I get the hot flashes."

"You want my knit cap? I have one in the truck somewhere."

"I'm good." Conrad hunkered his shoulders closer to his ears and tightened his jacket around his torso. "Don't fuss over me so much."

"I only want you to be comfortable."

"You know, Aiden, I was surprised you called me back, letting me come here."

Gazing off at the wall of emerald hills and the glistening slashes of lake caught between the trees, Aiden said, "Why surprised?"

"I just was."

They were silent, staring. "Let's walk one of the trails a bit into the woods," Aiden said, wanting to change the subject. "Might warm us up some."

Conrad jumped to his feet. "You lead the way."

They moved ahead, and Conrad mentioned something about grizzlies and mountain lions.

Aiden snickered. "Montana has predators, all right. But don't worry." He patted his side pocket. "I have a loud alarm on my keychain. I doubt we'll need it. Of all my time in the Montana backcountry I've only run across tracks."

"We never did see anything like a bear on the trails back east," Conrad said.

"There was that time we saw the baby deer drinking from a creek. And there was that fox, remember?"

"At that campsite in western Pennsylvania. He was so sly looking. I understood at that moment why they say, sly as a fox."

Conrad reached into his jacket pocket and withdrew a pack of cigarettes. Aiden held back from expressing surprise. Conrad had smoked occasionally while in college and in Chicago, but mostly when out at bars or parties. The act seemed abnormal surrounded by the natural beauty of rural Montana. To scar it with artificial smoke, with a stench that masked the fresh pine scent, disturbed Aiden.

He kept his qualms to himself and acted as if he didn't notice Conrad's dragging on a cigarette and stuffing the pack of Salems back inside his jacket.

"We never did get to northern Michigan like we planned," he said, blowing out a cloud of smoke. "Even after moving to Chicago."

Aiden eyed his sneakers, the toes damp from grass that grew on the seldom-used trail. He wished he knew beforehand they might go for a hike; he would have worn his boots. "Like you once said, the real world of jobs changes a person's priorities. Sometimes dreams have to be put on hold."

"You've fulfilled your dreams, haven't you?"

Aiden looked straight ahead. He sensed Conrad's eyes on him. Smoke from his cigarette whiffed under his nose and he turned away to avoid it stinging his eyes. They hiked farther into the woods. The vegetation cover grew denser, yet the new growth trees, thin and standing about only twenty feet, provided less shade. Intermittent splashes of sun fell on their shoulders and exposed necks. They rounded a bend in the trail heading eastward and Aiden appreciated the smoke from Conrad's cigarette shifting away from him.

"Most of my dreams are fulfilled," he said finally. "I still hope to make more of a difference in my writing one day. So far, I get stuck writing about silly things, like fashion trends. I'm looking forward to writing my latest article. Should be more significant than some of the other stuff."

The sun blinded them a moment before ducking behind more branches. Conrad said, "Maybe now it's too late for me to fulfill my dreams."

Aiden never really knew what Conrad's dreams were, yet he needed to encourage him. "Don't say that, Conrad. You've done lots of things. You earned a college degree, joined the ROTC program. Many people only dream of accomplishments like that." Aiden breathed. "In a way, if not for you, I wouldn't be here."

Conrad glared at him. "What do you mean?"

"The last time we spoke in Maryland, when you told me I was living in a fantasy world, you sort of spurred me to follow my dream and come to Montana. You're responsible for me being here and running into Daniel."

Conrad drew on his cigarette and smoke oozed from his sardonic grin. "Aren't I a great guy?"

"You opened a new world to me when we started backpacking," Aiden confessed. "I'll always be thankful for that."

Conrad dragged on his cigarette until the end burned bright and the smoke ceased curling upward. Blowing out smoke, he crushed the cigarette with the sole of his sneaker and flicked the butt into the trees. Aiden ignored the inconsiderate action. He'd seen people toss their smokes into the unspoiled wilderness before. At least Conrad possessed the intelligence to put it out first.

Noticing that Conrad was breathing heavy on the incline, Aiden suggested they turn back for the car. They hiked along silently. Closer to the trailhead, the shiny surface of the lake appeared. Reflections from the thickening layer of clouds moving across the mountains from the west gave the lake a silver sheen.

"Have you told your family about your illness?"

"You can say the word cancer, Aiden. I told them a few weeks after I found out."

"And?"

"Makes them uncomfortable, like they're indebted to me. You know, they are uptight about things like that, especially when I'm concerned. We never even hug each other. I wish I hadn't told them. Now they feel like I'm trying to squeeze them for sympathy." Conrad cringed. "I'd never want that from them."

Conrad told him many stories about his indifferent family. A mother who never worked a job her entire life. A father who seemed on an endless conveyor of temporary or part-time jobs. Two brothers who drank too much. A sister who married at seventeen, pregnant with another man's child. Conrad, the only college graduate among them, was, perhaps, the black sheep because he was so much more refined. And, of course, he was gay.

Conrad fell contemplative and he tightened his jaw. "Aiden," he said in a hushed voice, "I need to know that you forgive me for what I did to you in Chicago."

"It's in the past," Aiden said, looking down the widening trail.

Aiden thought he'd gotten over his time with Conrad in Chicago. He left Aiden cold and hard. Aiden couldn't imagine doing that to someone he loved. Each time Conrad forced him to relive those bad times and the hurt he caused him, he realized he carried around much of it, like an overstuffed backpack filled with thorns.

"I was a bum, as my dad would say," Conrad said, his eyes roaming about the lake but seemingly seeing nothing. "I didn't even understand how much what I did might have hurt you. I was so self-centered."

"You can't change the past, neither can I. What happened happened. I forgive you, okay?"

"Is it that simple?"

Aiden swallowed the crisp air. "Shouldn't it be? You asked for forgiveness. I'm giving it to you."

Uncomfortable with what might be Conrad's last declaration, Aiden breathed easier upon spotting his black truck. He pressed the key chain's remote unlock, although he knew he didn't have to since he hadn't locked the doors. Fingering his keychain, he was tempted to blast the alarm into the forest to punctuate what he hoped would be an end to any further discussion of his and Conrad's Chicago life.

"We better get back," he said, opening the door. "Rain's coming soon."

And so Aiden and Conrad climbed into the truck, and they drove eastward, and back to home.

Chapter EIGHT

THE heavy beating of rain against the rancher's windows accompanied them while they ate. Aiden watched Conrad wash down two bites of his fajita at a time with milk while Daniel poked at his dinner. Aiden reasoned Daniel ate little because, in part, he disliked Mexican food. But Aiden recalled when, back in college, he and Conrad ate Mexican at least twice a week.

Their hike into the Salish Range had stimulated Conrad's appetite, and Aiden was glad to see him clean his plate. How much time before the radiation treatments would destroy his desire for food?

Daniel shifted in his seat. He and Aiden exchanged questioning looks across the table. Daniel dabbed his mouth with his paper napkin and pushed aside his half-full plate when Conrad served himself seconds.

Daniel scooted out his chair and stood. "I best get to work in the garage. I have stools needing preliminary work."

"But it's raining out," Aiden said. "You can't work out there now."

"No worries. I'll take the umbrella. Besides, the garage is more weatherproofed in some ways than this old house."

With the master of the house gone, Ranger trotted over from his bed by the hearth and sat beside Conrad. He ogled him, licking his snout with his long, pink tongue. Conrad seemed to relax and eat even more once Daniel left.

He smiled with cheeks full of food and patted Ranger on the head. "He's a stern one," he said after swallowing.

"You mean Daniel? That's just his exterior," Aiden said. "He's about the kindest man I ever met."

"Guess that's the Amish in him," Conrad said, spooning rice into his mouth. "I hear they are strict."

"Some are, some aren't. They are just like anyone else." Aiden recalled Daniel telling him that once.

"No surprise you'd fall for a guy like that." Conrad raised his eyes from his plate and grinned. "You're almost as old fashioned as him."

Aiden forked the food around his plate. "It's more than that."

"He's a big guy. You always liked those types too. I've lost some weight myself, what with the cancer. You probably no longer find me attractive."

What difference did it make, Aiden thought.

Grinning, Conrad said, "I was thinking of getting a pass for a local gym while I'm here. You and Daniel belong to any?"

Aiden peered toward his half-eaten tortilla stuffed with fajita steak and veggies. "We do so much physical labor around here, backpacking, skiing, I haven't thought about things like working out at a gym in a long time."

"You still look in great shape." Conrad continued forking food into his mouth. "The doctors said I should exercise on days I feel up to it. Eventually, the good days will come farther and farther apart. I should enjoy them while I can."

Aiden called for Ranger to sit by him and quit bothering Conrad. "I can show you some of the gyms around town after your radiation treatment."

Conrad wiped his mouth and rested against the back of the chair. "Sounds like a good plan. You can work out with me. Remember how we used to work out all the time?" He rubbed his belly and smiled. "We'd go to classes, then get a good workout and shower, afterward dinner. We went nonstop."

Aiden checked his widening smile from getting the best of him. "What else is there for college students with no responsibilities?"

Conrad's gaze turned faraway, and the blue of his irises sparkled in the recessed lighting. Leaving him space, Aiden cleared the table. In the kitchen he hand-fed Ranger a few treats of leftover skirt steak. He peered through the rain-smeared kitchen window to the garage. A dim light filled the small windows to Daniel's woodshop.

The evening moved ahead. Aiden worked on his laptop at the dining table, eager to research more about strip mining near Glacier National Park. Daniel remained in his woodshop. His hiding reminded Aiden of their first meeting in Henry, when Daniel tried to evade him by staying in his woodshop there.

With no television, Conrad picked up a book from the console. He stayed quiet most of the evening, turning a leaf of the book every few minutes. Like with Ranger, Aiden enjoyed his presence filling the house with extra warmth.

"This is an interesting book," he said after another hour passed.

Aiden read the title from the dining table. "You never read *Huckleberry Finn* before?"

He shook his head. "Was never big into reading."

Aiden remembered disliking that feature of Conrad. Daniel read more than he'd have guessed for someone with an eighth-grade education. In fact, *Huckleberry Finn* belonged to Daniel.

Conrad tapped the book. "Huckleberry and Tom remind me of you and Daniel."

"How so?"

"You live like it's the 1800s."

Aiden chuckled and Conrad tossed the book where he found it on the console. He wandered to the window and watched as the rain changed to a light sleet mixed with snow. Aiden, gazing at his back, caught Conrad's reflection in the glass. Hands tucked in pants pockets, he appeared relaxed, contemplative.

"Would you like to play a game? Maybe some cards?" Aiden asked him.

Still staring out the window, Conrad sighed and said, "I think maybe I'll turn in." He eyed Aiden. "Tomorrow's the big day. My first appointment at the clinic."

Aiden provided him a tight smile. They said goodnight, and despite having appreciated Conrad's presence, Aiden was glad to have a moment alone with Ranger. Daniel entered the house several minutes later.

"You're not going to stay in the woodshop the entire time he's here, are you?" Aiden said to him.

Daniel set his boots aside and kissed the top of Aiden's head. "Good night," he said, and he wandered down the hallway.

THE next morning, Conrad sat at the dining table Aiden had laid out with a platter full of pancakes and bacon, but Conrad's appetite resembled nothing like the night before. He nibbled a strawberry Pop-Tart and nursed a glass of orange juice. Aiden guessed he felt nervous about his first day of radiation treatment. This time Aiden chose to stay silent on the subject unless Conrad spoke about it first.

"Daniel already gone again?" he asked with Ranger panting beside him.

"He has a lot of work to do and wanted to get an early start."

Conrad examined a piece of droopy bacon. "I think he's trying to avoid me."

"He isn't, Conrad. He's really busy." Aiden scooted aside the paperwork he was working on for his article and provided Conrad more attention. "Once you get to know each other, you won't feel that way. He's the one who insisted you come."

Conrad stared along the length of the table, his eyes wide and shiny. He finished his Pop-Tart in silence, deposited his empty glass in the sink, and announced, "I guess we better go. Unless you want me to look up the bus schedule or call a cab."

"Don't be silly."

"I could drive myself."

Aiden had pondered the notion. Shaking his head, he said, "You don't know your way around. Besides, you said you wanted to see a few gyms after your treatment."

"I have a ten-thirty appointment and should probably arrive early to fill out whatever paperwork. You can run errands while you're down there. I don't want for you to waste your time."

Aiden experienced the first genuine pang of empathy for Conrad, surpassing his other discomfort. What must Conrad be thinking before undergoing a series of radiation zaps? Aiden smiled to lessen the nervousness—both Conrad's and his own.

"Don't worry," he said. "I won't be wasting any time. I'll bring along my work."

During the drive into the Valley, he attempted small talk, suggesting the rain from last night had been good for the budding spring flowers and trees.

"I'll look forward to the scenery more on the way home," Conrad mumbled.

Tongue-tied, Aiden clutched the steering wheel. The drive into the Valley seemed to take hours. They remained mostly quiet. Conrad sighed as Aiden braked for the first traffic light.

Stopped at the intersection, Conrad gazed around for what seemed the first time since getting into the truck. "It's a bigger town than I expected," Conrad said. "I didn't get to see much of it the other night in the dark."

"It's growing every day," Aiden said. "If we turn left, Whitefish is twenty miles up the road, and if we continue toward Glacier National Park we head into Columbia Falls. Altogether the Flathead Valley has about one hundred fifty thousand people. It's the fastest growing region in Montana."

Conrad braced his hand against the dashboard when Aiden moved through the green light. "You can barely see the mountains down here," he said, with an unsettling alarm to his voice.

"It's a spread-out valley," Aiden said. "That's why people began populating it. Started as ranch country. We see what's left of that on the outskirts near where we live. We can show you the really big mountains of Glacier, if you like. Anytime you'd like to go, we'll take you there."

"I bet that's something to see. Let's go now and skip my appointment."

Aiden white-knuckled the steering wheel, watchful of the traffic that picked up once they passed Meridian Road. "You know you can't do that."

Conrad beamed Aiden a warm smile. “I’m only joking. It’s a date, then. I’ll look forward to seeing the national park. It’s one of the big things on my to-do list while I’m here.”

“Good.” Aiden smiled back, relieved Conrad was trying his best to brighten the day. “I promise it’ll be an experience you’ll never forget. Nothing like backpacking the East Coast.”

Stopping and moving through a dozen more traffic signals, Aiden found the Flathead Valley Cancer Center, a two-story modern structure on the edge of downtown Kalispell. On the other side of the road sat the United Community Church, which had a small rainbow flag displayed on its roadside sign. Seeking a church of their own to attend after moving to their present home, he and Daniel discovered the church while driving. They had attended two services but, although appreciating their gay inclusiveness, were put off by the radical political ideology expressed by the ministers and many of the congregation. They hadn’t attended any church since. And despite Daniel’s adherence to a belief in God, he seemed fine with keeping their faith in the privacy of their home, which Amish custom dictated anyway.

Aiden pulled into the clinic’s parking lot. By the number of different license plates, the clinic attracted patients from a wide area: Montana, Idaho, Washington, and many from Canada. A passenger van with Alberta tags blocked four parking spaces. Aiden found a free space near the back, set the brake, and turned off the ignition.

Conrad placed a hand on Aiden’s arm. “I’d rather do all this on my own. You understand, don’t you?”

Some challenges a man must face alone, Aiden figured. Perhaps most. He struggled to say something reassuring. “When do you want me to pick you up?”

“I’ll text you when I’m done. Go about your morning business. I won’t mind waiting around if I get done early.”

“I guess I could go to Glacier Park and do some research. I have my laptop with me.” Aiden hesitated and thought again. “But are you sure I shouldn’t come inside with you and meet the staff? I mean, maybe, since we’ll be, you know, caring for you, there’re things we should know.”

Conrad shook his head, his eyes squeezed closed. "I'm sure they'll give me brochures and whatnot. There isn't much to it anyway. Don't worry. You're already doing the most anyone can expect." He jumped out of the truck and slammed the door shut. At the window he wiggled his fingers and shouted, "Have a nice day, Aiden."

Aiden waved back and slowly pulled out of the parking lot. At the traffic signal, he caught sight of Conrad waiting by the sliding glass doors, as if frightened to enter, like a child on his first day of school. Before the stoplight turned green, he saw Conrad turn and glance at him. Next Conrad squared his shoulders and stepped inside.

Chapter NINE

LIKE Conrad, nearby Glacier National Park was poised to face its biggest challenge for survival. Twenty miles north of the Canadian border, a coal-mining company was looking to blast the MacDonald Mountains, which could affect the waters of Glacier and, thereby, damage the park's ecosystem and natural formations. If allowed to mine, the company, in a matter of a few decades, might turn the park, a national treasure, into nothing but a swamp, rampaged by gook, fallen trees, and debris.

Aiden's concept for the article had come to him last summer while he and Daniel, taking a relaxing break after a weekend of backpacking Piegan Pass in the eastern edge of the park, attended a ranger-led outdoor seminar on the park's ecosystem. The ranger mentioned that the park's future lay in the hands of the company mining for bituminous coal and gas. With a familiar sarcastic lilt to his voice, the ranger said few politicians on either side of the border seemed to care.

Curious, Aiden did more research at home and happened upon an obscure blog from an ecologist at the University of Montana. But his was the only mention of the strip mining near Glacier Park that Aiden found.

Months later, Aiden was surprised no one had yet to leap on the story. Even his and Daniel's former progressive church across from Conrad's cancer clinic had failed to act, or had been unaware of the problem. Outside the ecologist's rather far-out blog and the park ranger's mocking of government indifference, the story did not exist.

When he decided to take on the story, Aiden contacted the ecologist and compiled ten pages of notes from their hour-long telephone interview. Dr. Christopher Vernal seemed grateful for a chance to vent, and Aiden could barely keep up with the environmental jargon he used to describe the strip mining's possible impact on the park.

The editor of the Flathead Valley's largest newspaper, the *Valley Courant*, expressed interest in the story. Norman Schooner said he'd pay Aiden sixteen cents per word. Not a mint, but at least it was enough to keep Aiden focused on a meaningful writing assignment while Conrad convalesced under foot.

With the horrible images of Conrad's radiation treatments behind him, Aiden cleared the heart of Kalispell and passed the airport where the landscape opened with expansive subdivisions and green pastures, until he reached the town of Columbia Falls, Flathead Valley's third-largest city.

Columbia Falls, the gateway to Glacier National Park, was famous for its log cabin stores and lodges, many of which were made of false facades and showcased schmaltzy plastic elk racks hanging above doors. The lush hills rose higher here, and the soaring snow-streaked mountains reappeared as fixtures to the landscape.

Round the first significant bend of Route 2, he turned left and drove past the park's welcome sign. The park was a few months from in-season and he entered without needing to wait in line. He proceeded easily along the Going-to-the-Sun Road and recalled the first time he drove that road alone and beheld the park.

It had been a dream come true, to experience the wild frontier, managed by a system that kept the land untamed and dangerous, yet approachable to the public. Among the towering red cedars, Aiden realized he could never turn back for Maryland or Illinois again.

The farther he drove into the park, the higher the snow drifts collected on the side of the road and along the north side of the trees. Farther up at ten thousand feet, officials would not clear Logan Pass until June or July.

Wildlife was scarce, save for magpies scrounging for fallen pinecones uncovered by snowmelt. Bears were probably still snoozing in their dens higher up in the mountains, away from danger. The short stretch of warmer weather might have rustled awake the boars, but they were unlikely to have made it down near the park's lodge and the campgrounds.

He glanced to his left at Sprague Creek Campground on the banks of Lake MacDonald. Two tents and an RV were set up. Soon, the weather would warm enough that he and Daniel could go backpacking and camping again.

Would it be proper to bring Conrad to what had become Aiden and Daniel's sacred ground?

At Lake MacDonald Lodge, he parked beside a snow pile as big as a hill and walked to the ranger station in the hill's long shadow. The air was nippy. He zipped his jacket and headed inside.

He remembered the ranger behind the reception desk from his first trip to Glacier. Handsome and youthful, he had greeted Aiden with a wide grin and solicitous manner, like he did now. Aiden was certain the ranger did not recognize him since he saw tens of thousands of people each season.

"What can I do for you?" the ranger said, leaning into the counter.

Fighting a sudden bout of bashfulness, Aiden said, "I'm Aiden Cermak, a freelance journalist living in the Flathead Valley. I wanted to ask a few questions about the strip-mining operation opening up across the border."

The ranger kept his smile, but shook his head rigorously. "You'll have to speak to our public relations officer or the superintendent, and I don't think either will be in until later in the day. Mornings are slow starts for us this time of year."

Another ranger, interested in Aiden by the arch of his eyebrows, rounded a corner and stood by the counter. "What's going on, Brad?"

"This man wants to interview someone about the mountaintop mining in British Columbia."

The ranger stood taller with his chin raised and bald head reflecting the lights above. "I'll speak with you." He extended his large hand for a shake. "I'm Ranger Craig Ellis. I work in the education division at the park. You want to step back here where we can talk?"

Giddy with expectancy, Aiden nodded a thanks to the shrugging ranger named Brad and followed Ranger Ellis into his office. Ranger Ellis kept his door open, and the atmosphere was relaxed, if not typical of a government agency knotted in red tape. Aiden glanced at the mounds of paperwork. Little resembled the solitude and rustic feel of a national park. It was a cold, heartless administrative office with concrete slab walls and a single grimy window that prevented a good view of the surrounding beauty. Aiden might as well have been in an office in Washington, DC, or Chicago.

Ranger Ellis shoved aside a column of files and clasped his hands under his chin. Even before meeting his eyes, Aiden sensed his displeasure. Not at Aiden, but at the turn Ellis's job had taken. At the governmental overload that came with civil service.

Right away, Aiden understood he'd learn more about the burden of an increasingly thankless job than strip mining. Like the ranger whom Aiden had first heard raise the issue of strip mining, Ranger Ellis scoffed at the pressure of political pandering.

At the ranger's suggestion, Aiden sat across from him. He folded his hands in his lap, providing the ranger his full attention. Aiden never took notes when interviewing people for his articles. He feared it might create a wall. When finished he'd type a quick synopsis of the interview in his truck, while still fresh in his mind.

From his experience, people on the street were easier to interview than blurry-eyed officials used to being misquoted. The public loved the attention. And Aiden learned early that many interviewees said what they thought the interviewer wanted to hear. The longer he worked at his job, the more he realized they were more desperate for approval than to express their true thoughts.

Eyebrows still arched high, Ranger Ellis's gaze roamed from the workload on his desk to Aiden. He continued to smile, accentuating his high cheekbones, which were already glossy with a thin veil of sweat. He needed a shave, and his oily day-old beard that traced his firm jawline glistened under the harsh overhead lights.

"What publication do you work for?" Ellis asked with a showy sigh.

"I'm a freelancer actually, but my story will appear in the *Valley Courant*. I'm writing about the strip mining of bituminous coal near Glacier Park, perhaps a series if I can get enough feedback."

"Go right ahead. Ask away."

"Can you tell me more about the mining? Do you feel it actually poses a risk to the park's future?"

"Coal was mined in and around the park before the national park system came into existence," Ellis said. "The Blackfoot mined it for baking their pottery and then the French fur traders came in and mined scant amounts, followed by the pioneers. Little could be attained by hand. Now we have massive machines that can rip a mountain of five thousand feet down to sea level in a matter of a few years. But how much of a threat? I can't answer that. It might even affect the entire Flathead Valley. The watershed could be threatened and ranchers would have to move out."

"What has the park done to try to stop it?"

Ellis leaned back in his chair. "We've filed the requisite paperwork with the appropriate government agencies on both sides of the border, stating our concerns. It's out of our hands at this point."

"Which agencies are those?"

"National Park Service, Parks Canada, EPA, the British Columbia Environmental Assessment Office, Montana's DEQ."

"DEQ?"

"Department of Environmental Quality. The usual gang of suspects. Hey, don't you want to write any of this down?"

"I have a keen memory. Don't worry. I won't misquote you. Can I call you if I need to verify anything?"

"Sure, why not?"

"I won't mention anything that you'd prefer remain between you and me," he said to reassure him.

"Go right ahead. Write what you want," Ellis said with a downturn of his mouth. "The power guys are used to our complaints anyway."

Aiden appreciated the ranger's sarcastic candor. He noticed park rangers had become more and more cynical when speaking about Uncle Sam and the peripheral governmental agencies. Bitter sentiments aside, Aiden needed more frank words.

"Do you think you've done enough?"

"Sure, we've done what we can."

The ranger's eyes, sparkling blue, told another story, one in which he feared his days at the park would soon expire. Not for speaking bluntly to a reporter, but because there might be no park in which to work. Aiden massaged his knuckles. "What responses have you received?"

"Nothing substantial thus far. Just a lot of promises. Political posturing." He stared directly into Aiden's eyes. "Go ahead and quote me on that too."

Aiden repositioned himself. "There're no politicians taking up the park's plight?"

"Not really. Those on Capitol Hill are too far from the action to care. The premier of British Columbia and the Montana governor seem to have shrugged off the issue." He peered toward the ceiling and rubbed his scalp. "There is one state senator in Helena who started to take on the strip miners as a kind of pet project, but I haven't heard from her since last spring. We've appreciated her work prior to that. She probably burned out. She was fighting a bigger machine than the state of Montana. Hold on a minute." Ellis shouted for his colleague and asked if he could remember the senator's name who worked to end the strip mining.

"Gloria Klamsa," Brad from out front replied.

"That's right. Gloria Klamsa. She's in the state legislature."

Aiden recalled coming across the name during his research. He was unsure how involved Senator Klamsa was or had been. He made a mental note to interview her next. "Can you tell me what's being done on the Canadian side of the border?"

"Same rigmarole. Lots of talking, little action."

"As the park's education officer, what do you tell visitors so that they might help?"

"We tell them the environmental facts. It's in our pamphlets and brochures. All about wildlife preservation and ecology. Nothing too controversial. We don't want to play alarmists and bum out their trips. For some, coming to Glacier Park is a lifetime dream fulfilled."

Aiden swallowed, tightening the fist in his lap. Venturing to Glacier National Park had been a lifetime dream for him as well. He left Maryland and Illinois behind, and found something special living with Daniel in the shadow of Montana's mountain ranges. He hated that they might become endangered.

"Has there been a large outcry from environmental groups?" he asked.

Ellis shrugged. "Some fringe radical groups make themselves seen and heard on college campuses or in Helena now and then, but they've been fairly quiet on this issue."

"What about Canada?"

"Environmental groups in Canada are less organized than in the United States. They don't have the same power in the courts as they do here. But like I said, the American groups haven't voiced much opposition either. At least not yet."

"Do you have any ideas why that might be?"

He sighed and leaned back in his chair with the screech of fake leather. He carried on his back a job that often came with more burden than any other department: the need to educate the public without coming across as a pessimist. "I wish I could tell you more. I guess bigger environmental activists are focused on global warming or climate change, or whatever they're calling it today. The stuff that gets big press. Ironically, compared with the strip mining, the melting glaciers are hardly a problem, especially if the worldwide climate shifts to colder as some scientists are predicting."

"I'd like to quote you on that, if you don't mind."

"Sure. I've been in the park department for twelve years. There's a hiring freeze so I don't think I'll be going anywhere unless the park goes first."

Drama upon drama. Controversy layered upon controversy, like the sedimentary rocks that had shaped the mountains of Glacier Park, much of which contained the bituminous coal sought by large corporate miners. Seemed everywhere one looked, contention was ready to jump out, even inside a pristine national park.

They talked at length about the science behind strip mining, which the rangers had referred to by the more scientific term, mountaintop mining, and Aiden listened to Ranger Ellis complain about government bureaucracy, an aspect of the job Ellis had never envisioned when he dreamed of being a park ranger as a boy. A half hour later, Aiden stood and left a business card with Ranger Ellis.

"Thanks for all your input," he said.

"My pleasure," Ellis said, pumping Aiden's hand. "Hope you get a big reaction with your story."

Back at his truck, Aiden took out his laptop and typed eight quick pages of notes from their interview while still clear in his head. After rereading the rough draft, he realized he needed to do much more preliminary interviewing. The Montana senator, Gloria Klamsa, might provide him with an entirely new angle. He considered a trip across the border to speak with the company officials. He found their address on the Internet, and they seemed to have offices all over the world, with headquarters in Alberta.

His cell phone dinged with an incoming text message. Conrad. Ready for pick up.

Aiden quickly packed his laptop and headed out of the park for the Valley. Twenty-five minutes later, he found Conrad waiting for him on a bench outside the clinic.

"I hope you weren't waiting too long," he said after Conrad climbed in.

"I told you I wouldn't mind waiting. Did you go to Glacier Park?"

"I spoke with the education officer there." Aiden studied Conrad for sign of change. "What was it like?"

"No big deal." Conrad shrugged. "I laid on a table and it was over before I knew it. Here." Conrad handed Aiden a bundle of pamphlets and brochures. Aiden eyed them before laying them aside and noticed the National Cancer Institute logo in the corners.

Feigning a smile, he remembered promising to show Conrad gyms, but figured he'd be in no mood to work out after his first bout of radiation. Besides, with the excitement of leaving for his first treatment, neither had remembered to pack a bag. Instead, he pulled onto Route 2 and, without knowing what else to say, headed back into the hills.

Chapter TEN

DANIEL spent the afternoon working on the console for the lodge in Columbia Falls. He expected to complete it in two weeks, ready for delivery by the local freight company. Earlier, Aiden texted him that Conrad underwent his first radiation treatment. Daniel imagined what it must have been like for them both.

Focusing on his console, he used the only plastic parts he allowed for his work. The lodge intended the console for storing plates and silverware, and Daniel had to construct the drawers with added reinforcement. That meant he needed artificial inlays in the drawer cavities. Although he hated what he called "falsh shticks," plywood would have proved too weak. He cut the rectangles using a special blade and ensured they fit before adhering them with carpenter's glue.

Next, he set the drawers aside to dry and calculated in his head the dimensions needed for the four legs. With a handsaw he cut the first plank, lined it up to the next, and repeated the steps two more times. He set them on the back table to cure and with nothing to do until the wood set he figured it was time to head home.

He closed the shop shortly after Phedra left and hesitantly climbed into his Suburban. Conrad would be at his home. And he'd be there for many evenings to come. Daniel barely noticed the tree branches hanging over the canyon-like road as he wound toward the house.

Ranger greeted him with his tail wagging and tongue lapping when he stepped inside. Smells from the kitchen warmed his heart. Yet, there sitting in his favorite easy chair and holding a beverage, was Conrad, smiling at him.

"Hi there."

He didn't look any frailer than when he'd last seen him. Nonetheless Daniel refrained from asking about his treatment, which he suspected was painful. "Hello," he said. "How are you?"

"Not bad considering everything. How's things at the shop?"

"*Goot.*" Why he had reverted to the Pennsylvania German for "good" to a man who wouldn't know German from Latin, Daniel didn't know. He patted Ranger's head and tossed a toy for him. Ranger raced down the hallway after it. Aiden came from the kitchen and kissed Daniel's cheek.

Daniel flinched, embarrassed to show affection in front of Conrad. He tried to smile off his discomfort. "You have a good day?"

"I went to Glacier Park for my interview while Conrad was at the clinic."

"And how did that go?" Daniel pulled off his boots and lined them by the door.

"Went better than expected. I learned a lot. There's a senator from Helena who might be useful. I'm going to call and see if I can interview her. I'll need more facts and quotes before I have anything publishable."

"Sounds like another good article."

Daniel headed for the bedroom. He undressed and, almost trancelike, stepped into the shower. He stayed under the hot rush of water longer than usual. He was used to quick showers powered by wind energy. Lathering himself with coconut-scented soap, he wished he had invited Nick for supper again. Was it too late? Would Aiden think he was purposefully creating another buffer between them and Conrad? Besides, Nick Pfeifer had his own life to live, Daniel speculated, although since Nick lived alone, he had no idea what kind of life that might be.

He stepped out of the shower, defogged the mirror with his fist, and scraped a blade over the five o'clock shadow budding above his upper lip, cringing at his reflection. He never did like ostentatious vanity. Yet as more of the fog cleared, he examined himself with attention. At twenty-nine, he appeared youthful despite the age lines forming around his eyes from working the oat field under the hot sun since he was a boy. While toweling off and dressing, he admitted with a flush that he had a strong, rugged look.

He dreaded heading out into the great room, where supper awaited along with their guest. He supposed Conrad wasn't too bad. He was a sick man and needed assistance. Or at least tender care. Everyone deserved that, didn't they? Aiden sure did seem to already lavish him with attention.

When he reentered the great room, dressed and refreshed from his shower, Aiden smiled at him from the kitchen. He was stirring a pot of something that smelled like venison stew. Aiden must have decided to defrost the elk meat that Nick had given them last autumn after his hunting trip to the Cabinet Mountains.

"Thought you fell through a black hole," Aiden said.

"What is that?" Daniel asked.

Aiden snickered. "It's something in outer space."

Conrad and Aiden laughed, and Daniel felt like a fool. He rarely got the strange references Aiden made about the modern world. He grew up with no television and had not experienced the world like Aiden and Conrad. But he figured in some strange way he encountered more.

His nose was correct, and despite his upset, he enjoyed the venison stew. While they ate, Aiden detailed his trip into Glacier Park, emphasizing the scenery and snow amounts more than what he had learned about strip mining. They finished supper and Aiden worked on his article at the computer console and Daniel sorted their taxes at the dining table. Conrad read Daniel's favorite book in his favorite easy chair.

The quiet somberness suffocated Daniel. He never did well with company. Not even when Aiden stayed with his family back in Henry before he understood his true longings for him.

Of course his feelings for Conrad had nothing to do with masked love and desire.

Insisting he needed rest, Daniel excused himself before the little hand on the mantel clock reached nine. He was in bed, sitting up against the headboard reading a carpentry magazine, when Aiden stepped into the bedroom about an hour later and shut the door. He brushed his teeth and slid under the covers.

"Did you remember to write Elisabeth back?"

"Yes and I had Phedra mail the letter during lunch." Aiden gave his typical nod and Daniel added, now that they were alone, "Has he given you any money for room and board?"

"I haven't asked. I'd feel awkward."

"Has he offered to pay gas for running him to and from the Valley?"

"Daniel, it's for his cancer treatments."

Daniel sighed. "And how did things go today with our guest at the clinic?"

"Brace yourself." Aiden reached into the drawer beside him and splayed a handful of pamphlets across the covers. "I read through most of them. You should too."

Daniel let his magazine fall facedown onto his chest and he reached for one of the glossy pamphlets. He turned it over in his hands, glanced over the writing and the corny photographs, and unfolded it.

"It's about caring for cancer patients and precautions to take," Aiden said.

"Precautions?"

"The medication Conrad is taking is toxic to people who don't have cancer." Aiden nodded toward the pamphlet in Daniel's shaky hands. "Read on. We'll need to buy some of what they call nitrile gloves for when we clean his bathroom or have to help him when he's sick."

Daniel gazed at the ceiling. "I'm familiar with those gloves. We sometimes used them when we were helping little Leah during the worst of her illness." Was he prepared to go through that again? With someone he didn't know? Or really care for? And without the aid of an entire community that often rallied to support one of their own? Tending to Conrad might be a task too big, even for someone used to death.

"At least he doesn't have AIDS," Daniel mumbled, peering at the pack of pamphlets.

Luckily, Aiden ignored his insensitive comment. Daniel reached for another brochure and breezed through it. This one was specific to non-Hodgkin lymphoma. The most alarming information was that the cancer drug Aiden said Conrad was taking could compromise a healthy person's immune system.

"They make the treatments sound more dangerous to those who are around the patient than the cancer is to the patient himself," he said to Aiden.

"You know how people are. Always trumpeting doom and gloom. I think they make it sound worse than it really is. We just have to be cautious, but not freak out if we get too close to his, well, bodily fluids." Daniel tensed, and Aiden continued. "I'll buy supplies tomorrow. I looked up nitrile gloves on the Internet and they are easily available at drugstores. Apparently there is an entire caregiver community out there. A multibillion-dollar-a-year industry."

Daniel thought again about suppressed immune systems and radiation treatments. "When should we expect him to suffer more from the side effects?"

"From what I read in the brochures it takes a few treatments before anything kicks in," he said. "Differs from person to person. Apparently the chemo meds aren't as bad as the radiation."

"Are you prepared for this?"

"I think it'll be okay. We can handle it. He needs us, Daniel."

Aiden hunkered down closer to him, spilling some of the slick pamphlets onto the floor, and drew off the covers. Daniel tried to conceal his partial arousal visible through his pajama bottoms.

"Aiden, he'll hear."

"I've thought about you all day long, wanting you."

Daniel gripped the bedcovers. "I feel like a *dummkop*."

"Why would you feel stupid? Conrad doesn't expect us to be celibate during his stay." In German, Aiden teased him in his typical manner, "*Ich will Sei*."

More worried now, Daniel whispered, "Did you speak of this with Conrad?"

"Of course not, Daniel. Why would I do that? Relax, okay. I won't take no for an answer."

He brushed aside Daniel's carpentry magazine and the lingering pamphlets, turned down the covers, and climbed on top. Already naked, he wrapped his arms around Daniel, and Daniel, giving in to his affections, embraced him tighter again his chest.

They made love, and the kisses and caresses dispelled Daniel's worries that they were ill prepared to cope with Conrad's cancer. The brochures Aiden sprung on him frightened Daniel more than enlightened him. But in the midst of lovemaking, life reared up pleasing and powerful.

After they finished, Aiden rolled over to his side of the bed and his breathing slowed. Daniel reached for a few of the pamphlets on the floor and read them in the moonlight that cut through the Venetian blinds. The pamphlets quickly took him from the physical pleasure of Aiden's body and back to the ugliness of death and disease.

CONRAD failed to show for breakfast the next morning. Worried his first radiation treatment might have made him sick, Aiden left Daniel at the table and checked on him. Conrad lay in bed, gazing at his laptop.

"Are you okay?" Aiden looked about the room. Conrad's belongings were scattered everywhere. Luggage sat partially unpacked. He noticed a drawer half open and overflowing with socks and underwear. Already the room smelled different. Like Conrad.

"One of those mornings," Conrad said with a tremulous smile. He set his laptop aside and clutched his stomach. "I guess I'm a bit nauseated."

"You want anything?" Aiden said. "Coffee, tea? Your favorite strawberry Pop-Tarts?"

"I'm good right now, thanks. Go ahead and act as if I'm not here." He winced. "Remember, I don't want to be a nuisance."

From what the brochures explained, side effects shouldn't show for a few days. But Conrad had been on Leukeran for at least a month.

"Don't be silly," Aiden said, eyeing Conrad. "That's why you're here, for days like this. You sure you don't want anything?"

"No, please, I'll be okay. Come back later, okay? In about an hour, I should be better."

"Try to get some rest. Let me know if you need anything."

Aiden returned to the breakfast table, which seemed achingly lonely even with Daniel seated next to him. Aiden recounted Conrad's condition to him. The uncertainty in Daniel's dark eyes made Aiden nervous.

Daniel wiped his mouth and stood. "I best get to the shop."

Aiden and Ranger saw Daniel to the door and they kissed him good-bye. Once again, Daniel left earlier than usual, and Aiden wondered if he wanted to escape the helplessness and despair of Conrad's illness. He said something about larger orders, but Daniel had larger orders for most of the year.

Ranger whined at the kitchen door. Aiden let him outside to do his business. With Ranger running in the backyard, Aiden cleaned the breakfast dishes. Then he remembered Conrad requested he look in on him. He prepared a tea service, along with an untoasted strawberry Pop-Tart. As he carried the tray to him, Conrad called out in a weak voice. Aiden hustled along, trying not to spill the tea. Conrad was sitting up and smiling.

"I was on my way in." Aiden set the tea service on the night table and poured him a cup.

Conrad sipped the tea. "This is good. Thanks."

Looking at him, Aiden wanted to stroke his perspiring forehead. He was happy to remind himself that he must avoid his bodily fluids. But surely cancer patients needed physical soothing more than anyone.

Being with Conrad at that moment reminded him of when Daniel's oldest sister Elisabeth nursed Aiden in bed after his sudden bout with the flu, during the time he and Daniel made their last trip to Illinois for Mark's Christmas wedding. She gave him tea also—the same kind, in fact. Chamomile with ginger. And with a damp cloth soothed his warm forehead and cheeks. It was during their talk that Aiden realized she must have known about her eldest brother's sexuality and that he and Aiden were more than friends.

She was the only one of Daniel's family members who kept in touch with Daniel, but she never admitted she understood about their relationship. Even to the more modernized Amish, discussing sex did not come easy, unless they were talking about their farm animals. Daniel would not have liked an open discussion of his personal life regardless.

Aiden sat on the bed next to Conrad and tried to mimic Elisabeth's salubrious gestures from that time. He wanted Conrad to feel secure and not embarrassed for his being ill. Conrad grinned, sat up higher.

"You've already been amazing to me," he said.

Aiden's cheeks warmed. "I haven't really done anything. You just got here. Now eat your Pop-Tart."

Conrad took two small bites, his grin unabated. "The fact that you let me stay here is enough. I'm indebted to you." He chewed and swallowed. "I only hope this'll be the worst of it."

"I've cared for you when you got sick before."

Conrad laughed, and covered his mouth with his fist to prevent food from falling out. "This isn't like those crazy college days after a night of binge drinking."

Aiden's face tightened as he tried to keep from laughing. He reflected over their short relationship together. His time with Conrad had been some of the most fun-filled he'd experienced, before turning into the worst.

"Do you remember how we used to spend mornings like this when we didn't have classes?" Conrad said. "Sitting in bed, watching TV, reading to each other from those lousy college textbooks, and well… other things?"

Aiden understood what Conrad meant by "other things." Those were some of the good memories. Many more were unpleasant. Cleaning up after Conrad's hangovers was hardly that bad in comparison.

Conrad lowered his eyes. "I really did blow it with you, didn't I?"

Was this Conrad's final confession? Aiden did not wish to discuss the past. He averted his eyes from Conrad and studied the shine to his tea. "I guess we both made mistakes. We were younger." Aiden refreshed his tea, nearly topping the mug to overflowing. Conrad, careful not to spill any, slurped the excess.

"We started to talk about what happened when we went hiking by that lake," Conrad said once he brought the cup to his lap. "Let's finish. We both know it's been a time bomb between us."

Aiden wished he hadn't brought up the past again. If only the walls might absorb the reality of their past—and present. He wanted to leave but gripped his hands on his thighs and willed himself to remain seated.

"I haven't met anyone like you before or since," Conrad went on. "That's why I thought of calling you to help me when I needed it. Of all the people on earth, even after everything I did to you, I knew I could count on you."

Aiden massaged the rough fabric of his jeans. "I'm glad you did," he said, his voice sounding faraway to him. Finally he slapped his leg and stood. "I was thinking of showing you some more of the sights, unless you don't think you'll be up for it?"

Conrad's blue eyes brightened. "I will be. I'm sure. I feel much better already."

"Finish your tea and if you're in the mood, we'll go do something."

He left Conrad alone and wandered into the kitchen. He poured a cup of tea for himself, and felt a combination of elation and dread.

Aiden made use of the morning by spreading out his work on the Glacier article at the dining table. With a tepid mug of tea by his laptop, he telephoned Senator Gloria Klamsa. He was shocked to hear the senator answer the phone.

She expressed enthusiasm for Aiden's research and provided him with more information on the strip mining than he found on the Internet or that Ranger Ellis offered. She ended each of her statements with "but we still have to learn more." Political legalese, Aiden assumed.

He clicked off and, for the moment, felt contented, perhaps even useful, fulfilling two important roles at the same time: one, caring for a fellow human being in need, and two, revealing the strip-mining operation that might injure one of the world's most majestic national parks.

He heard Conrad close the door to the hallway bathroom followed by the sigh of the pipes. Aiden cleared his work from the table. He would have to find a way to entertain him. And then after that, each of the days he stayed with them.

Hair damp and glistening, Conrad wandered into the living area where Aiden sat petting Ranger.

Conrad smiled at him. "You ready to get out of here?" Aiden itched to focus more on his article, especially now that he had additional notes from Senator Klamsa's interview, but he had promised Conrad adventure. Conrad, in this case, came first.

Chapter ELEVEN

IN THAT first week, Conrad became a fixture in Aiden and Daniel's home. The time living with him transpired like an awkward storm cloud pushing over the mountains. An additional gnawing expectation materialized.

Dimness replaced the sharp flashes in Daniel's ebony eyes, but what alarmed Aiden most was Daniel's avoiding Conrad. Each morning he insisted on leaving early for his shop and returning home close to seven, saying he needed to finish backlogged projects. Aiden understood Daniel wanted to divorce himself from the drama played out at their nascent home. Aiden discovered that whenever Daniel had little control over a situation, he'd rather disappear than feel the emasculating effects of helplessness.

Again on Sunday, Daniel worked several hours in his garage workshop. Aiden explained to Conrad that spring was Daniel's busiest season. Despite Daniel's apathy, Aiden concentrated on Conrad's wants and needs. With no television, Conrad spent much of his time watching shared files or movies on his laptop, usually while in the living area, under Aiden's nose. They spent little time apart.

On Monday Aiden carted him to the cancer clinic for a third time. Aiden never knew which days Conrad was to undergo radiation until the night before and one time the morning of.

Like the first two times, Conrad insisted Aiden drop him off. Aiden understood his need for privacy. He spent an hour at the public library working on his article until Conrad texted him. As usual, Conrad was waiting for him outside on the bench.

At home Conrad complained of backaches and stomach cramps, but he was able to sit on the easy chair and waste time on his laptop. Aiden was glad he had his article to keep him busy while Conrad sighed and shifted on Daniel's favorite chair. Conrad found a good friend in Ranger. Later in the afternoon, they played outdoors for a half hour and when they came in, Conrad gave Ranger a treat from his special cupboard.

Conrad appeared healthier Wednesday night when Nick showed for dinner. That time it was Aiden who invited their good neighbor.

Nick, a welcome distraction for them, brought cheer to a growing gloominess in the quiet home. Perhaps he charmed Conrad more. After they ate, Nick and Conrad convened on the sofa with their shoulders near touching and talked about Michigan and life in the nation's capital.

Nick's lazy Oklahoma accent deepened the more he chatted with Conrad. Cleaning the dinner dishes, Aiden and Daniel glanced at each other and shrugged.

"I've got great news," Nick said once Aiden and Daniel joined them in the living space. "My wonderful friend from Albany Ridge is finally coming for a visit. He'll be here next week. He has business in the Flathead Valley. It's been a long time since I've seen him."

"Why don't you both come over for dinner while he's here," Aiden said. "Anytime is good."

"Sounds like an excellent plan. I'll make sure of letting Farzad know. I'm sure he'd enjoy meeting you. He'll be staying at a hotel in town. Refused my offer to put him up, although I have more than ample room." Nick looked past them and out the darkened dining window toward where his lonely ranch sat hidden behind the line of trees straddling the road. "Said he wanted to be closer to his work. He was always a private man."

That makes two of you, Aiden wanted to say. Instead, he offered Nick more coffee. They spoke the rest of the night about the coming spring, Daniel's orders for furniture, a little about Aiden's article on strip mining. Unlike last time, they avoided talk of Conrad's illness.

Conrad was the first to see Nick to the door when he announced he needed to leave. Nick patted Conrad's shoulder. "You take care of yourself, young man. See you soon."

"Bye, Nick." Conrad waved after him.

Later that night in bed, Aiden said, "I'm glad Conrad and Nick are becoming good friends. For both of them."

"Maybe you can see if Nick wants to spend more time with Conrad."

Aiden gaped at Daniel. "But you said no playing matchmaker."

"Matchmaker?" Daniel snickered. "I'm thinking more of filling Conrad's free time. From what I've seen he has plenty of it. Too much. Besides, I have doubts of your assumption Nick Pfeifer is like us."

"But Nick knows we're gay," Aiden ventured to say. "And clearly he doesn't mind. None of the other neighbors have talked with us much here. Surely they know we're a couple."

Daniel squirmed under the bedcovers. "Even Nick says that they don't talk to him much."

"See, that's what I mean. We're all the same to them. Nick's probably gay."

Daniel furrowed his forehead. "Then why wouldn't he tell us?"

"He's private, like you said. We never told him about us in so many words, have we?"

"People here are more reclusive. That's why they move here. It was that way when we lived closer to the Swan Range. But none of that matters." Daniel made a sweeping motion with his right hand. "I still can't imagine spending my time doing nothing. If we are to care for Conrad, then we should encourage him to spend time outside of the home with others. And Nick must want more company. He can't always come over here. He's lonely."

The word "lonely" flopped from Daniel's mouth like an egg falling from slippery fingers. Blatant truths were often so real there could be no shying away from them. Daniel, like Aiden, did not like to equivocate. He might avoid a subject but once he fixated on one, he did not fabricate nonsense. He was raised in a culture where such thinking was considered phony. Nick was one of the loneliest men Aiden ever came across, and he accepted there was no point in whitewashing Daniel's insight.

The old glint returned to Daniel's eyes, and Aiden knew exactly what he was thinking. There were many topics uncomfortable for Daniel to broach, even in front of Aiden, but his eyes, like deep ponds, never lied. Wouldn't Daniel, growing up gay on an Amish farm, know more about loneliness than any of them?

"Sometimes loneliness makes us seek more of it," Daniel said, his coffee-colored eyes wide, "as if we're ashamed what others will think if they learned the truth."

Aiden laid his head on Daniel's broad shoulder. "Nick doesn't strike me as someone who worries much about what others think about him. That's what's so baffling. He should be surrounded by friends. He's so outgoing, but he hides so much too. I'm glad his friend from school will be visiting."

"Nick has many secrets," Daniel surprised Aiden by admitting. "The Amish aren't the only people who feel uncomfortable talking about their private lives."

Aiden shifted his eyes to get a good look at Daniel. He noted his reddening cheeks above his beard. "Maybe in the mountains," Aiden said, "in places like Montana, people are more at peace with who they are with no need for shouting to the world. Maybe that's why they seem so secretive."

Daniel's cheeks darkened further. "I figure that might be true. Meanwhile, best get some sleep." He reached up and switched off the light. "Our days have gotten longer with Conrad here, don't you think? Much longer than what the spring alone has brought."

IN THE middle of the night, Daniel awoke to a strange stirring down the hall. He sat up and turned on the table lamp. Aiden was not in bed. He checked for a light under the bathroom door. Empty. The alarm clock read half past two. Soon after, Aiden, his face drawn and sleepy, slumped into the room. He mumbled for Daniel to switch off the light and hunkered under the covers without any more words.

Daniel ogled his dark form, waiting for him to explain.

"He's sick," Aiden said to the murkiness with a grainy voice. "I probably shouldn't have allowed him to stay up so late with Nick."

Daniel stared at him. "Did he throw up?"

He sensed Aiden nodding. "The worst of it was over before I got there. He's sleeping now. He looked so healthy and full of energy before bed. I guess that's how lymphoma treatments work. One minute you're fine, the next…."

"We don't need to take him to the hospital?"

"Of course not."

"Did you wear the gloves?"

"I took all the precautions."

"Maybe we can hire an at-home nurse. Even the Amish sometimes use them when absolutely necessary."

"There's no need for that. I'll care for him."

"I worry about you." Daniel's voice fell to a raspy tone. "I don't want you to get sick too. You read the brochures. If you expose yourself to cancer drugs and radiation, you can increase your resistance to any cancer drug if you… if you were to ever get cancer in the future."

"People treat cancer patients every day, they don't all fall ill," Aiden murmured into his pillow. "You don't have to worry. But I can't help but think, Daniel, what if… in the worst-case scenario… what if he dies here. What if we're his hospice care and the last people he'll interact with?"

"Maybe we should speak to his doctors. I feel we should know more."

The sheets rustled, and Aiden cuddled closer. "What else is there to know? He's here, and we have to help him."

"And for how long will that be?"

Aiden breathed. "I have no clue."

Daniel felt Aiden lift his head, and in the murky shadows, he could see his molten amber eyes. "I don't like that he's sick or watching him growing weaker, Daniel." His head fell warm against Daniel's chest and his breath tickled Daniel's flesh. "But he does need us, both of us."

Aiden fell quiet, and Daniel stroked Aiden's back while his words vibrated deep inside his gut. "Figure he's the type that might need someone to help him even if he didn't have a life-threatening illness," Daniel whispered toward the ceiling, hoping perhaps someone more potent than the both of them heard his sober words.

Chapter TWELVE

TWO mornings later, Daniel, to Aiden's dismay, again finished breakfast ahead of Conrad's slumping to the table. He kissed the top of Aiden's head, but Aiden stopped him before leaving. "I need to ask you something," he said.

"You want me to pick up more of Ranger's food?"

Fearful that what he was about to request might cause Daniel to buck and fight, he inhaled and spoke straight through. "I need to do important research for my article today. It'll require that I travel. I feel badly about leaving Conrad alone. Can he please spend time with you at the shop today?"

"You can leave him by himself a few hours." Daniel turned for the front door. "He's not a baby."

"But, Daniel, I'll be gone most of the day."

"Take him with you."

"I'm going into Canada. I have a deadline coming up and I can't put off this research any longer."

"What about Nick?" Daniel said. "Didn't we sit up two nights ago wanting him to spend more time with Conrad?"

"Do you think he'll mind?"

"He seems smitten with him. Go ahead and call."

Rehearsing in his head how to ask him to babysit with Conrad, Aiden speed dialed Nick's cell phone while Daniel waited. He might suggest Nick show Conrad around his ranch and teach him the art of horse breeding. But the phone went straight to voice mail. Aiden did not bother to leave a message.

Turning to Daniel, he said, "He must be at some horse auction out of range." He gave Daniel a pleading look. "Please, Daniel. Just for one day."

Daniel sighed. "If you feel that it's necessary. I'll find a way to keep your patient busy. But I still say he can stay in the house alone and find something useful to do."

Aiden kissed Daniel on the lips and his beard tickled his chin. "Thanks, Daniel. Don't worry about waiting for him to wake up. I'll drop him off on my way."

After Daniel's truck disappeared down the road, Aiden tiptoed down the hall and pressed his ear against the door to Conrad's bedroom. He heard stirring. Aiden retreated into the kitchen and prepared him something to eat. Conrad appeared alert and healthy when he came to the breakfast table.

"Good morning, Conrad."

Conrad sipped his steaming tea Aiden placed before him. "Good morning. That's what I needed, a good, long sleep."

While Conrad ate a Pop-Tart and microwaved french toast and sausage, Aiden brought up the subject of Conrad spending the day with Daniel at the shop. "I feel bad leaving you alone today while I'm working," he said, sitting across from him. "Since you're feeling better, why not spend the day with Daniel? You won't mind, would you? Daniel said he'd love to show you how he works. You've asked about it enough times."

Conrad focused on his empty plate coated with syrup. "If you want me to. But I'd rather stay here."

"I'd feel better knowing you were being looked after. Isn't that why you're here? I help Daniel at the shop a lot. You'll like it. It'll give you something to do."

"Why don't I come with you?"

Aiden feared he'd suggest that. He wanted to work alone, without worrying about Conrad for a while. He wasn't seeking to shuck Conrad off on Daniel. He merely needed to focus on his work without interruptions. He was going into a foreign country, and Conrad would be too much of a hassle.

Aiden had a prepared reply ready. "I don't think that's a good idea. I'm going to be gone most the day, driving over a hundred miles round-trip on choppy roads. You won't like it at all."

Conrad shrugged and gazed out the window. "Whatever is easiest for you. I don't want to be an inconvenience."

Aiden forced a smile and gulped his orange juice. "I'm thinking about what's best for you."

They cleaned the breakfast dishes in silence, and Conrad took his time getting ready to leave. During the short drive to the Rose Crossing village center, Conrad appeared solemn.

He stayed at Daniel's shop long enough to say hello to Phedra. She seemed delighted with seeing Conrad again after their brief meeting at Beadsman's Deli. Daniel looked overburdened by Conrad's presence. Aiden could do little about that. It was Daniel's turn to mind Conrad awhile. Aiden needed to clear his head for what might be the most important fact-finding expedition of his entire career.

Forcing his mind away from Conrad and Daniel, he hopped in his truck and headed toward the border. He was forced to take roundabout US 2 to 89 since the Going-to-the-Sun shortcut through Glacier Park was still closed by heavy snows. He meandered along the hill country on the eastern edge of the park, and headed north into the Blackfeet Tribe. He stopped about ten miles before the border to fill his tank to avoid Canada's exorbitant fuel costs and the pain of trying to convert liters into gallons.

Crossing into Canada was no easy matter. He had to pull off at the shared border station, like truckers at weigh stations. There were no ostentatious US flags welcoming drivers traveling from the north. A lone maple leaf fluttered in the wind on the Canadian side.

Tourist season was a few months away, and Aiden was the sole driver crossing northbound that morning. On the other side, he noted the American agents, who carried weapons, unlike their Canadian counterparts, showcasing more alertness. The US border agent interviewed a pair with Saskatchewan license plates. Behind them a line of five cars formed, all but one with Canadian tags.

The Canadian border official approached and motioned for Aiden to lower the window. She was emotionless, exhibiting the typical government agent expression—impassive, narrow-eyed—and robotic in her movements.

She asked him a slew of questions with a monotone voice. Aiden told her he was doing work for half a day and then would return to Montana before sunset. It was clear English was not her first language, and she seemed more ill-tempered with Aiden for his American accent than he should be for hers. Both asked each other to repeat themselves after each utterance. She went on to ask a series of questions: did he possess guns, ammunition, pepper spray.

The Canadian guard, who appeared Punjabi, maintained a lazy sneer, which Aiden associated with boredom and discontent. She checked his identification, vehicle registration, passport, back license plate, and returned his government documents. With a quick nod of her head, he drove across the imaginary line separating two nations.

He headed north through Alberta, chasing flat clover fields that kept the cold earth warm until the late spring planting season. Signs turned from mileage to the metric system and warned of random road stops. A fresh dusting of snow coated the hard dirt side roads that lead to unseen farmhouses. The even plateau settled around him, and to his distant left, where lay the two national parks shared by the United States and Canada, he watched the big sky expand and throb with northern intensity. A dark mass spanned the distant horizon, but could hardly be distinguished for the Rocky Mountains.

Tar seals crisscrossed the winter-battered road and jerked Aiden's pickup truck with rhythmic bounces. Dwarf alders and shrubs filled his vision. The high road, near parallel with the remote mountain peaks, carried him farther into the northlands, and soon lulling hills rolled him forward.

He relied on his Magellan GPS system to guide him to the strip-mining company's regional headquarters, about an hour north of the border. Traffic on the Canadian side was light. There were few establishments to stop and ask for directions should he get lost. Before long he turned into a long narrow gravel road and came to a locked gate with a prominent sign which read: "Private Property: NO TRESPASSING."

Aiden parked the pickup next to the gate that surrounded the facility and walked to the small guard station. The guard stepped outside and met him halfway.

"What do you need?" he said in a thick western Canadian accent.

"I spoke with someone about an interview a few days ago," Aiden said. "I was hoping to speak with the president of the company, Mr. McGregor."

The guard looked skeptical. He was tall with big round dark eyes like an owl's. "I don't have any information about any visitors today."

"Is there any way I can talk to Mr. McGregor or someone else inside? Just to see if they'll let me in?"

Shaking his head, the guard said, "Don't think so." He glanced over Aiden's shoulder to his GMC truck with the Montana tags. "What do you want here?"

"I work for a group of investors who are interested in strip mining," he lied. "They send me out to interview people to access if they're good bets. I'm sure I spoke with someone here the other day and they agreed to an appointment."

The man regarded Aiden a moment. "Wait right here." He left Aiden standing in the middle of the gravel road. The two-story facility, made from the local sandstone, partially obscured by surrounding conifers, looked like any other industrial building. Aiden peered around. The landscape stretched forever. The Rocky Mountains were farther west, out of sight.

He took out his digital camera and snapped a few pictures before the guard rushed to him.

"Hey, you can't take photos. Stop that or I'll have to confiscate it. You get out of here now. No one recalls talking with any investors."

"Can you speak with me?"

"That's not possible. Now get away from here."

Aiden took one last look at the facility before turning for his truck. At least he was able to get a gander at the place, to absorb what type of company wanted to strip mine for coal that could forever alter the face of Glacier National Park. He knew it was a long shot to speak with anyone. But his day wasn't quite over.

His Magellan led him southwest, toward the national parks. The company was setting up its mining operation along the Flathead River in the MacDonald Mountains.

Within an hour he made his way into British Columbia, crossing the snow-ridden Continental Divide, and, relying on bits of information he found on the Internet, he tried to locate the field office. After several wrong turns and being chased by a nasty hound that bit at his tires, he followed a gravel road down a sharp embankment and was relieved to see more gates and barbwire fencing. The mining site.

Behind the impenetrable fence, large bulldozers and mining equipment sat idle like a dinosaur exhibit. They were still in the preliminary stages. The company might begin work as early as the start of summer.

He stopped before clearing a bend in the driveway, hopped out of the cab of his truck, and snapped a few pictures of the site. Back behind the steering wheel, he hadn't a chance to move forward in his pickup when two men with a fierce dog emerged from nowhere and impeded Aiden's passage. One of the men motioned for Aiden to lower his window while the man holding back the snarling hound waited a few paces behind him.

"This is private property," the robust man with a rough voice said.

Aiden smiled and feigned a helpless look. "I think I might be lost. What's going on here?"

"None of your business."

"I'm kind of curious now that I'm here. Could I speak with someone in charge of operations? Could I speak with you, even?"

"Take off."

"I only want to ask questions, not accuse anyone of anything. Why do you have so much security?"

"We have to keep out people like you. You've got rogue reporter written all over your face."

The second man struggled to hold back what Aiden guessed was a Rottweiler. "Pete, don't talk to the guy. Send him on his way."

The man named Pete turned back to Aiden. His suntanned face softened. "There's nothing for you here. You better take off. You know how to get back to the border from here?"

Aiden persisted. "How long have you worked here, Pete?"

"We been set up for a year, waiting for the go ahead. Now get going."

"Do you like working here, Pete?"

Glancing about with frantic eyes, Pete said, "I had better jobs."

"Pete!" The man with the Rottweiler jockeyed closer. Pete stood in attention and leered at Aiden with squinty blue eyes.

"Look here, you have to take off or we'll call out the municipal boys. They're on our side of the law. Don't you think otherwise."

The Rottweiler seemed eager for action. Aiden grinned. "Thanks, Pete." He handed him a business card. "Please give me a call if you think you'd like to talk. I'm available anytime."

Pete eyeballed the card dangling between Aiden's fingers. The hound reared up as if he wanted to bite a mosquito, and jerked his handler off balance. With his partner's attention momentarily distracted, Pete snatched the card and slipped it in his shirt pocket. "Take off from here!"

Aiden backed out of the driveway, but before heading for the main road for Montana, he meandered his way around the dirt roads that wound higher into the mountains, hoping to get a better view of the mining operation. Most of the ancient logging and mining roads led to dead ends. Weeds and spindly bushes reclaimed the roads that at one time conveyed man and machine. His truck bounced and heaved until he feared he might snap his neck.

He parked near a small northern vista and peered through a thick grove of blue spruce where he spotted an unnatural orange color. Using his binoculars, he realized the orange was part of the plastic dust shield draped over barbwire fencing. Hidden behind had to be the secretive strip-mining site. On the other side, trees had clearly been felled to make way for workers and equipment.

By his estimation, the mining site spanned the size of the average Midwestern farm. He lowered the binoculars and glanced up at the sweeping mountain range that stretched into Glacier National Park, recalling the huge mining equipment he saw where Pete stood guard. An operation so vast and with enough heavy machinery might take down a mountain in a matter of years, like Ranger Craig Ellis warned. He snapped several pictures and climbed inside his truck.

Satisfied he'd seen enough, Aiden found Route 93, on which he headed for the Montana border, where he'd most likely encounter a far worse rigmarole to enter the United States than he faced crossing into Canada.

DANIEL steadied the auger bit over the oak wood and drilled three quick sessions to form a small burrow. Next he placed a wooden divot into the groove and hammered it in. He repeated this step five more times to attach the console's first leg to the table frame before Conrad's wandering distracted him.

"If this is boring you," he said, swinging around the table so that he could focus on the second leg, "I can find something for you to do."

"Sure, I'd like to help out. What else will I do while I'm here?"

Daniel nodded toward the far corner. "There are stacks of plywood that need to be set upright so I can judge their sizes. Do you mind? That is, if you're up for it."

"I'm up for it. No problem."

"Try to group them based on size and width. They aren't too heavy."

"I'm not worried about that. I can handle it."

"There are some canvas gloves on the table over there."

Conrad slipped on the gloves and worked at his task without dropping too many of the boards, allowing Daniel to return to drilling grooves for the dowels. They both worked without speaking until Conrad seemed to grow bored with his task.

"Do you like spending time alone like this each day?" he asked, laying the boards one by one against the wall.

Daniel hammered a dowel in place. "I always prefer to work in solitude."

"The Amish are like that, I guess."

"Like what?"

"They like to be isolated."

"Depends on the Amish."

Conrad snickered. "That's what Aiden said." After Daniel finished drilling three more grooves, Conrad, his breath shortening as he worked, asked, "What's it like to be Amish?"

Daniel lifted the auger bit, blew off the shavings, and wiped his brow with the back of his hand. "It's just an orthodox religious denomination. Nothing special."

"It is different, you have to admit. Must have been tough being gay and raised in such an austere religion."

The door was shut tight and Phedra by the cash register could not hear their conversation, thank goodness; still, Daniel did not wish to get personal with this man. "For sure it was difficult."

"Does your family know?"

"I figure they do by now."

"Aiden said something about you not being able to see them anymore. They call it the shunning, don't they?"

Daniel aimed the auger into the wood and drilled. He almost went through the leg and he quickly switched off the drill. *Des is shlecht*, he cursed himself. Squinting his right eye into the groove, he figured he hadn't wasted good wood. He continued drilling two more grooves and inserted the wooden dowels.

"*Ya*," he said, pausing between hammering, "they call it the shunning. But I've been shunned for leaving the Church, not for anything else."

"I don't talk to my family much either, but for me it's my own decision." Conrad stopped stacking the plywood and glanced out the garage door windows. "They are not the most pleasant people."

"Sometimes it's for the best, one way or the other."

Shrugging, Conrad set back to stacking the boards. "You should write a book."

"And why would I do that?"

"People would be interested in reading what it was like to grow up gay and Amish. Maybe Aiden will write it. He's the writer in the family, right? You can tell him your story."

Daniel had never imagined Aiden using his God-given gifts as a writer to reveal their secrets to the world. He'd have to confront him and make sure that never happened. He pushed the drill harder, wood chips flying off the flute.

"I'd love to read about how you guys met. Aiden hasn't told me much about it."

"It's a long story."

Conrad chuckled. "That's what Aiden says too. Here we are alone all day. I have time. Go ahead. Tell me."

Daniel had no intention of disclosing to Conrad—Aiden's ex-boyfriend—how he and Aiden had battled their emotions to overcome the unbearable desire to be near each other against enormous odds when they first met in Illinois. Even if he had followed through with his second marriage to Tara Hostetler, he would have lugged around his love for Aiden like a sack full of melons until the day of his death. Like their lovemaking, that part of their relationship was for no one else's ears. But he saw no harm in telling Conrad how they met.

He lifted his head from his work and eyed Conrad for the first time since assembling the console. "Aiden had come to Frederick County in Illinois to write about the Amish."

"That's how you met? Really? That's so cute."

Reluctant to reveal too much emotion, Daniel continued. "I suppose I could see his kindness and loving nature, and that's what drew me to him." That and his honey-glazed eyes and raven-black curly hair, he wanted to say. He grinned and studied Conrad. "Aiden saved my family, did you know that?" Proud of what Aiden had done, Daniel chose not to hold back from recounting the events that proved Aiden an exceptional man. "He swerved his car in front of an oncoming pickup that would have crashed into our buggy, filled with my entire family. We might have all been killed."

"I had no idea it was anything that dramatic."

"Aiden is a wonderful man."

"Did you two fool around in the middle of Amish country after that?"

"Fool around? Nothing like that." Daniel turned his back to Conrad and began drilling. His arms moved up and down in fast rhythm that kept his mind focused and away from the ire that threatened to erupt against Conrad. "Is that your business?" he said above the vibration of the drill as it came to a stop.

"I'm only curious. I think it's hot. But you're right, I guess. It's none of my business. No doubt why you guys took to each other, though. You're both hot and down-to-earth."

The word "hot" again. Daniel heard the term often but was unsure if it meant something he wanted to be. "*Dank u*," he said, reverting to Pennsylvania German.

"Did Aiden ever tell you how he and I met?"

Daniel inhaled the smell of heated wood and cautiously glimpsed at Conrad over his shoulder. "I don't think he bothered with details."

Conrad continued to build several disorganized piles. "We met in college. I think he saw me in my ROTC uniform and it was love at first sight. We really hit it off."

Turning back to his work, Daniel felt Conrad shift behind him. The room currents moved to his left, giving Daniel a chill along his spine.

"I guess he told you how we broke up?" Conrad went on, his voice closer.

"Not in so many words, but I pieced together the story from what he's mentioned of the past."

"I'm a different person now," Conrad said with a haughty tone, which caused Daniel to rear up on the drill and nearly break off the bit. "If I knew then what I know now, I'd never have left him. You're a lucky man, Daniel."

The silence Daniel craved suddenly irked him. A vacuum-like stillness sucked out the energy. His limbs grew weak and tired.

In a flash, Daniel envisioned what Aiden might have experienced while living with Conrad in Chicago. He almost wanted to defend him, as if Aiden were forging through the anguish again. Conrad and Aiden had been engaged in Englisher terms. Like Daniel and Tara Hostetler back in Illinois. But Tara Hostetler never moved in with Daniel and Aiden and demanded most of their time.

"I don't believe in luck," Daniel said. "I do feel that, despite everything, God has smiled upon me."

"God?" Conrad made a huffing noise, similar to the sound a bear makes when angered. "No offense, but it's hard for someone like me to believe in a god."

"Shouldn't you believe in Him more so now?"

"Why should I? My life has been horrible. Yes, I take responsibility. But if you'd known my family. I was given nothing. I entered the world on my own. I suppose I'll leave it that way too."

"You don't worry about eternal damnation?"

"Don't tell me you still believe in all that stuff. I mean, okay, I can deal with thinking there's a god. But to think you're here to reserve a spot in a fantasy place called Heaven, especially after how your life is. You're gay and have been shunned. According to most religions, we'll both rot in hell."

Daniel suppressed an anxious grunt. "Because others have kept us from their lives does not mean that God will. He does not shun." Or so Daniel had to believe. Not for his sake alone, but for Aiden's. How could a man—someone willing to sacrifice his life and now give up so much for his former boyfriend—be forsaken by a loving god?

To his surprise, Daniel sounded similar to his old minister and nemesis, his cousin on his mother's side, the Reverend Amos Yoder, yet without Daniel's broadminded undertones. Preaching wasn't Daniel's strongest point. Being a reclusive man, he stewed in his own thoughts and beliefs and likewise allowed others to wallow in theirs.

Thinking of Aiden for inspiration, Daniel realized he must go easy on Conrad. He was a man battling serious illness. He'd seen even the Amish bemoan God for bestowing them with hardship or taking from them someone they loved. His father, who he once overheard confess to Daniel's mother that he'd rather not pray for a few days after the death of Leah, turned his back on God before.

"You really are Amish, aren't you?" Conrad said, his voice back to its somewhat dull tone while he set the last of the boards against the wall. Daniel noticed he'd done a haphazard job and would have to rearrange them.

"I figure I'll always be Amish."

"That why you still keep the beard?"

Instinctively Daniel touched his freshly trimmed beard. "It's part of my identity."

Phedra knocked on the door and popped her head inside. "I'm going to lunch now, okay?" she said in English, most likely for Conrad's sake. She eyed him like she had earlier. Her brown eyes wide and expectant. Conrad grinned at her.

Aiden's ex-boyfriend seemed the type with a big enough ego that he'd enjoy the attentions of any interested suitor, including a Hutterite woman. Daniel conceded he was good looking. Cancer had yet to eat away at his sharp features and thick reddish-blond hair. Phedra, at the age she yearned for courtship, returned his smile. She bowed out of the room after Daniel okayed her leaving for lunch and he returned to fastening the console legs.

"You're lucky, I have to admit," Conrad resumed saying, standing by his side.

Daniel restrained a slight shudder. "So are you, if you think about it."

"How so?"

"You have treatments that likely will save your life, administered by highly trained and caring professionals. And you appear no worse for wear." He adjusted the torque, lowered the auger bit, and burrowed two grooves. "My sister took ill when she was only six," he said after drilling. "I know what illness is like. I lived with it back in Illinois." He peered at Conrad from feet to head. "You can walk, you have the strength to stack piles of wood, and you still have a nice head of hair."

Conrad stroked his hair. "They say it could happen any time. Sometimes it takes weeks, sometimes days. So you like my hair, huh? You hope I don't lose it?"

Daniel eyed him one last time before returning to his drilling. "I've seen worse mops," he mumbled.

Conrad chuckled and he helped Daniel hold the underside of the table while Daniel hammered the dowels in place.

Chapter THIRTEEN

THE first of April marked two weeks Conrad had lived with Aiden and Daniel in Montana. Early that morning, Aiden drove Conrad to his sixth radiation treatment. He was still exhausted from his trip into Canada the day before. Most of his day had been spent on the road, and he did not wish to drive any more than necessary. But Aiden could not ask that Conrad take a bus that would require he walk half a mile to the main road for the line into downtown Kalispell. And he worried the radiation treatment might leave him too rattled and unfocused to drive himself from the clinic.

While in town waiting for Conrad to finish, Aiden shopped at one of his favorite specialty stores to find something for his mother's birthday to send her in Maryland. She was to hit the big sixty. He purchased his items and drove in a daze to meet Conrad at the clinic. He waited in the parking lot and worked on his Glacier project.

With his notes scattered over the front seat, he mulled over his trip to Canada. The strip-mining operation might have practiced clandestine operations because they tired of aimless snooping, or maybe there was a reason people poked around and the company sought to keep their plans from prying eyes. Although Canada was hardly a foreign nation like Afghanistan or even Mexico, it was still a sovereign country with unique laws that would make it difficult for Aiden to compile much information.

He jotted down questions that he might ask experts to elucidate his current findings and worked on his laptop to structure his article, leaving blank spaces where he would later insert information. An old journalist's trick—one he was embarrassed to confess to—that he learned from a journalism professor in college. Facts can come later, she said. The gimmick threatened the unbiased writing, but Aiden trusted that he'd stick to the truth.

He became so engrossed in writing, he nearly banged his head on the ceiling when Conrad knocked on the passenger window and beamed him a smile. He hopped inside and buckled the seatbelt.

"Hi there," he said. "Having fun?"

Aiden cleared aside his work. "That didn't take long," he said, turning the ignition. Each time after Conrad received proton beams, Aiden would check him for signs he looked different. Conrad never did look worse for wear. Often he appeared more refreshed, not lethargic and despondent.

"Only took about a half hour this time," Conrad said. "No one was ahead of me. Here, I got you something." Conrad handed Aiden a candy bar, and Aiden took it with a light chuckle. "I got it from the vending machine."

"Thanks." Aiden pocketed the Snickers and drove out of the parking lot. "I'll save it for dessert."

"Can you can give me a lift to the store before we head home? I need a few things."

"Wish you had told me before," Aiden said. "I was already at the shopping center. I could've picked up whatever you needed." Aiden made a U-turn and headed back toward town. "Feel free to put whatever things you need on our list on the refrigerator for next time," he added.

"I don't want you to pay for it, though."

"How are your funds?"

"I have enough," Conrad said, staring out the window. "For me a few bucks should hold me off a while. Who knows how much I'll need if I only have a few short years left?"

"Conrad, don't talk like that. You can't be so negative."

"Not negative, honest."

"The treatments are helping, right? Have you had any new tests?"

Conrad shrugged. "Tests? Not yet."

Aiden pulled up to the drugstore and sat in the truck while Conrad dashed inside. He texted Daniel at the shop that they were finished with Conrad's treatment, and running some errands. Daniel responded a few minutes later: "OK."

The rest of the morning Aiden worked more on his article at the dining table, trying to ignore Conrad's moping about the house. He encouraged him to play with Ranger outside. With the house silent, Aiden took a break from work and enjoyed one of his quiet meditations, gazing at the view outside the dining window and nursing a mug of lukewarm coffee. A short time later, Conrad and Ranger rushed inside and Conrad began rummaging in the kitchen. "Is there anything to eat?" he sang out over his shoulder.

Aiden brought his feet to the floor and sat straighter. "Leftover stew."

"Tired of stew. You have any more salsa and chips?"

"There's some in the cupboard right next to you."

Conrad poured chips and salsa into bowls and carried a tray to the living area. Ranger followed on his heels. Ranger's warming up to Conrad had at first pleased Aiden, but as he went about returning to working on the draft to his article, a sense of burden and lonesomeness grabbed his shoulders.

Conrad's grumbling wasn't helping. "What's up for the rest of the day?" he said with a full mouth.

"Shouldn't you be taking it easy so soon after your treatment?"

"All that zapping has me itchy and antsy. I don't feel like lying around."

"You have to take care of yourself," Aiden told him. "I know how difficult it's been for you, but you have no choice." Aiden noticed him feeding Ranger chips. "Please, Conrad. You can't give dogs food like that. Ranger has a sensitive belly and we never feed him from the table." He bit the pencil and thought hard. "Since you're feeling better, I can take you into the mountains again if you want."

"For an overnighter?"

"I was thinking more of a day hike. I guess we could arrange an overnighter sometime if Daniel wants to take the time off. Maybe we could go one weekend and he can let Phedra run the shop."

"I don't want to take him from his work. He's very dedicated. I saw that firsthand. Maybe you and I could go alone."

"I'm not sure we should."

Conrad jumped to his feet. His smile faded and he wobbled. Clutching onto the sofa, he knocked over the lamp to keep from falling. Aiden rushed to his side. "Are you all right?"

"Just a little dizzy."

"Here, sit down." He helped him back to the sofa. "You shouldn't get up so fast."

"I'm okay. I just need some fresh air. Give me some space, will you?"

Conrad brushed Aiden's hands away and stomped outside. Aiden allowed him some alone time while he cleaned the mess Conrad left in the living area. He righted the lamp and brought his food to the kitchen before Ranger tried for seconds. Ranger scratched at the front door. Aiden let him out and stepped onto the landing behind him, but first he reached for a jacket from one of the coat hooks.

Conrad sat on the landing, smoking a cigarette. Aiden studied his back a moment without announcing himself. He looked forlorn and helpless. The shadow of the house kept them cold. "Here." Aiden draped the jacket around Conrad's shoulders.

Conrad pulled the jacket firmer around him. "Thanks," he said, releasing a cloud of white smoke toward the pine trees.

"Should you be doing that?" Aiden said, commenting on his smoking for the first time.

Conrad gazed up at him, his forehead wrinkled. With lethargic eyes, he peered at the cigarette between his fingers. "What difference does it make? They say it takes about twenty years to get full-blown lung cancer from smoking. I won't make it beyond that time. Might as well enjoy a few vices. Besides, it can sometimes help with the nausea."

Aiden sat beside Conrad and brought up Montana's legal medicinal marijuana law passed several years ago. Perhaps Conrad might get a prescription.

"It's easy to come by from what I hear," Aiden added. "You just need a doctor to sign a paper saying you fall under a whole slew of ailments. Even backaches are a legal reason for medical pot. They sell it near everywhere now. I even saw some at a drive-thru coffee stand once."

"I don't want that." Conrad shook his head with a sharp frown. "It's against my beliefs. People are allowed beliefs, aren't they? Doesn't your religious boyfriend have them too? I was in the ROTC in college, remember? We don't smoke illegal drugs. I can handle a little nausea."

"But it's not illegal, I just told you that." Aiden snickered. "You're just hung up on an old media image. It's no worse than those cigarettes you're smoking. Or the medicines you take, or the alcohol you drink."

He eyed Aiden. "Don't try to convince me about pot," he emphasized with a sneer.

"I'm not trying to preach," Aiden said. "I don't smoke it either. I don't like feeling out of control. But if it would help me like any other drug, I might consider—"

"I won't smoke pot!" Conrad drew on his cigarette until the end burned bright orange and faded to a dull red.

Aiden let a breeze carry away the awkward moment along with the exhaled smoke. Aiden held back from saying he foresaw Conrad's collapse long ago, perhaps before he followed him to Chicago and moved in with him. He was always yearning for too much, thinking of only himself. He was destined for a crash, cancer or not.

Now he had no one to turn to but an ex-boyfriend who felt more pity for him than love. He dug for that same feeling from when he realized the courage it took for Conrad to face his lymphoma.

Conrad snickered and shook his head. "That's the third time I've snapped at you in less than fifteen minutes," he said. "You'll forgive me, right?"

Aiden softened his tone. "Sure I will. I was just trying to suggest something helpful. No one is trying to force you to do things against your will. Your treatment is your business. Even the literature says so."

Ranger circled an aspen sapling, urinated on it, and kicked duff with his hind paws. The wind shifted and Aiden was grateful he did not get a face full of Conrad's cigarette smoke.

"I've been a pest coming here," Conrad mumbled, tracing his finger in the dirt. "I'm embarrassed."

"No reason to be. I'm glad you came."

Conrad jerked his head toward him. “You are?”

“There’s a chance we might become good friends after all this.”

Conrad gazed at his stocking feet. “Won’t it be too late?”

“You have to be more positive, Conrad,” Aiden said. “Positive thinking is important in your treatment. I read about these things when I do research for my articles.”

“Are you going to write about me coming here?”

“Why would I do that?”

Conrad smirked. “Isn’t that what writers do? I told Daniel you should write about his life. Wouldn’t it be more interesting than mine?”

“I have no intention of profiting off my relationships with my boyfriend or my friends.”

“You are my friend, right? You do like me, don’t you, Aiden?”

Aiden provided Conrad a tight smile. “Of course I do. Would I let you come here if I didn’t?”

“But after everything I’ve done—”

“Is that so important now?”

Conrad wiggled his toes. “I’m just in one of those moods. Feeling sorry for myself, wishing things were different.” He glanced up at the towering hemlock next to the porch and sighed. “And bored out of my mind.” He gazed back through the trees toward the mountains rising in the distance beyond Nick’s ranch. “Hey, are there any bars in town?”

“The Kalispell area has many bars, why?”

“I mean gay bars.”

“There are some establishments known as gay friendly but the area is too small for exclusive gay bars.”

Conrad studied the burning end of his cigarette, inhaled one last time, and grinded the butt into the grass. Ranger rushed up to him and demanded petting. Conrad draped an arm around him while Aiden stroked his furry hindquarters.

“There you go.” Aiden chuckled. “That’s better, isn’t it? You two just need some attention.”

Conrad echoed his chuckles and, hugging Ranger firmer, leaned closer into Aiden’s shoulder.

Chapter FOURTEEN

"MY HAIR!"

Daniel jerked his head toward the sound of Conrad's wailing. Aiden tossed aside the towel he was using to dry the supper pots and pans and leaped down the hallway. Daniel left his tax work at the dining table and followed after him.

"My hair!" The shouts were coming from the hallway bathroom. "My hair—"

Aiden swung open the door. Daniel pressed closer behind him to get a good look. With tears staining his face, Conrad peered at them from the floor where he sat trembling on his haunches. In his cupped hand, he revealed a mound of strawberry blond hair.

"It's… it's falling out. I'm losing my hair. I'm losing my hair."

Aiden dropped to a squat beside him. "It's not so bad, Conrad. Really, it isn't."

"How can you say that? Look!" He held the hair higher for Aiden and Daniel's eyes. "It's clumps of my hair!" Conrad began sobbing and Daniel wanted to leave, embarrassed to witness a grown man fall apart. Already wracked with guilt for having saddled Aiden with the brunt of Conrad's care, he forced himself to remain by the door and stare.

Aiden lowered Conrad's hand and helped him to his feet. "Try not to worry too much about things like this, okay? You knew this might happen. It'll pass. Your hair will grow back."

"It's horrible, Aiden. It's horrible."

Aiden forced the hair from Conrad's hand into the sink and eyed Daniel on his way escorting Conrad out of the bathroom. Daniel shook his head in empathy, his mind cluttered with misgivings. He helped by tearing off a few squares of toilet paper and taking the hairs out of the sink and flushing the crumpled ball down the commode. He rinsed the sink and returned to the dining table.

He was never gladder for taxes. The task enabled him to keep his mind focused and away from Conrad, whose condition seemed to go from good to bad, one moment to the next. Several minutes passed and Aiden dropped onto the sofa with a lengthy sigh. Daniel nudged aside the tax forms and sat beside him.

"He's sleeping," Aiden said toward the cold, empty fireplace. Ranger was lying on the sofa, and together he and Aiden massaged his scruffy fur.

"That's good," Daniel said, staring at the dead fireplace along with Aiden.

Somewhere in Ranger's fur, Aiden and Daniel found each other's hands. They locked fingers.

"Are you okay?" Daniel asked.

"Me? I'm fine. It's Conrad who's losing his hair."

"Things might get worse."

"I figure they will." Aiden released Daniel's hand and stood. "I'm going to leave the pans to soak until the morning. Good night." He lumbered down the hallway and Daniel heard the bedroom door close with a dull thud.

Aiden was fast asleep by the time Daniel spent another hour on the tax forms and crawled under the bedcovers. He hugged him from behind and found himself desperate to absorb Aiden's warmth. He slumbered like that, a position he normally would dislike for sleep.

The next morning they ate breakfast without discussing Conrad's episode from the night before. Conrad was still asleep when Daniel kissed Aiden good-bye. He bypassed the shop and drove straight into Kalispell to pick up a cutting tool he'd been wanting for many months, but thought was too extravagant.

During the drive, he kept harping on why—why did Conrad's caregivers have to be him and Aiden? Daniel never knew anyone to be devoid of friends. And family? Daniel lost his—but was that his fault? He hadn't created the unwritten centuries-old *Ordnung* that required anyone who left the Amish Church to be shunned.

He drove past the cancer center. Squat and wide, the clinic to some was their last bastion of hope for an extended life. Leah, his little sister, had outlived doctors' prognoses. In the end, death prevailed. She never lived long enough to see her ninth birthday.

The hardware store, a monolithic building the size of an Amish farm with a parking lot to match, stretched before him. He parked and beelined inside. The bright lights swept thoughts of Conrad and death from his mind, and, like a boy in a toy shop, he roamed the aisles, delighting in the vast array of tools and gadgets.

Despite his plain upbringing, Daniel and his fellow Amish had an innate love for Englisher inventions. They used what they could get away with, eschewing what took them far from home, like cars and tractors. Little that mattered to Daniel now.

He spent a half hour looking around and found his object of desire in the back, a newfangled handheld contraption that made cutting intricate details far easier and with fewer mistakes. Created by a team of scientists at the Massachusetts Institute of Technology, the tiny tool actually had a computer inside that photographed a "map" of the design so that it knew precisely where to cut the wood. Too costly when it had first come out, the tool's price had finally fallen to within Daniel's budget. Besides, he was due a treat.

At the checkout, he pictured Aiden and Conrad. What were they doing at that precise moment? Poor Aiden had his hands full with a grown man suffering from cancer. Aiden barely complained about his new and daunting task, not even after dealing with one of Conrad's bouts with midnight sickness.

They had to care for Conrad as they would a newborn baby. And like many fathers, Daniel wondered how many times he had slept through the night without hearing a sound. He realized he needed to aid Aiden more. There was no turning Conrad away at that point. The more Daniel helped Aiden, the easier it would be for everyone.

As he carried his purchase to his parked truck, he considered his own advice from days before. Nick Pfeifer might help in giving Conrad extra attention. They seemed to have enjoyed each other's company. Perhaps he'd volunteer to drive Conrad into town for his treatments and give Aiden a break from that burdensome chore.

He was nearing the cancer clinic again. A man in a white doctor's coat stepped outside from the sliding glass doors. He darted around the corner. At the next traffic signal, Daniel glanced in the rearview mirror and saw the doctor light a cigarette. Ironic, he thought.

Phedra had opened the shop and was tidying the shelves when he stepped inside. Early morning sunlight highlighted the wooden knickknacks he'd made when he had enough free time apart from the larger items. The cedar scent and hushed stillness of his business gave him that subtle shiver that he anticipated each time he entered his shop.

"*Gudde moren.*"

"*Guder mariye*, Phedra."

"You have an order placed already this morning," she said in English. Daniel stopped surprised and took the message from Phedra's small, pale hand.

"This is *goot*," he said after reading it. "The lodge in Columbia Falls wants more furniture, before I have even delivered their console." He looked at her and grinned. "I will charge them an arm and leg and they won't refuse."

Phedra giggled and Daniel headed for his workshop. He tacked the order on the bulletin board and opened his new purchase like a boy on Christmas morning.

He studied the manual for his new digital toy and practiced several cuts on old plywood for the rest of the morning. He was amazed at what he accomplished. He chuckled aloud when he cut a perfect replica of a United States map.

AIDEN washed several loads of clothes while Conrad rested in his bedroom. The task was extra burdensome with the addition of another person living with them. Aiden folded clean towels and carried an armload to Conrad's hallway bathroom, relishing the warmth against his chest and the fresh lavender scent. He stepped inside before it was too late to see Conrad standing naked by the shower, drying off. Aiden averted his eyes, blushing.

"I'm sorry," he said. "I thought you were napping." He quickly laid the towels on the counter, keeping his eyes from Conrad and his reflection in the mirror. "I just wanted to give you some clean towels."

"Aiden, don't act embarrassed. You've seen me naked before." Conrad stood upright, the towel dangling from his hand.

Aiden tried to chuckle. He backed out, scurried to his room and sat on the edge of the bed. He hadn't seen Conrad undressed in many years. He used to find him irresistible. He had been shocked that Conrad still had a fit physique. He'd lost weight, but the skin pulled tight over his muscles. A body more resembling someone twenty, not thirty. The treatments had failed to render him into an emaciated bag of bones. Maybe that would come later. He'd only begun radiation three weeks ago. Now that Conrad lost some of his hair, Aiden thought about how sad it would be once the deterioration fully kicked in.

Inhaling, he returned to the laundry room, reloaded the dryer and washer and folded more clothes. Conrad, dressed in casual jeans and sweatshirt, walked in behind him. "Well, what did you think?"

Keeping his head focused on folding, Aiden said, "Think about what?"

"You know what. The old body not so bad for a balding sick man, huh?"

Aiden's face burned. "I didn't really notice."

Conrad chuckled behind him. "I was working out stronger than ever when I realized something was wrong. At first I thought I was overtraining." Aiden heard him sigh. "I had no choice but to get a checkup. That's when they took blood tests and concluded I had lymphoma. Guess soon enough I'll be a shriveled mess. I'm going to enjoy my health while I have it."

Aiden turned to him and smiled. Sickness made for wise men, he surmised. Conrad lived in a world vastly different from him and Daniel. A world with one foot in life, the other in death. One way or another, everyone struggled with the same predicament.

"That's a good attitude, Conrad," he said. "I'm glad to see you've adjusted to the idea. And try not to worry about your—" For the first time Aiden noticed Conrad's buzz cut. "Your hair. When did you do that?"

Conrad stroked the stubbles. "Before my shower. I bought a clipper at the store that time you took me. Don't worry, I put down some plastic bags and cleaned up. This way you won't be able to notice the bald spots as much."

Aiden scrutinized his head. "I can hardly tell."

With vacant eyes, Conrad reached for a shirt and began helping Aiden fold. "What other choice do I have?"

Suppressing that horrible impression of pity, Aiden said, "If you're feeling up to it, we can do something fun today like you wanted."

"Like go to the gym?"

"You think you should?"

"Didn't you just hear me? I feel great right now. I should probably get as much exercise in as I can before, well, before I won't be able to."

Aiden folded one of Daniel's T-shirts, using his chin to hold it in place. "Let me finish up with the laundry and then we can head back into the Valley. There're a few gyms I know of."

Conrad dropped a Polo shirt midway through folding it into the laundry basket. "I'll switch into my workout clothes. Do you know of any gyms with a pool?"

"I think so."

"We'll do a swim after, okay?"

Aiden nodded with his chin pressed to his sternum and Conrad dashed off.

Aiden finished the laundry, and by three o'clock they were at Valley Sport, the closest gym in Kalispell with a pool. Aiden had reservations about going, but once he started his workout and his body heated up, he was glad to get in some weight-bearing exercises after going without for so long. Aiden spotted Conrad on the bench press, noticing that he was shakier than some of the others. How long before he wouldn't be able to lift a towel off the floor?

They worked out another hour, then Aiden followed Conrad into the locker room. He was surprised when Conrad changed into a Speedo, or that he bothered to pack a bathing suit for his Montana trip.

He avoided looking at his body again, which was pale and dusted with a modest amount of blond hair, the way he remembered. The buzz cut accentuated his rigid jawline and slim physique. He looked like a human bullet. Aiden slipped on his board shorts and together they found the wet area.

It was the middle of the workweek and, like the gym floor, the natatorium was near empty. One older man sat in the Jacuzzi. The setting sun filtering through the wide windows splashed pink and yellow off the flat surface of the pool. Aiden unraveled the white terry cloth towel he brought along from the locker room.

"Looks like you haven't lost your figure," Conrad said. He dove in, splashing Aiden. He reemerged from under the water and wiped his face with his hands. "Whoa! Feels good."

Aiden eased himself in. The tepid water washed over his limbs, stiff with blood from the heavy workout session. For lap swims, Conrad's skimpy Speedo seemed practical, while Aiden's board shorts were less so. Aiden did the breaststroke since he tired too easily when swimming freestyle. He could barely keep up with Conrad, who always showed more endurance in water.

After several minutes, Aiden's lungs throbbed. He swam to the edge of the pool and hoisted himself up. Sitting with his feet dangling in the water, he watched Conrad swim a few laps. His sleek jaw rose high above the water's surface with each breath. He pulled back the water with his arms, pushed forward, his protruding backbones pumping like pistons. He swam five more laps before he stopped in the middle of the pool and blew water from his mouth.

"I can't go on," he said, breathing heavy. Sunlight glistened off his wet shoulders and facial stubble that now looked like flecks of gold. He climbed out of the pool, placed his hands on his hips, and cocked his head back and forth to shake water from his ears. "Ready for a shower?"

Reluctantly, Aiden followed Conrad into the one large shower room. They washed off the chlorine a few paces apart. Aiden kept his back to Conrad, but he couldn't help but catch a few glimpses of Conrad's concaved butt cheeks while the suds trickled down his body.

Conrad was in good spirits—and shape. He caught Conrad peeping at him, and he spun quickly to rinse off.

Darkness met them in the parking lot. Aiden hadn't been aware of the passage of time. When they returned home, Daniel was on a ladder by the porch, illuminated by a spotlight. He was sawing off the branch of the cottonwood that threatened to wallop the front landing since the day they bought the rancher. He peered down at them. "Have a good time?"

Aiden flushed. "We went to the gym and had a swim. I meant to text you but I guess I forgot. Looks like you're working hard as usual."

"Chores have to be done. I put this off long enough."

The sawing sound ushered Aiden and Conrad inside. Aiden headed straight for the bedroom and quickly gathered his soiled gym clothes for the laundry room. From there he beelined for the kitchen and started dinner. He decided to make Daniel's favorite. Roast beef with boiled potatoes and carrots.

Chapter FIFTEEN

SUN washed over the south-facing green slopes of the Livingston Range where the Packers Roost Trail switchbacked above Mineral Creek. Bighorn sheep grazed on the lichen shoots closer to the creek and barely glanced at the three hikers. When Conrad slipped on the talus and sent a spray of harmless scree hurdling toward them, the herd kept their curvy horns pointed toward the earth.

Daniel led the trio, and he stopped to ensure Conrad had not hurt himself. Aiden, holding the caboose position, reached out to steady him. Daniel hiked several paces and waited at the next switchback. He swallowed a few gulps of the lukewarm water through the hydration tube on his backpack. Daniel and Aiden bore the burden of their load for the overnight trip into Glacier National Park, while Conrad wore a small backpack containing mostly foodstuffs.

Aiden encouraged Conrad to keep hiking at a steady pace. Daniel watched their sluggish ascent. He was happy to be outdoors and hiking, especially after sending in their tax forms. He made more money and would pay more to the government too. Temperatures hovered in the low fifties, which was perfect for a mildly rugged excursion. Watching Conrad huff along, Daniel wished Aiden had heeded his suggestion that Nick, who would be watching Ranger, spend the weekend sitting with Conrad too.

Two days ago Daniel sat up in bed listening to Aiden explain the need to take Conrad to Glacier National Park—for all of their sakes. The weather service predicted a calm April weekend, and the wondrous outdoors beckoned everyone, including the infirmed. The backpack trip would give Conrad newfound confidence, Aiden insisted. Daniel could not disagree. Life really wasn't so horrible on America's backcountry trails.

After Daniel gave Aiden the wooden cutout of the US map he made with his new computerized cutting tool, Aiden set it aside and rummaged through their stash of topographical maps from the chest in their bedroom. Daniel was surprised Aiden picked Packers Roost for their hike with Conrad. They hiked the same trail when he and Aiden ran into each other by chance, nearly a year to the day after they met in Illinois.

Reason told Daniel that this was one of the few trails inside Glacier Park clear of snow in April, a good two months from prime tourist season. But why not backpack the Swan Range, or closer to their house in the Salish Range?

Glacier National Park rose as the gem of northwestern Montana. Who wouldn't want to travel there? Daniel conceded that visiting the Flathead Valley without seeing the national park would be like visiting Henry, Illinois, and ignoring the Amish.

He gazed westward at the ribbon of trail they had eaten up in the past three hours. Normally they'd cover the moderate seven-mile trail in half the time and would have been setting up camp by now. They needed to go extra slow for Conrad's sake. Although he was no novice (Aiden explained how Conrad introduced him to backpacking), his cancer and the treatments weakened him.

Conrad and Aiden reached Daniel. Conrad, huffing and puffing, smiled and wiped sweat from his forehead. He had begun wearing a skullcap to conceal his spreading baldness. Daniel noticed his body changing too. He was thinner. Yet he had a youthful appearance, not as sickly as one might have expected. His borrowed hiking pants hung low in the seat, but when he bent over to adjust the old boots Aiden lent him there was no denying some muscle tone remained.

"This is some hike," he said, standing straight. "More than what I was used to back east. Remember, Aiden?"

"We had some pretty decent switchbacks," Aiden said, coming up behind Conrad. "Like that trip in Boiling Springs."

Conrad released a breathy chuckle. "That was our first big climb."

"We were so competitive," Aiden said, snorting. "Who was the strongest? Who was the fittest? Who could reach the summit the fastest? Male combativeness," he said with an uncharacteristically sarcastic deep-voiced grunt. "We began to compete for everything."

"You've got the upper hand this time. I wasn't sick then."

"You're hanging in okay," Aiden assured him with a pat on his shoulders. "Drink some water and rest a minute."

The thick stench of skunk rose up from the forest below. Daniel moved ahead, placing his hand on their single protection, an eight-ounce canister of capsaicin bear deterrent. He pressed along the trail, not bothering to look back to see if Aiden and Conrad followed. He advanced upslope to the next switchback. Again, he did not look back.

Weighted by his sixty-pound pack, he took to the trail steadily. Fresh sweat beads broke loose and singed his temples. He wiped them away, inhaling the scent of pine. His farm-honed plain sense of smell told him snow lurked close by. That meant they were nearing the plateau and the north-facing slopes covered with leftover snowfields that did not melt until midsummer. Their campsite would be only a few miles from there, an easy downhill trek.

He focused on the pine trees that leaned into the slope and tried to garner strength from their sturdy pillar-like trunks and erect branches that offered their green foliage to Heaven. They had such purpose and vitality. Seeing Conrad slouch as he rounded another switchback, Daniel wondered—what did he have? Disease? Death?

Or perhaps Conrad had Aiden as his dependable pillar.

The view to the right provided Daniel with the resurrection to appreciate life and Aiden. The mountains, purple and proud, rose above the emerald charm of the park. This was what Aiden and Daniel wanted in coming to Montana. Away from home, Daniel and Aiden might breathe easier helping their sickly guest. Daniel understood that Aiden's idea coming to Glacier was as much for Daniel as it was for Conrad.

The path is to be prepared in the wilderness, states Mathew in the New Testament.

The sound of Aiden and Conrad conversing with each other trickled up the trail. Their voices were light and, in between Conrad's heavy breathing, full of amusement. Once the trail leveled off at eight thousand feet, an opening in the forest provided Daniel an opportunity to stop and wait for Conrad and Aiden to catch up before their final descent into their campsite. About fifty yards from where Daniel stood, a family of mule deer drank from a small puddle left behind from snowmelt.

Aiden and Conrad's voices grew louder. "My legs are burning," Aiden said once he reached Daniel. His smile filled the small glade. Daniel could not help but allow Aiden's boyish enjoyment to infuse him.

Aiden circumvented Conrad and Daniel and snapped a few pictures of the mule deer with his digital camera. Next, he insisted on posing everyone for group and couple pictures. Aiden took one of Conrad and Daniel, Conrad took one of Daniel and Aiden, and Daniel took one of Conrad and Aiden, and Aiden set the camera, with the timer on ten seconds, on a low tree branch to snap a photograph of the three of them.

Sunrays cutting through the tree branches from the west and casting a golden haze about them told Daniel they needed to keep hiking if they were to have enough daylight hours to set up camp and make supper. Keeping to the rear this time, Daniel nudged them along.

As the trail narrowed, their voices became muted, and eventually they ceased speaking. They advanced step by step through an ankle-high snowfield. Daniel focused on the goal at hand, which was to reach camp. A few paces ahead of him, Aiden swung his arms wider and his head pressed forward, blazing through the bushes, which changed from north-facing dwarf pines to taller blue spruce and red cedars. With the shallow snowfield left behind, they turned eastward and picked up speed toward camp.

"We have the entire place to ourselves." Aiden's voice echoed in the expansive clearing once they broke through the towering trees for their campsite. "Not a soul here. I only wish the park allowed dogs so Ranger could have come with us."

Aiden dropped his hefty backpack against the trunk of a massive red cedar. Same spot where he and Daniel surrendered to their longing inside Aiden's tent for the first time. Did Aiden remember that special moment? Had he claimed that spot for a reason?

Blue eyes sparkled at him from the edge of the forest. Aiden, like an excited boy, circled the designated camp area, ogling Daniel. No doubt he did remember their fateful meeting from a few years before and, by the look in his eyes, was reliving their encounter. But no room for romance with Conrad present and the three sharing a tent.

Conrad sat on a rock outcropping, smoking a cigarette and staring off through the forest, the small of his back curved, while Daniel and Aiden unfurled the tent, laid out the tarp, and erected the tent poles.

Daniel grabbed a few toiletries from Aiden's pack and cookware and food from the bear canister they'd retrieved from the ranger station, and he and Aiden hooked their three backpacks on tree nodules far enough out of reach from pesky forest animals.

Aiden started supper in the preparation area while Daniel washed in the nearby creek. The sound of snapping twigs drowned out the gurgling of the running water. From the trees, mule deer spied on him. He rinsed his hair and washed his face and beard, unconcerned about his new company.

The deer family followed him near camp, making sure to keep to the edge of the forest. They were waiting for the men to finish their meal and disappear inside their tent so that they could flush out of the woods and forage for crumbs.

When Daniel cleared the creek trail for camp, Conrad and Aiden were bent over a boiling pot of water. They brought along freeze-dried lasagna, and with the changing direction of the wind Daniel smelled the spicy tomato sauce. Instantly his stomach growled. He handed Aiden the toiletries so he could wash and swapped places with him. Conrad followed Aiden down the creek trail.

Daniel had supper served when they returned. They ate about fifty yards from the tent while sitting on fallen trees, and chatted about the beauty that surrounded them. Despite his present misgivings, Daniel imagined building a cabin on that spot and living like a frontiersman. He had escaped there prior to his first marriage to Esther, and then again before he was to wed Tara Hostetler. During that last breaking away, Aiden and Daniel had met and soon expressed their love, the kind that required no justification, even to God, Daniel dared to believe.

Once they had eaten, cleaned their supper ware, and collected enough firewood for a fire later that night, Aiden asked Conrad if he was up for a hike to the old stone fire tower.

"How far?" Conrad asked.

“Only a short twenty-minute hike. The side trail is right over there. There’s still enough daylight left to get there and back with time to enjoy the view.”

Taking the lead, Conrad said that if Aiden was up for an extra hike, so was he. Daniel dragged behind. The hike took longer than usual, since Conrad stopped several times to catch his breath. About forty minutes later, they reached the top—the apex of the Western Continental Divide.

As usual, the panoramic view from the fire tower snatched Daniel’s breath. Conrad did not seem interested in the three-hundred-sixty-degree spectacle of blue glaciers and awakening waterfalls glistening in the light of the weakening sun. Nor did he appear impressed with learning the fire tower was older than the park.

Daniel, wanting a moment to appreciate the scenery alone, stepped away from Conrad and Aiden. The western peaks, extending higher than those on the eastside of the park, blocked the wind at that hour of the afternoon. Not until nightfall would the winds rush down the mountains and fill the plateaus with a chill. He experienced a near out-of-body experience, seeing God’s glory around him. Did he dare say he beheld the world from Heaven’s perch?

Aiden and Conrad moved to the stone steps. They sat shoulder to shoulder, gazing toward the west where Mineral Creek, like an icy blue ribbon, meandered through the glacier carved valleys. Taking small, hesitant steps, Daniel rejoined them.

“What do you think of our backyard?” Aiden asked Conrad.

Conrad squinted toward the sun. “This is what you’ve always dreamed, Aiden. Looks like you found your little bit of paradise.”

Daniel listened. They did, indeed, stand in the midst of paradise. But uncertain emotions returned. He glanced down at Conrad’s skullcap. His shoulders, pointing through his long-sleeved hiking shirt, hunched forward with an annoying indifference. Perhaps the severely ill, beaten by invading disease and intrusive treatments, lacked the concern for earthly things, like mountains and streams.

Then he remembered little Leah, barely able to move a muscle, and how her face would beam when given the simple gift of a faceless Amish doll.

Conrad stood with a stretch and wandered toward the talus slope. Aiden warned him to watch his footing. Daniel used to caution Aiden about his step. Nowadays, Aiden seemed more capable and less the klutz he remembered from when they first met.

Aiden trailed after Conrad while Daniel hovered in the background. Above the rustling wind and the barking osprey, Daniel overheard bits and pieces of their one-on-one conversation.

"Don't forget to take your pills before you go to bed tonight," Aiden said.

"I would have left them at home like I wanted if you hadn't forced me to bring them."

"You can't skip those pills, you know that."

Conrad said something, but it was lost in the wind. Aiden said, "It's a fact of life you have to get used to. I'll get you one of those pill planners to make it easier. My grandpa had one."

Daniel realized that Aiden had thought his last comment about his grandfather was perhaps insensitive and wished he hadn't said it. He recognized the tilt to his head, and the staring off and away. The same posture he took whenever overcome by embarrassment.

The wind and barking osprey swallowed Aiden's next comment. Conrad shook his head over and over toward his borrowed boots. "Aiden, I… I… I wish things were different. I really wish things were different."

Aiden draped an arm around his back and patted his shoulder. "I know you do. I do too. But we can't change what's happened. We can try to shape what's to come. Taking your medicines, keeping positive, that's all part of that."

A shadow of a smile appeared on Conrad's face when he turned to Aiden. Daniel stepped back a pace, but stopped himself, unsure why the sense that he was intruding should attack him there, in Glacier National Park, near where he and Aiden first consummated their commitment to each other.

"Just look at the beauty, Conrad," Aiden said louder, pointing toward the purple crags rising above the emerald expanse. "I remember the first time I saw it. I couldn't believe it. Remember how it was when we hiked to Annapolis Rock overlooking South Mountain? This is one hundred times more breathtaking."

"God speaks through nature." Daniel stood behind them now.

Aiden jerked around and brought his arm to his side. "Daniel, you scared us."

"I didn't intend to."

Aiden waved him closer. "Come stare at nature with us."

"I can see plenty from here."

"More talk of God, Daniel?" Conrad snickered. "Okay, you can have your god."

Daniel allowed Conrad's comment to pass over him. He was a sick man who railed against the goodness that Daniel's Anabaptist God represented. His slur came as gently as the scree that trickled downslope when Conrad, agitated and forlorn, kicked his feet.

Nonetheless, Daniel wanted to escape him for a while. The howling winds in the forest below, which often brought lonesomeness, called Daniel forward. He turned for the trail back to camp.

Behind him, he heard the steps of Aiden and Conrad move off the overlook. He kept a steady pace down to camp without looking back. No other hikers claimed the five campsites reserved for backpackers while they'd romped around the tower. Strangely disappointed, Daniel set about forming a fire teepee.

"Come on, Conrad." Aiden's voice traveled among the trees as he and Conrad entered the camping area. "The woods aren't always about silent introspection. Let's have fun."

Aiden's enthusiasm filled Daniel with dizzying warmth. Moments like that would pull him to Aiden and, surrounded by towering trees and woodland animals, he'd kiss him fully, unconcerned if any unexpected hikers saw. Not that trip. Not with Conrad near glued to Aiden's side.

Daniel struck a match and laid it to the shreds of newspaper they packed, thinking about Solomon's proclamation to "live life to the fullest." Solomon also warned that "death is certain… the Great Equalizer."

Aiden maintained an upbeat attitude as the three gathered about the growing fire. Regardless of the circumstances, Daniel made the best of their excursion. The sharp slices of pink sun disappeared beyond the western peaks and the sky turned indigo. The flames reached higher and illuminated their blank faces.

The honking of Canada geese flying above penetrated the sudden quiet of evening twilight. The geese were on their way to Lake MacDonald or one of the thousands of glacier lakes that dotted the park. Aiden's gaze dropped northward, toward the old fire tower.

"I wonder how much longer we can enjoy this," he said, surprising Daniel with his sudden somber tone.

Daniel spied him through the flames that cast shadows over his face. The light lines around his mouth and nose seemed to deepen. "What do you mean?"

"How long before everything in Glacier Park turns into a swamp," Aiden answered Daniel. "How long before the strip-mining operation destroys everything?"

No one spoke. With the passing of the geese, the forest descended into utter stillness. Not even the gentlest breeze or the crackling fire interrupted their sober contemplation.

Then Aiden sat strong and flexed his shoulders. "Why worry about what might never happen? It's a beautiful night, isn't it? Wasn't it me who said to give up on all this philosophical shussliness?"

Daniel smiled through the fire at Aiden's use of "shussly," an old Amish word Daniel often used when he wanted to describe something that he found silly. Light chatter replaced the severe quiet. Aiden mentioned his and Daniel's fishing excursions, and he also recounted the many backpacking trips he and Conrad took years ago.

The Appalachian Trail sounded like an interesting place to Daniel, but he could not fathom anything matching the grandeur of what surrounded them now, even in shadows. He was happy to be there. Still, as night brightened with the rising moon, he wanted to prolong climbing into the tent with Conrad.

When Conrad stood and stretched, for a moment Daniel relaxed, glad that he might make his way inside the tent first. Then Aiden stood along with him, his bones cracking against the night. Both announced they were tired.

Daniel was about to let them go alone, but Aiden squatted down beside him, laid his droopy head on his shoulder, warmed by the waning fire. "You ready, Daniel?"

Daniel tossed the stick he'd been using to poke at the fire into the flames. "I guess I could use some sleep."

The sleeping arrangements were as awkward as Daniel had imagined. Though they had a four-man tent, there was barely room for three adult males, especially with Daniel's six-two frame. Conrad claimed the sleeping bag farthest from the tent flap. He was tucked in by the time Daniel followed Aiden inside.

What did other people do in similar situations? Would his parents or Mark and his wife sleep with an old lover in one tent?

By the time Daniel unholstered the bear spray and removed his boots, the sound of Aiden and Conrad's slow breathing indicated both had fallen fast asleep. He heard the mule deer encroaching on their campsite and beginning to fidget around the doused campfire. Soon, the nervous rustling drew Daniel into a jittery sleep.

He awoke to a green glow, glad to find his tentmate, Conrad, missing. He took the opportunity to kiss Aiden's cheek. A kiss would have to do. Aiden stirred, but remained snoozing. Daniel quietly unzipped the tent flap. He was fully dressed, for he had felt strange stripping naked the way he normally would before slinking inside his zero-degree bag. He slipped on his boots, holstered the bear spray, and crawled outside.

He looked forward to experiencing the first chill of dawn and the smell of crisp pine. Instead, his senses were assaulted by the stench of cigarette smoke.

Conrad sat on a log, smoking. The wind directed the smoke into Daniel's face. He scrunched his nose.

"Good morning," Daniel said, lacing his boots and trying not to sound disgusted with Conrad's habit.

Conrad dragged on his cigarette and blew out a cloud of smoke. "Good morning. Sleep okay?"

"Good enough, considering."

Daniel walked off his stiff muscles. This was his and Aiden's first overnighter since autumn and his legs and back muscles had cramped up. He moved farther away from Conrad's cigarette and pulled down their backpacks from the red cedars. At the food preparation area, he warmed the butane stove for breakfast, one eye peeled for Conrad.

Aiden awoke, and the sound of his happy chatter filling the somber morning chill warmed Daniel's spirits. He smiled at him across the campground and hoped Aiden would notice him and smile back. Instead, he went straight to Conrad, who stood and stretched. At least he had the decency to flick his cigarette butt into the cold fire pit with the ashes from last night's fire.

It wasn't until Daniel, Conrad, and Aiden began to dismantle the tent, waiting for the water to boil, that Daniel gave thanks that they had planned for a one-night trip. An extra night sleeping with Conrad in the tent would have pushed him to his limits.

Lighter on his feet, he left Conrad and Aiden rolling the tent and he attended to breakfast. They ate oatmeal and drank hot green tea as the sun crowned the eastern snow-capped peaks. Daniel gazed around at the panorama of pure nature: sky, mountains, trees, earth.

With their backpacks secured, they headed for the trailhead and Daniel's awaiting truck. They came across the same skiff of snow shielded by blue spruce and juniper groves. Daniel waited impatiently for the sun to rise higher above the tree canopies to warm his chilled muscles. The dampened earth hushed the snap of leaves under their boots, and their early morning trek was all the more serene and purposeful.

The mostly downhill trek took half the time as the hike in, and the sight of the shiny burgundy Suburban through the trees at Packers Roost Trailhead before lunchtime brought the typical sense of accomplishment for Daniel. Nothing could replace the pride Daniel felt after completing a rigorous hike.

Nothing, perhaps, other than the love he bore for Aiden, who was presently occupied helping Conrad slip off his small backpack and ensuring he had enough water to drink.

Chapter SIXTEEN

WHEN they returned from Glacier Park, a horrible hacking caused them to pause just inside the front door. Aiden dropped the gear in his arms and, without taking off his Birkenstocks, rushed to the kitchen. Daniel found him on his knees, stroking Ranger's head and whispering reassurances. "Daddy and Poppy are here. You're okay."

Several piles of vomit, mostly foamy bile, were scattered across the kitchen floor. Daniel cared little for the mess. He was more concerned with Aiden's reaction. Ranger had hacked up before, usually pinecones, but never had Daniel seen him experience such sickness.

"We'll have to take him to the vet," Aiden said, his golden eyes wide with distress.

"It's Sunday. None will be open."

"We can take him to an emergency hospital."

"An emergency hospital?"

"For pets, Daniel. There's one in the Valley."

Conrad came up behind them and stared. "Is he okay?"

Neither answered. Aiden waited with his hand on Ranger's back and comforted him until Ranger stopped heaving. He seemed over the worst of it and, with his tail between his legs, scurried for the security of his bed by the hearth. Daniel scooped up the vomit piles with paper towels and examined them while Aiden peered over his shoulder.

"What do you think he's been eating? His bowl's full of food."

"Hard to tell," Daniel said.

Aiden glared at Conrad. "Did you feed Ranger anything before we left?"

"Sorry, Aiden. Guess he did eat some of my breakfast when I wasn't looking."

"I've told you never to feed Ranger people food. You can't feed dogs stuff like Pop-Tarts and nachos, especially not Ranger."

"That was twenty-four hours ago," Daniel said, standing upright. "Maybe he got into the trash."

Aiden dashed out the kitchen door. Meanwhile, Conrad wandered toward his bedroom. A moment later, Aiden stepped back inside the house. "Trash cans are perfectly intact. No sign of rummaging. Besides, he's never dug through the trash before. Do you think he's been getting sick all weekend?"

Daniel peered through the kitchen's pass-through at Ranger. "We'll ask Nick when he comes over."

Aiden scrolled through his smartphone, most likely looking for an ER vet. He spoke with someone and clicked off. "The Flathead Veterinarian Emergency Clinic is open twenty-four hours," he said. "We better get going."

Daniel shrugged, unable to imagine taking one of his old farm animals to such a place. "Someone should stay here and unpack."

"Come on, Conrad," Aiden shouted in his roughest voice. "You're coming with me and Ranger."

While Conrad and Aiden were at the vet, Daniel mopped the kitchen floor, stowed the hiking gear in the third bedroom they used mostly for storage, and set up the tent in the backyard to air-dry the condensation that had accumulated overnight. Aiden and Conrad returned three hours later. Ranger went straight to his hearthside bed and lay down.

"How is he?" Daniel asked.

Aiden tossed paperwork onto the dining table. "They said he probably ate something that upset his gastrointestinal tract. They gave him a shot to help with nausea and subcutaneous fluids for dehydration." Still visibly upset, Aiden went to Ranger's side and stroked his head. "Everything's okay. Everything's okay," he kept cooing.

Nick Pfeifer shouted "hello" from the footpath, and Daniel opened the front door for him. "Come the house in, Nick."

"You all been home long? I just got back from the horse auction. Sold one of my mares."

Aiden sat upright. "Did you know Ranger was sick?"

"He threw up sometime around Saturday afternoon," Nick said. "I cleaned up a couple of piles. I was about to take him to the vet but reckoned it had passed. Did he vomit again?"

"The kitchen was full of it," Aiden said, turning his attention back to Ranger. "I'd never seen so much vomit."

"When I fed him this morning everything looked okay." He ogled Ranger and Aiden by the hearth. "Poor fellow. Come to think of it, he hasn't had much of an appetite all weekend."

"Did he get into something you might have eaten, Nick?" Daniel asked with a reserved tone. He did not wish to come across as accusatory.

Nick shook his head and shrugged. "I never once ate a thing while over here. Didn't even drink a glass of water."

"Maybe he got into something out back," Daniel said, more out of consideration than belief.

"I usually played with him after he did his business. I don't recall seeing him get into anything. But you know this time of year. All kinds of critters come out in warmer weather."

"We took him to an emergency vet," Conrad said. "You should've seen the place. Like a real hospital. Almost as big as the clinic."

"Wish I could have done more to help," Nick said. "Sometimes my horses get sick like this. No real explanation. The vet gives antibiotics and a shot to make them feel better. But I suspect they'd get better even without medication."

Daniel patted Nick's shoulder. "He'll be okay. He's a sturdy dog. Thanks for watching over him, Nick. We know he was in good hands."

"My pleasure." Nick acted like he wanted to leave but he stopped closer to the door and said, "Might as well tell you. I used your hallway bathroom once and while I was washing my hands the sink backed up on me." He snickered. "Seems all hell broke loose while you all were gone."

"It's always like that," Daniel said.

"I also wanted to remind you about my friend coming for dinner tomorrow, but I feel bad about that now."

Aiden looked up. "That's tomorrow?"

"We can cancel if you want."

"That's not necessary," Aiden said. "I'm looking forward to meeting him."

"I hope Ranger will be better by then. Poor fellow."

After Nick left, Aiden's face grew red. He stayed by Ranger's side while Conrad showered down the hall and Daniel read through the vet bill. Three hundred and sixty-six dollars!

With Conrad finished showering and out of the way, Daniel hunkered over the hallway bathroom sink and tried to unclog the drain. Fast-acting drain cleaner failed to work. Annoyed by the steam left from Conrad's shower, he griped while tinkering with the snake, sliding it in and out and wrenching it sideways to dislodge whatever was trapped inside. He wiped sweat from his forehead and contemplated what to do next.

Conrad strolled out of his bedroom and Daniel heard him ask Aiden for something to eat.

"Make sure he doesn't get any of your food, Conrad," Aiden said, his voice stern. "I'm going to take a shower." Several minutes later, Aiden, towel wrapped around his waist, poked his head inside the hallway bathroom. "How's it going?"

"Looks like hair clumps."

"My dad's a plumber. I picked up a few tricks if you want some help."

Daniel scowled at him. "You could put some clothes on before traipsing around the house."

Aiden chortled. "I just got out of the shower. We're all guys here. No big deal."

Daniel did his best to fix the sink and was wiping his tools when Aiden stepped back into the bathroom, this time fully dressed. "I have to run to the village store to buy some things for tomorrow night. Can you keep an eye on Ranger and Conrad?"

"Can't you take Conrad with you?"

"I guess I could. I'll see if he wants to tag along again. He might be too tired after the hike and going with me to the vet hospital."

Daniel was glad when Conrad said he'd like to go with Aiden. He sensed Conrad was as uncomfortable being alone with Daniel as Daniel was with him. He appreciated the quiet Sunday evening with all his work complete. The tent was cleaned and stowed and the bathroom sink appeared fixed, at least temporarily. He wanted to telephone Phedra to ask her how the shop had gone on Saturday, but did not want to disturb her on the Lord's Day. Being Hutterite, she was as orthodox as Daniel. Or at least as orthodox as Daniel had once been.

Ranger appeared no worse and lounged on the sofa beside Daniel while Daniel sipped root beer. It was at that moment Daniel realized how Conrad had become such a part of their world that he no longer wondered when he'd leave, but how they would learn to make do with him as a permanent member of their household—like they had Ranger. Until a few hours ago, Aiden hardly complained.

Daniel took a sinister pleasure reliving how Aiden snapped at Conrad and warned him not to feed Ranger scraps from the table. It was selfish to feel such pleasant sensations while Ranger suffered. The good feeling grabbed Daniel nonetheless. He struggled to keep from smiling.

MONDAY afternoon Daniel came home from the shop and found Aiden alone in the kitchen preparing for Nick and his friend's visit. "Where are our boys?" he asked.

Aiden nodded toward the window. "At Nick's. Nick came over again to apologize for Ranger, and he invited Conrad to help him run his horses."

"Ranger too?"

"He was so excited about tagging along I figured he could run around over there now that he's his old self."

Daniel wrapped his arms around Aiden and held him tight to his chest. Aiden leaned back and clung to Daniel's arms. "You haven't done that in many weeks."

"Haven't had the chance," Daniel said. "Do you realize this is the first time you and I have been alone inside this house in a month?"

Aiden held Daniel tighter. "I still feel horrible for having lost my temper at Conrad yesterday. It was the first time I exploded at him." Light from the recessed lighting caught Aiden's honey-brown eyes when he turned to gaze up at Daniel. "You should've heard the lecture I gave him while driving Ranger to the hospital. I hate how I treated him, especially with him being sick."

Daniel forced a compassionate smile. He wished he had ridden along with them to witness Aiden scolding Conrad. "This is normal for caregivers," he said. "I saw even my parents go from lavishing Leah with attention to yelling at her for the slightest slipup while she was at her worst. Try not to worry over him for now. He's with our good friend Nick, enjoying a sunny afternoon caring for horses. He's forgotten all about your lecture."

Aiden rested his forehead on Daniel's chest. "I guess."

Daniel recognized Aiden's sulking tone. "I think you're jealous."

"Jealous?" Aiden nudged Daniel back and grimaced. "Of whom?"

"Ranger. Conrad. Ranger's your baby and lately he seems to have taken to Conrad, and Conrad is spending more time with Nick."

"That's nonsense. Why would you say that?"

"Because it's the truth. You are a very caring man, Aiden Cermak. People and animals come into your fold and you like to hold on to them."

Aiden refocused on the stove and stirred a pot that smelled like it contained stewed tomatoes. "Am I suffocating?"

He flashed over his shoulder one of his hurt looks and right away Daniel wished he hadn't teased him. He shuffled closer and placed his hands on Aiden's shoulders. "You have a lot of love to give."

"It does make me think about things," Aiden said. "I value our time together and our life here, but, well…. One day don't you want to have kids, Daniel?"

They had been through the child talk before…. Daniel experienced parenthood, but for only a few months. Before God chose to take his baby son from him. He thought about that boy now. Zachariah would be almost three. Walking and talking, following his father around the woodshop or smitten with the farm animals, like Daniel was at that age.

Now he stood planted in another world, far removed from plain farms, Amish hausfraws, and barefooted children. Could his present and former worlds commune together?

"I too wish I had something fragile to care for," he muttered more for his sake than Aiden's. "But often, I worry more over those things that are the strongest. Why do you think I have fallen for you, Aiden? You are the strongest man I've ever known. You, and not those weak-kneed types, are the ones who should be watched after."

Aiden embraced Daniel again. "I feel the same about you," he said. "I remember when we met in Glacier Park. You looked so fragile standing under those towering hemlocks and red cedars, yet you were so sturdy. I couldn't help but think, regardless if you rejected me again, that I'd spend the rest of my life defending you and men like you."

Daniel and Aiden held onto each other until the silence of the house awakened with a deafening jolt and Daniel grew self-conscious. He broke off and said, "What can I do to help for our supper party tonight?"

"Maybe you should fix that bathroom sink."

"Still backed up?"

Aiden nodded. "I tried to fix it but it won't drain. I had to tell Conrad to use either our bathroom or the kitchen sink until it's working properly."

"I'll see what I can do. Maybe I just need to use some more drain cleaner and let it sit for a while."

The door opened and slammed shut, followed by the sound of Ranger's tags jingling.

"Your babies are back," Daniel said.

"Ha-ha."

Daniel kissed Aiden on top of his curly head and strolled down the hall, away from Conrad and toward more chores for their coming guests.

Chapter SEVENTEEN

PROMPTLY at seven, Nick and his old prep school friend arrived for dinner. Farzad Qajar was as debonair as Aiden had pictured him. A hint of rust showed in his salt and pepper hair, trimmed to accentuate his square jaw and highlight his large ebony eyes. Dressed in a dark suit and open-necked white shirt, Farzad looked ready for a reception at a country club rather than their small gathering in a modest Montana rancher.

He was fiftyish, about Nick's age, and demonstrated the manners learned at an elite private school. Aiden wondered how to ask him to take off his shoes, but he began to slip off his black loafers before Nick kicked off his cowboy boots. Aiden supposed Persians, like other Asians, were accustomed to removing their shoes before entering a home.

While Farzad looked everyone directly in the eyes during the handshakes, he glanced away from Conrad, as if shocked by his frail appearance. Conrad, a fresh buzz cut to conceal the expanding bald spots and his shape lost inside his wool sweater and chino pants, slumped back into the easy chair, either unaware or unconcerned by Farzad's subtle spurn.

Farzad's cheeks darkened, perhaps tinted by the heat from the fireplace. Aiden was right in believing that he was a man who might require special attention. Then he recalled the story of how Nick and his school buddies taunted Farzad for his royal bloodline, and how much Farzad had savored being treated like one of the boys. Aiden made a point to do the same.

"What can I get you guys? We're fully stocked. Name it and we got it."

"I'll have my usual scotch and soda tonight," Nick said.

"I'd like a vodka and orange juice, if you have any," Farzad said, giving Ranger an obligatory head pat when he sniffed him.

"I said if you name it, we got it," Aiden said with a singsong voice, and he retrieved their drinks while Daniel led them into the living area. They rarely drank anything alcoholic besides beer, but Aiden wanted to prepare a grander spread for Nick's special friend. Yesterday while shopping, Aiden telephoned Nick to ask what his friend's drink was, but Nick couldn't recall, so Aiden bought a bottle of nearly everything.

From the kitchen Aiden listened in on the conversation, and now and then he glanced through the pass-through. Daniel, seated on the rocker, asked Farzad how he was enjoying his visit. Farzad mentioned the amazing beauty of the area and how, if he knew better, he would have come earlier and extended his visit.

"Business means nothing when surrounded by such scenery," he said. "Next time I will bring my family."

"What business brings you here?" Daniel asked.

"I'm attending a software conference. This area is booming with small start-ups. Once I graduated from Dartmouth, I started my own company, which now seems like many years ago."

"Dartmouth?" Conrad exclaimed. "That's a fancy school."

Pouring the drinks, Aiden grinned. Since his scolding yesterday, Conrad had sulked and acted more reserved. But he always perked up in the company of Nick.

Aiden brought in the drinks on a tray while Farzad stated he enjoyed attending Dartmouth, but learned more from on-the-job training after graduating. "Nothing can replace real life experiences," he said, taking a drink from Aiden's tray. A subtle scent of spicy cologne emanated from under his sleeve.

"Farzad was one of the trailblazers of the software innovations in the early nineties," Nick said, the second to reach for his drink. "Now he heads one of the largest computer companies on the East Coast."

"I'm fascinated with people who run their own companies," Aiden said, sitting on the floor by Daniel's feet once he served everyone. "Daniel has a woodshop here in Rose Crossing."

"Carpentry? Wonderful." Farzad sipped his screwdriver. "I've always admired those who can use their hands."

"I learned my trade on the job too," Daniel said.

"It might interest you to know, Farzad," Nick said, "that Daniel was raised Amish."

Farzad's dark eyes grew wider. "You don't say. Amish?"

"And in many ways he's still very much Amish," Nick said. "Just look at his beard."

Aiden knew Daniel did not like to talk about his being raised Amish. It led to why he'd left. Although to some, the answer was clear. Two men living together in a home far from any large city most likely were gay. Aiden was unsure how much Nick had enlightened Farzad or if he were astute enough to figure out Aiden and Daniel were a couple. Behind Aiden, Daniel cleared his throat. Gazing up at him, Aiden couldn't help but chortle.

"I know about the Amish in America but have never met any face-to-face," Farzad said. "I'm quite interested in learning more about your former ways."

"I'm just as interested in your life," Daniel said. "Do you dislike having your photograph taken too? I hear that is the case with Muslims like with the Amish."

Farzad laughed. "We're interested in each other's cultures, yet I suspect we share many similarities, like hating to have our pictures taken. It has to do with the belief that only God should make human images."

"We also think of it as haughty," Daniel said.

Aiden noticed Daniel glimpse toward the mantel where his and Daniel's portrait sat. Farzad also caught Daniel's swift eye movement, and his own eyes stopped on the photograph taken inside Glacier National Park, with Aiden and Daniel smiling and arms wrapped around each other. Farzad roved his head toward Aiden and Daniel, then back to the photograph. His lips moved, but no words emerged. He turned his gaze to his lap and he seemed to flush.

"What's Iran like?" Aiden said, wanting to sweep away any sudden awkwardness, whether real or imagined.

“I wish I could tell you something,” Farzad said, his smile returning. “I came over when I was young and can recall only fragments. Most of what I remember could have taken place in New Jersey or Oklahoma.”

“I filled in the boys about your famous family, Farzad.”

“I’m proud of my family’s heritage but that means nothing here in America,” Farzad said. “I prefer it that way. I’ve made my way like anyone else. You see, my family’s fortune was taken from us, and the relatives I lived with in Iran only had so much. Once I left Albany School, I was to find my own way, like any American. And I’m proud to say as of two years ago I finally became a full-fledged US citizen.”

“What do you know,” Nick cried. “Why didn’t you ever say anything before, Farzad?”

“I suppose I didn’t want to be prideful.” He flashed Daniel a light smile. “I am Amish that way too.”

They all joined in congratulating Farzad and raised their glasses to toast the newest American among them.

Farzad lowered his eyes and his cheeks darkened in typical Far Eastern modesty. “My wife, three daughters, and two grandchildren are all American. I told myself, it’s about time I become one too.”

He again glanced around the house, this time showcasing an unabashed sense of curiosity. His inquisitiveness eclipsed his earlier reserve. Aiden imagined suddenly Farzad’s daughters having given him quite a headache growing up in suburban America. Briefly, Aiden yearned to ask for details.

But he squashed his inquisitive reporter’s desire to know every dirty secret. Living with Daniel, he learned to appreciate the value of a person’s privacy. Aiden thought Farzad might make an interesting interview subject if destiny brought them into each other’s company again.

“Where in Iran are you originally from?” Aiden asked him.

“North of Tehran.” Farzad’s bashfulness returned. His face shined from the firelight. He set his glass in his lap and licked his lips. “I was raised by friends of my aunt and uncle after they left for France. I was supposed to meet them there but then the Shah was exiled to the United States and a new bout of anti-Americanism engulfed Parisians, most of whom were hostile to the wealthy, and prompted my relatives, like most of their class, to flee for America. You know the French. While they were protesting America's involvement in Vietnam, their own military was massacring millions of Algerians. My family thought it best that I get as far from the ruckus as possible and they enrolled me in a school in the middle of the United States. Albany Ridge School, where I met Nick."

"Must have been scary living through a revolution," Daniel said.

"Like I said, I don't recall much about it," Farzad responded to Daniel's sincere statement. "But I assure you I could not have been afraid. It's not in my family to fear. Don't assume that my responsibilities as a businessman mean I cannot defend myself. I learned Varzesh-e-Bastani, Iranian martial arts, soon after I could walk."

"We never knew about this in school." Nick snickered. "We ribbed him for being from royalty and yet little did we know how close we came to him beating us into pulp. He never once threatened us with his skills, or shared his abilities. What do you all think of that?"

"I was afraid of hurting you," Farzad said with a chuckle. And the company laughed. With Nick, Farzad seemed more relaxed, almost submissive to him, perhaps reliving the schoolboy taunts that had come at him with good intentions.

"We were such innocent, silly kids back then," Nick said with a downturn of his mouth.

"And now you're successful entrepreneurs," Conrad said, his voice revealing the slightest suggestion of sarcastic envy.

"And who isn't who graduated from the Albany Ridge School?" Farzad said.

Nick shrugged and chuckled. "I'm an old horse farmer, barely able to sell a broomtail. What success am I?"

"You've done more than that, Nick Pfeifer. Don't you tell your friends here about what you've accomplished?"

"Why would anyone care? I've done nothing special."

Aiden became more intrigued with Nick than he did their exotic guest, and he could tell that Daniel, with his coffee-brown eyes pinned on Nick, had also grown interested. Their neighbor was a welcome addition to their lives, yet they knew very little about him. As gregarious as he was, he seldom spoke about his life before moving to Montana.

They waited what seemed a long while for Farzad Qajar to continue to reveal more about Nick. Conrad jumped in, unrestrained by Aiden and Daniel's tacit understanding that Nick favored his privacy. "What did he do before raising horses?"

"Nick was one of the most successful prosecutors in Tulsa," Farzad said with a gentle nod of his head. "You never mentioned it, Nick?"

An attorney. Aiden never imagined. They knew he'd gone to Stanford, but when Aiden had asked him what he'd majored in the night he spoke of his former college days, Nick had only mentioned he received a "useless" degree in the humanities. Farzad revealed a new side to Nick, and Aiden felt as if he had two strangers—perhaps three with Conrad—gathered around him.

Nick flushed. He looked toward the fireplace and Aiden noticed his knuckles turning white where he grasped his glass. "I remember those days," he said, shaking his head toward the flaming and smoking logs. "I'm glad I gave it up for something simpler." Then he swept everyone a tremulous smirk. "I was just a regular old working stiff living in the suburbs of Tulsa."

"Not so regular," Farzad interceded. "In addition to being an attorney, he owned two successful restaurants before selling them off in a sudden fit to hide away here in Montana. He gave up so much. But for what reason, I never figured out."

Nick waved off Farzad's comment. "My ancillary businesses were a drain. Besides, it was time to give up the rat race." He raised his chin and declared, "Life demands more from us all than business, right?"

The word *life* punctured the air, brandishing a sharper edge than in normal company. Conrad sat among them. He slid farther into his chair and disappeared more into his clothes. Of the five men, he alone would understand the priorities of life.

Nervous energy seemed to coalesce among the small party. Farzad massaged the condensation on his glass with his free hand. Nick stared down the hallway as if seeking an escape route. Conrad gazed at his sunken lap. Daniel's shoulders rose to his ears. Aiden said he'd check on dinner and figured the sooner they ate the better.

Removing the lamb roast from the oven, Aiden heard Farzad ask Daniel more about his woodshop. Daniel told him about his many clients, from young families eager for high-quality craftsmanship to fancy lodges, which required authentic pieces to match their rustic surroundings.

"And you, Conrad," Farzad said. "What is it that you do?"

"I'm a computer guy, like you," Conrad chimed.

Aiden shouted through the pass-through, "He's one of those guys who can fix anything computer related. I've tried to learn but I never can."

"Do you work here in Montana?"

Aiden noticed a hesitation. Daniel spoke on Conrad's behalf with his deepest baritone, "He's visiting."

More silence followed, and Aiden realized Nick hadn't mentioned to Farzad the intimate details of Conrad's illness or Aiden and Daniel's domestic situation. Nick spoke up, his voice unusually loud and jovial. "He wanted to get away from the rat race too, Farzad."

"I'm here for some recuperation, you might say," Conrad replied with a snigger.

"Conrad's from Washington, DC," Nick added.

"You came as far as I have."

"Daniel and Aiden have been kind to let me stay here," Conrad said to Farzad.

Farzad hollered toward the kitchen, "And what do you do, Aiden?"

"I'm a freelance writer," Aiden said, stirring the warmed garlic mashed potatoes. "I write articles on just about anything as long as they pay me."

"He's writing about Glacier National Park now," Conrad said. "Something about the environment."

Aiden plated the lamb roast on a platter that he used for fancy occasions. "It's somewhat involved, but there's a strip-mining corporation across the border setting up operations that might adversely affect the park, and possibly even the entire Flathead Valley."

"I hope you can expose them for what they are," Farzad said. "The power behind such large companies can be difficult to contain. It takes power to fight power."

"Bully the bullies," Conrad sang, and sipped from his drink. Struggling to stand, he said, "I'll go see if Aiden needs help." He sidled next to Aiden in the kitchen and whispered in his ear with the stink of gin, "This is turning into a fun night."

Aiden held back a chuckle and said under his voice, "It'll be over soon enough, don't worry. Go tell everyone dinner's ready."

The five men gathered around the table and Daniel led a prayer, one that each of them could interpret to meet the needs of his own faith, or lack of one. Afterward they passed the serving bowls and platters, hand over hand. Farzad served himself scant amounts. Aiden suspected he was being polite by refusing too much. His plump lower lip trembled with each bite. He became quiet, provided an uneven smile around the table.

"This is wonderful, Aiden," Nick said. "You've outdone yourself. Best lamb I've ever tasted."

"It's very good," Daniel said.

"Glad you guys like it. Eat up. There's plenty."

"Forgive me, I'm confused," Farzad said, still picking at his food. "Who is it who lives here?"

"Aiden and Daniel both live here, Farzad," Nick said, eyes on his plate. "I told you that. And Conrad is a friend of theirs."

"So none of you have a wife?"

Aiden's hand froze in the midst of doling himself mashed potatoes. He could see that Farzad had directed the question to Daniel. They sat facing each other across the table, like two seated chess pieces.

"I was married once," Daniel said bluntly. "I even had one son."

"I don't mean to pry. It's just that…."

"My wife and infant son were killed in a tornado in Illinois a few years ago," Daniel stated.

Farzad stayed quiet. Conrad, who had never learned the details of Daniel's past, dropped his fork on his plate with a resounding clink. Nick had known about Daniel's life in Illinois, for Daniel had volunteered this intimate detail of his Amish past to him one winter night over hot chocolate before a roaring fire. Nick had seemed genuinely stricken. It was then Aiden and Daniel knew they had found a true friend in their solicitous neighbor.

"And now you live here, with Aiden?" Farzad said.

"*Ya.*"

Aiden hurried plating the food. He saw that Farzad had again glanced at their portrait on the mantle.

"I see," Farzad said. "It's just that…." His words trailed off into a mumble.

Nick attempted to jump-start the conversation. "Wonderful choice of wine," he said, raising his glass of cabernet sauvignon and examining the deep blush that shimmered under the overhead lights. "Has a sweet, woodsy taste."

"Thought it might pair well with the lamb," Aiden said, parroting Nick's tone. They sounded like bad actors in a horrible TV commercial.

Daniel cut into his meat, focusing on one of his favorite meals. Aiden figured by the rise of his shoulders that he wished Aiden had never invited Nick's friend over for dinner.

By the hearth, Ranger held his head high, eager for treats. He'd become pushy about getting scraps from the table lately and Daniel had scolded him more often than not.

"You should try Aiden's Mexican cooking," Conrad said, as if trying to get a rise from them. "Tasty stuff, you bet."

"I've never had the pleasure of trying one of his Mexican suppers," Nick said.

"I'll have to invite you over next time we have one," Aiden said.

"Aiden's suppers warm the belly and the soul," Daniel said.

"Speaking of warm, Farzad tells me they've already had temperatures in the eighties back east." Nick forked a healthy piece of lamb into his mouth and glanced around the table. "We won't see temps that high until about June, huh, Daniel? Daniel is our expert weatherman, Farzad."

Farzad lifted lethargic eyes from his plate. "Oh?"

"Being raised on an Amish farm makes you sensitive to those things, right, Daniel?"

"I figure that could be. Dad had the tongue for changing weather, though."

"A tongue?" Conrad asked.

"We used to say he had a taste for the weather."

They chuckled, all but Farzad. Nick added, "Tell us, Daniel, when do you foresee the weather warming up for good?"

"Unsure," Daniel murmured toward his plate. "There's still yet snow in the higher elevations."

"We get some strange weather here, don't we, fellows? Take September. Can be our hottest month, just when you'd expect things to cool off."

Aiden swallowed a bite of lamb. "I think it has to do with the craggy mountains, Nick. Heat gets trapped in the rocks and by the end of summer they act like heaters. It's something to experience when you backpack in the woods. At night, you can actually feel the heat rise off rock outcroppings and even the coldest nights can be warmed by them."

"I've noticed that," Nick said. "Much cheaper than Flathead Electric."

Shaky laughter rolled around the table. Only Farzad remained mute.

"I'm sorry," he said, finally. "I can't…."

"Farzad!" Nick reached for Farzad as he stood with a harsh skid of his chair. "Where are you going? We're in the middle of eating."

"Forgive me, Nick. Forgive me, everyone. I don't wish to be impolite. But my faith, my bloodline, my very existence prevents me from accepting this. I know that for some it is okay, especially for young people. Even in my home country, I hear they are less prone to condemnation. But I cannot." He turned for the door, leaving behind a trail of spicy cologne, and said over and over under his breath, "I must leave. Please forgive me. I must leave."

He slipped on his loafers and was grabbing for the door handle when Nick leaped from his chair. "You wait right there, Farzad Qajar. I don't give a damn how much you apologize, you are still a guest in my friends' home. You are showing your ignorance."

Farzad, frozen by the door, slowly turned to face his old friend. His complexion reddened with deepening anguish. Aiden never saw a man show such pain on his face. "One man's ignorance is another's convictions," he muttered. "I'm going to the hotel. I'll call for a taxi with my cellular outside. Don't bother to show me out."

"Don't be a fool, Farzad. I'll drive you. Stay put." Nick yanked his jacket off the hook and turned to Aiden and the others, his gray eyes full of regret. "I'm very sorry for this. If I had known—"

Left at the table, Daniel, Aiden, and Conrad sat quiet and stunned. Aiden glanced around. Daniel kept his head down, his cheeks redder than the cabernet sauvignon. Conrad poked his food, scratched his naked scalp.

"He was a load of laughs," he said, releasing the tension.

"I sensed that might happen," Daniel put in.

It wasn't until the last drop of gravy was slurped up with the store-bought rolls that a light chuckle rippled around the table, changing to a full-blown howl. Even Ranger jumped up, tail wagging like a willow branch in the wind, and found the entire evening ridiculous.

NEAR ten o'clock, while everyone relaxed before the fire and appeared to have forgotten Farzad Qajar's outburst, Aiden answered a light knock on the front door. Nick stood on the landing wringing his hands, looking sheepish and ashamed.

"Come on in, Nick." Aiden opened the door wider.

Nick stepped in, smiled shakily at Daniel and Conrad seated in the living area. "I suppose my reaction was almost as bad as his," he said to them. "He got me so angry. I had no idea he harbored such prejudices. I tried to talk sense into him, but he is a stubborn man."

"Your friend has a right to his beliefs," Daniel said from the sofa.

"You are good and understanding men," Nick said with a trembling smile. "But it angers me there are people like Farzad in the world."

"Would you like me to fix you a plate?" Aiden asked him. "You didn't get to finish your dinner or have any dessert. I bought a cherry-rhubarb pie from a local Amish bakery."

Nick shook his head. "Sounds tempting. But it's late. Maybe tomorrow. I just wanted to apologize. And to promise next time I'll be sure to bring a dinner guest with less passion for his views."

"We weren't offended," Aiden said.

"No worries, Nick," Daniel said.

"He was a hoot," Conrad declared from the easy chair. "Best dinner party I ever attended."

Shaking his head, Nick tried to chuckle. "I wish I could be as casual about this as you all." He stared at them, his mouth opened slightly. His Adam's apple quivered with a strange expectancy. "I better get home," he said at last. "You fellows have a good night. Sorry again for the trouble."

"Good night, Nick," they shouted after him.

A half hour later, Aiden lay in bed and watched Daniel change into pajama bottoms while trying to hold back from expressing his suspicions that Nick had wanted to offer more than apologies. Nick concealed something. The same sensation Aiden experienced from the other times whenever in Nick's company. "I wonder what Nick's true beef is," Aiden finally said.

"You don't think he was merely upset by his friend insulting us?"

"Seems more to it than that."

"Nick was for sure boogered by it more than us," Daniel said.

"You agree with me and think he's gay, don't you?"

"I don't understand why he wouldn't tell us if it's true. He clearly has no issues with it."

"I just can't figure it out," Aiden said.

Daniel tested the elastic on his waistband. “Stop trying to. People have a right to their own business.”

Daniel hunkered under the bedcovers. Once settled, Aiden leaned into him and said, “Do you ever resent being with me?”

“Every day of my life.”

Aiden gaped. “What?”

“Sometimes I think it’d be much easier to live a sad, empty life than one filled with so much love. Brings a lot of heartache.”

“But honestly, Daniel. Do you sometimes feel weird about our relationship?”

Daniel set his gaze on the opposite wall. “Sometimes I think it’s unusual to be with a man, despite it being my nature.”

Aiden accepted Daniel’s frankness, devoid of empty sentiments. Crinkling his forehead, he said, “Did Farzad make you feel bad about yourself tonight?”

“I’d rather dine with an honest enemy than a condescending ally,” Daniel said.

Aiden considered Daniel’s words. “I feel the same.”

Daniel kissed Aiden’s cheek. “Good. Now let’s get some sleep. I need to get up early in the morning.”

Aiden snickered. “Like Nick said, you’re still very much Amish, aren’t you? You like to rise early, you wear a moustacheless beard, lots of things like that.”

“I reckon old habits die hard. Does any of that bother you?”

Aiden cuddled closer to Daniel, clung to his powerful bicep. “Not in the slightest. I love your old-fashioned ways. But you’re nothing like Farzad. You’re an understanding, strong, sensitive man. Not a sanctimonious religious kook.”

“That’s good to know.” Daniel switched off the light and gave Aiden one last kiss before rolling to his side. “Have good dreams, Aiden.”

“You too, Daniel. Good night.”

But Aiden did not slide under the covers and close his eyes along with Daniel. Instead, he stared into the darkness, and stayed up at least another hour, wondering….

Chapter EIGHTEEN

AFTER seeing Daniel off for work the next morning, Aiden watched Nick cross the road from his horse ranch. At the door, Aiden greeted him and offered him to step inside, but Nick raised his hand and shook his head.

"I just wanted to make sure you all were doing okay after last night's incident," he said, patting Ranger, who had left his bed to say hello.

"We aren't bothered by people like Farzad, Nick," Aiden emphasized. "Don't mention it again."

"He was easier to get along with than Aiden," said Conrad, who was sitting on the floor and tying his shoelaces with a scowl on his face. "Aiden insists I'm a sick, helpless man and shouldn't drive myself to my treatments."

Aiden tried to laugh off Conrad's exaggerations. "We were just heading out to the clinic, Nick."

"Don't get angry at him for worrying about you," Nick told Conrad. "He's only looking out for your best interest. But to fix your troubles, why don't I drive you this time around?"

Conrad's beaming face took Aiden by surprise. "Okay," Conrad said, jumping to his feet. "But you'll have to find somewhere to go while you wait. I won't have anyone holding my hand. Not even you, Nick Pfeifer."

Nick chuckled. "I understand, young man. I won't baby you. I'll just be your ride."

Conrad, grabbing for his jacket, brushed past Aiden and headed straight for Nick's truck, parked in his driveway across the road. Aiden and Nick exchanged looks and shrugs, and Nick, snickering under his breath, followed after Conrad.

Aiden shut the door and sighed. He gave Ranger a dog biscuit from his special cupboard and, with a smile, watched him trot back to his hearthside bed. Happy to have someone else chauffeur Conrad, Aiden returned to his strip-mining article scattered across the dining table, where he'd been working before Conrad announced out of the blue he had a radiation appointment in an hour.

The idea of Conrad driving alone had worried Aiden, especially that morning. During breakfast, Aiden noticed even more his emaciated physique, which had become almost feminine with curves and protruding adolescent boy hips. He pictured him back in college filling out his gray camouflage ROTC uniform. Was the lymphoma winning the battle of life versus death?

For the first time, Aiden understood his mother's old saying, "If you have your health, you have everything."

Aiden figured people would surrender a fortune in exchange for wellness.

He tried to keep a positive attitude while he wrote, but the doubts nagged him. The same doubts since the afternoon he first recognized Conrad's voice on his cell phone.

He realized the awfulness of their situation when he returned home from Glacier Park and cleaved to Ranger, arched and vomiting bile in the kitchen. Many times in the darkest hours of morning, Aiden held Conrad's head after he'd gotten sick. During those times, his heart coasted elsewhere. Not so with Ranger. With his arms thrown around his furry waist, Aiden near fainted from anguish that he might lose his beloved pet. Yet he snapped at Conrad, more worried that Ranger suffered from food poisoning than whether he hurt Conrad's feelings.

Pity was such a nasty emotion. The past few weeks, his devotion to Conrad had transformed into a labored redundancy. The occasional midnight sicknesses made Aiden yearn for the time when Conrad's treatments would end and he might leave them.

He sketched out a third draft, realizing midway that he needed additional information for his article to sound more professional. He attempted to call the mining company again, but their phone number he'd found on the Internet rang and rang without answer. Frustrated, he sat back in the chair and gazed out the window.

The aspen trees were filling out, and sun highlighted their bright green crowns. Briefly he wished he'd gone with Conrad for an excuse to get outside. Their backpacking trip stirred inside him the need to spend more time with nature. Nonetheless, it was good Nick and Conrad had become special friends.

Watching the jays gather in the front yard to feed off the pine seeds, Aiden supposed Daniel was right. Why fixate about Nick when his private life was none of their affair? Farzad was another enigma. A swarthy, charming man, he had found Aiden, Daniel, and Conrad undesirable dining companions. In some ways, Aiden felt sorry for him. Deep down, despite his royal bloodline, he was a simple man enslaved by age-old fear and ideology.

Aiden was about to turn back to his article when his cell phone rang with the generic ringtone. He reached for the phone on the table. "Hello?"

"Aiden Cer… Cermak?"

"Yes, this is him."

Aiden leaped to his feet when he heard the name of the caller. "Of course I remember you, Pete. How are you? What can I do for you?"

"I'm down in Kalispell right now. If you still want to meet… I can meet with you, but only if you can come right now."

"Where are you?"

"You know where the Lion Burger is at on Route 93?"

"Yes, I'll leave right away. It might take me about thirty minutes, so please don't leave. Promise?"

"Okay. But hurry it up. I can't wait too long."

Aiden rushed to gather his work and make sure Ranger had fresh water. He texted Nick and asked if he would mind keeping Conrad company until he returned. He snatched his laptop, packed it in its case, and jogged for his pickup without worrying to read Nick's response. Aiden knew he'd comply.

He cruised into Kalispell in record time, passing the cancer clinic without a glimpse, and pulled into the parking lot for Lion Burger about four miles south on Route 93, where Pete Campbell from the strip-mining company said to meet. With sunny skies and temperatures in the low sixties, Pete sat outside, stuffing his face full of fries. Aiden steadied his anxious pace and approached him.

"Hello, Pete. It's me. Aiden Cermak."

The hefty man with a bronzed face glanced up from the fiberglass picnic table. His shirt, unbuttoned to expose the stark white tan line of his wrinkled brown neck, was stained with grease. "You want something to eat or drink?"

Aiden sat across from him. "No thanks. I was very glad you called. What made you decide?"

Pete stopped eating long enough to gaze toward Aiden, but not directly at him. His clear blue eyes squinted from the bright sun. He looked much the same when Aiden first met him at the British Columbia mining site. The only difference was he appeared more at ease while eating at a Kalispell eatery than when he had stood guard before locked, barbwire gates.

"I kept the business card you gave me," Pete said. "I thought about tossing it out, but couldn't." He spoke with a similar accent as Americans from that part of the country, but some of his words—like "out" and "couldn't"—sounded more reminiscent of the British. "I was coming down to the States for a medical checkup and to do some shopping anyhow, so I thought I'd go ahead and ring you up."

"I'm glad you did."

"The good doctor says I need to lose about thirty pounds, but here I am eating like a hog. I love this place. I eat here every time I come into Kalispell. They could use a chain of these up in Canada. Man cannot live by donuts alone, you know."

Aiden watched him eat. His eyes held little of the suspicion and worry from the last time Aiden saw him. "Why are you seeing a doctor? Is your health okay?"

Focused on one objective—his hamburger and mound of fries—he barely glanced at Aiden while he answered. "I was diagnosed with prostate cancer about three years ago."

"I'm sorry." Was everyone sick, Aiden wondered.

Pete shook his head. "I'm getting good care. I have to visit my oncologist three times a year to keep tabs on things. My doctor in Canada prescribed the one I go to in the States."

"The Flathead Valley Cancer Center?"

Pete nodded, his mouth stuffed with fries. "That's the one, you bet. My wife won't come down here with me anymore. She hasn't crossed the border since two years ago. Says she hates all the hassles. Border officials scare her to death. So I come down alone, see my doctor, shop a little, gas up." He lifted his basket of food. "And to eat."

He settled the basket under his nose and continued to eat. His expression reminded Aiden of Ranger when he concentrated gnawing on a pig ear. Aiden suppressed a chuckle.

"I'm guessing you weren't looking for a lunchtime companion since your wife no longer travels with you," Aiden said. "What did you want to speak to me about, Pete?"

Pete bent four fries onto his tongue and washed them down with a gulp of soda. "Did you know that most of the world's strip-mining companies are Canadian owned?"

"I think I read that somewhere on the Internet."

"They've leveled entire Philippine islands, a dozen Mexican towns, large chunks of Central America. Locals sometimes hold huge protests. They riot, burn US flags. Canada, America, what's the difference to them? But nothing stops these companies."

"Have you seen this firsthand?"

"I worked a site for another company in Guatemala about ten years ago. Hated what I saw, but I kept to my work, guarding the place. After that I refused any more foreign assignments, despite it paying twice as much."

"What did you see, Pete?"

"Squatters were keeping the company from coming into the hills. Natives who lived literally in grass huts. Didn't take much to torch their homes to the ground. But the locals came back looking for blood. The government, on the company payroll, sent in the military to shoot on the spot anyone who prevented access to the hills. I could hear gunfire now and then, but I never saw anyone actually shot." He shook his head toward his basket of food. "I'll always remember those huts going up in flames. Guatemalan soldiers sprayed them with flamethrowers. Sometimes with people inside refusing to come out. Women screaming, babies crying. Horrible."

"And this is the same type of mining company you work for now, setting up mining across the border from Glacier National Park?"

"I'm guessing they all operate on the same level. If they run into squatters, they call up the government, the government calls up the military, and the squatters, usually natives, are forcibly removed. If they refuse, they kill them. I heard one company had soldiers blow up an entire village in the Philippines. Weren't no men around to defend the place because they were off fighting some religious war on another island, or something of that sort."

He paused to scratch his expanding forehead, bronzed like the craggy peaks of the Swan Range rising east of the city. Throughout his speech, he maintained minimal eye contact with Aiden. He appeared tranquil, perhaps too much. Indifferent to the consequences of his meeting Aiden, or to the horror he recounted brought about by corrupt governments and hyper-aggressive corporations.

"Some of these companies can sway entire elections in places like the Philippines and Central America," he continued with a shrug. "Now if the natives down here in the US start to protest, we have craftier ways of dealing with you."

Aiden waited for him to take another swig from his soda. "How's that?"

Pete wiped his mouth. "Nothing is as it seems, you know that, don't you? You understand everything is an illusion, right?"

"There're reasons for keeping things secret, I guess," Aiden said, unsure in which direction Pete wanted to steer their interview.

Taking a break from eating, Pete looked Aiden in the eye for the first time. With a confident shake of his head, he whispered, "I'm not the only one who's come forward about all this, you know. Lots of the guys have. Just so you know, nothing has ever come from it. I'm guessing nearly everyone is on the take. Even reporters like you. I suspect some of them start investigations just so they'd get a promise of a bribe."

Aiden studied Pete's blue eyes. He swallowed. "Then why bother to speak with me?"

Pete leaned back, patted his round belly. "I don't know. Maybe guys like me talk just to clear our conscience. Maybe I trust you, for whatever reason. Where you plan on publishing your article?"

"The local newspaper here in Kalispell."

Pete bent back his neck and gazed at the periwinkle sky. "Hope you have better luck with a small town newspaper. None of the giants ever cover it." He leaned forward and toyed with a forlorn french fry, droopy and soggy from the grease that settled on the bottom of the parchment paper. "What can we do?" he said, popping the fry into his mouth. "The world slumps ahead whether the bad guys are punished or not."

Aiden checked his wristwatch, mindful of needing to get back to Conrad and relieve Nick of his duties in reasonable time. Most likely they had returned home. "You mentioned about taking care of us locals down here in craftier ways. What did you mean exactly?"

"Companies can't use brute force in the United States or make open-faced threats against the government like they do in places like Guatemala and Mexico. That'll get too many people upset."

"Then how do mining companies silence dissenters down here?"

Pete kicked away the tiny warblers scavenging by their feet. "The media, politicians."

"By buying and selling them?"

"Talk around the mine is they use politicians to give the illusion they're fighting the company, but it's all a ruse. Kind of like how companies post fake five-star reviews of their products on the Internet, pretending that it's unbiased. And it goes all the way to Ottawa and Washington, from what I've experienced." Pete tilted his head and scrutinized Aiden. "You been talking to someone named Gloria Klamsa?"

Aiden clutched the table's edge and sat taller. "Senator Gloria Klamsa?"

Pete gave a quick nod. "She's supposed to be adamantly opposed to the mining across the border, right? She's on your side, right?

You've been talking with her about the evils it will do to the environment, right? Well, she's on the take, like most politicians. We have them in Canada too. Real pigs. I think her efforts were sincere at first, but the company threw enough money at her, under cover, of course, and she piped down real quick."

Pete revealed more. Lots more. About how other strip-mining companies were planning to open sites in Colorado and Arizona. Encroaching inside the United States itself.

Aiden devoured what Pete told him. "And environment groups? Have they caused any headaches for these companies?"

Pete laughed, nearly spitting. "You'd think they'd be the loudest, but they're not. Hardly make a peep. Invisible except for a handful. Maybe a while back they were more vocal, but not so much these days."

"Even when people like you come forward?"

"I have my own theories about that." Pete swallowed the last of his food. "You do too, if you think about it. Why isn't the media attacking senators like Gloria Klamsa, huh? Or all over my company's headquarters in Alberta? Where are the bleeding hearts when Guatemalan natives are torched alive in their own homes? Why not blast the cover off the entire scheme? You know the answer. We might be wrong. Who knows? But I think we're right."

Aiden could not turn his eyes from Pete. He watched him dab at his mouth, work his tongue around his gums to loosen any food caught between his teeth.

"My father used to say the only difference between Canadians and Americans was attitude," Pete said finally. "Americans look at the world through the eyes of pioneers, he'd tell me, while Canadians are more like loyalists."

Aiden never considered it before, but he asked anyway. "You think so?"

"It don't make too much difference. I'm right about that. Who am I to care?"

"You care, or you wouldn't be here talking with me."

"Okay, okay, I care. But caring has little to do with anything. I'm not going to lose any sleep over what I can't control. You shouldn't either. Listen, don't let this eat you up inside. It's not worth it."

"Saving Glacier Park and perhaps many other places around the world isn't worth it?"

"Let's say Glacier Park and towns like Kalispell are turned into swamps," Pete said with a rise to his voice. "Is that going to keep people in Toronto or Boston from their Sunday afternoon coffees? No, it won't. Not ever. Why should you worry? Go ahead, but don't bother crying over it. Enjoy your caffe latte."

Intermittent traffic from nearby Route 93 rumbled above the resulting silence. Pete's words stymied Aiden. He failed to find a proper response. Despite the excitement building in his chest about uncovering an uglier side to the strip-mining business than anything he imagined, Aiden suddenly wished he were with Conrad. He'd rather face the uncertainty of cancer than the sureness of human depravity.

"Something else you should know," Pete said, fixing a sudden stare on Aiden, which caused Aiden to flinch. "We start blasting in the MacDonald Mountains next month. Sites are already marked."

"Doesn't give us a lot of time, does it?"

"Not much for you. Go ahead. Write your article. See if anybody worries enough to stop the mining. You know the reason why no one will. Think about it."

Aiden recalled his interview with Ranger Craig Ellis, Glacier Park's education officer, a nature-loving man who dreamed of working in the national park system since he was a boy. Ranger Ellis expressed the same odd combination of concern and cryptic impassiveness. A chill traced along Aiden's neck. He searched for sign of a breeze, but the day was as still as any he remembered since moving to northwestern Montana.

Aiden tried to find folly in Pete's sober words. He was an insider. But enough that he'd understand the workings of politics and big corporations like an expert? What were his true motives, if he had any? Did Pete really care, or was he just another weasel looking for a payoff? He had spoken authoritatively, from the position of someone who'd witnessed brutality. Aiden could not refuse the potency of his admissions.

Maybe like with Conrad, Pete's cancer made him more astute.

One thing Aiden knew: an elaborate scheme was playing out on both sides of the border for no reason than fast money, much of it at taxpayers' expense. Both Americans and Canadians were being taken. It would be up to Aiden—and his valuable First Amendment rights—to see that he at least hobbled, if not ended, the fiasco.

He also understood that Pete's disclosure would require much more research. He couldn't print Pete's isolated testimony. He'd have to dig for more firsthand accounts and reactions from those Pete had said suffered or those he accused of bribe taking.

Pete stood. "It's been nice talking to you, but I better get going. Long trip back north and I still have to face border control. Gets worse in the afternoons." He dipped his fingers into his shirt pocket and withdrew Aiden's business card. "Here. I won't be contacting you again."

Aiden took the greasy business card from Pete and thanked him with a firm handshake. He understood the risks Pete took to meet him. "I won't use your name in my articles, Pete, I promise."

Pete snickered. "Of course you won't. You could be an accessory after the fact if you did."

Aiden accompanied Pete down the footpath and watched him drive off in his Ford Escape. After that, he sat in his truck in the Lion Burger parking lot and, contemplating a moment, typed five pages from the information Pete told him. Once he returned home, he chose to keep quiet about what he learned. He sat on something hot, and intended to let it simmer before serving it to the world.

But he found no one home to reveal his exciting news to even if he wanted. The house sat still and empty. Even Ranger was gone. Across the road, one of Nick's horses neighed. Aiden opened the front door and peered out. The stench of livestock from Nick's ranch seemed extra thick.

He stared across the road a good while, almost forgetting about his astonishing interview with Pete. Through the trees Whitey, Nick's prized mustang, and her most recent foal ran back and forth on Nick's property, playing almost like dogs.

Out of the trees Ranger appeared, dancing circles around the foal. His low-pitched bark echoed against the deepening sky. He heard fluctuating laughter and the baritone of Nick and Conrad's voices. Sighing with both relief and dismay, Aiden shut the door and headed for the bedroom.

Chapter NINETEEN

SATURDAY afternoon, Conrad, his bright-blue eyes shiny like fiery gemstones, strolled in from another visit with Nick. "Do you mind if I take one of the trucks out tonight?"

Aiden, seated at the dining table, stopped poking at his laptop keypad and looked up. "Didn't we already decide you shouldn't drive?"

"You decided, not me. I'm a grown man, Daddy."

Daniel, newly home from the shop and sorting through the mail by the front door in his stocking feet, gawked at him. "What do you want with one of the trucks?"

"I was thinking of hitting those gay-friendly establishments in Kalispell Aiden was talking about. I'm craving nightlife. I did some Internet searching of my own and have a few places in mind."

"Are you up for that?" Aiden said, trying not to sound too condescending. "Especially after getting a little sick last night?"

"I'm clearly much better today and I plan on having some fun. Real fun. Can I have a house key too? I'll probably be home late and I don't want to wake you guys."

"Is Nick going with you?" Aiden asked.

"Nope. Why would you think that?"

Aiden shrugged. "Just wondering. You've been spending a lot of time at his ranch lately."

"You're not interested in coming along, are you? No offense, but we see enough of each other. I thought I'd give us all a break."

"But you don't know your way around town," Aiden said, determined to change Conrad's mind.

"I can figure it out using my smartphone."

Aiden and Daniel traded frowns. "If you really feel you're well enough," Aiden said after gauging Daniel's reaction and realizing they would have no chance to convince Conrad otherwise. "I guess it'll be okay, but just for a little while."

"I'll be all right," Conrad said as he headed down the hall.

Daniel gazed at the mail in his loose fingers with weary brown eyes. Aiden's hesitations continued to dog him too. While Aiden worried about Conrad driving alone, especially at night, he realized Daniel's concerns centered more on Conrad taking one of their trucks. No way would Daniel allow Conrad to drive his beloved Chevy Suburban.

And that night, despite their qualms about Conrad's leaving in Aiden's pickup, Aiden and Daniel took advantage of their rare privacy. They made love like they hadn't in weeks. They spent most the evening grappling each other in bed. Daniel showed his uncommon aggressive side. Afterward they camped out by the coffee table to watch a download on Aiden's laptop, a romantic gay romance called *Big Eden* set near, of all places, Glacier National Park.

In the middle of the movie, Daniel, his arms wrapped loosely around Aiden's shoulders, articulated Aiden's nagging thoughts. "If he's feeling good enough to go out on a Saturday night, why does he need us to care for him?"

Aiden organized his words before speaking, wanting to convince himself more than Daniel. "He's having one of those good days, like he said. We should actually encourage him. That's part of our responsibility as caregivers."

Daniel said nothing else on the matter.

They watched the rest of the film, tidied up the kitchen, and climbed into bed at midnight. Aiden asked about the latest letter from Elisabeth. Daniel recounted the Henry and Schrock family news. Life back in Illinois Amish Country trotted along at its typical unhurried, but purposeful, pace.

Soon after, Aiden fell fast asleep until the front door opening and shutting followed by the rattling of Ranger's collar awoke him. He glanced at the digital alarm next to the snoozing Daniel. Two thirty-five. Last call in Montana was two.

Conrad stomped down the hallway. Aiden perked his ears toward the bedroom door, wondering if Conrad had been inconsiderate and brought home a one-nighter. They should have stipulated before he'd left that he couldn't invite anyone home.

The sound of streaming urine seemed endless. Finally, Conrad flushed, followed by his bedroom door shutting. Ranger's collar stilled, and Aiden could tell he settled back on his bed by the hearth.

Satisfied Conrad had come home alone, Aiden laid his head back on the pillow and lay awake for some time before yielding again to sleep.

DANIEL and Aiden were finishing Sunday breakfast when they heard Conrad fiddling in the bathroom. Daniel got up from the table and slipped on his boots. "I'll be out in the garage shop," he said, and he left out the front door before Conrad appeared.

Conrad came into the kitchen without his skullcap tight around his head as they'd become accustomed to seeing, and Aiden gaped. His head was now completely bald, reflecting the overhead lights. Aiden looked away, barely able to utter a good morning. Conrad, on the other hand, seemed in good spirits.

He tore into a fresh box of strawberry Pop-Tarts. "I put your car keys on the coffee table. Not much going on last night," he offered. "Your gay-friendly taverns are more like watering holes for dirty old men."

Aiden shuffled to the refrigerator to put away the milk. "That's usually the way small towns are."

"Funny thing, I thought I'd feel conspicuous with my bald head, so I wore my skullcap. When I stepped into the first bar, half the men were bald. I went to two other places, and the same. I took off my cap and no one noticed." He chewed on a bite of Pop-tart and snickered under his breath. "I thought there'd be some hot cowboys looking for Saturday-night action."

"Lonely ranchers meet each other online these days, I guess." Was that how Nick spent his lonely hours, Aiden mused.

"They're almost as bad as what I saw at the bars," Conrad said.

Aiden sighed. "I've never been in the chat rooms or bars here. No need to. I'm with Daniel, remember?"

"You're being smug."

"I don't mean to be," Aiden mumbled. "Just stating a fact."

"Where is Daniel, anyhow?"

"Out in the woodshop."

Sunday was one of those cold May mornings and Aiden noticed the beginnings of a headache creeping upon him—as if Conrad's late-nighter had transferred onto him, which happened often while the two had dated. A contact hangover, Aiden used to call it. Conrad was always a partier, even after he and Aiden moved together as a couple to Chicago. Their first night in the new city, Conrad dragged Aiden to the local gay bars. Aiden tolerated the outings for a few weeks, then balked, allowing Conrad to satisfy his appetite for drinks and socializing three, four times a week.

Conrad poured orange juice and carried his glass and a second Pop-Tart to the dining table. He munched on his small breakfast while Aiden cleaned the kitchen. Without a word, Conrad deposited his empty glass in the sink and disappeared into his bedroom. Daniel entered through the kitchen soon after. He stood stiff, turning up his nose, mimicking Ranger when he'd run outside in the mornings and catch scent of Nick's horses. "Conrad come out?" he said, slipping off his boots.

Aiden nodded. "He just went back to his bedroom. I thought you were going to hide out in your woodshop all day."

"Hide out? Why would you think that? I wish I had more of my work to keep me busy here."

Nonetheless, for most of that Sunday, Daniel came and went between the garage and the house. Aiden never bothered to ask what he was doing. He suspected he was organizing for spring cleaning. Once the weather warmed permanently for the season, they would borrow Nick's ride-on mower and spend weekend after weekend on yard work. Aiden couldn't dream up anything nicer, but he hated thinking Daniel was shutting down again, hiding away.

Conrad, too, kept himself scarce. He spent most of the day lying in his room, goofing off on the Internet, while Ranger lay beside him, despite Aiden requesting that he stay off the bed. Ranger seemed to take a watchful concern for their convalescing boarder. He kept by his side more and more. Aiden was both glad and resentful. Like he had feared back in March, Conrad, indeed, disrupted much of their lives.

He never did anything to encourage Conrad to leave. Just the opposite. Although the midnight diarrhea and nausea was something he could have lived without, the worst was when Conrad acted belligerent, like a moody adolescent. Aiden reminded himself his illness and the side effects of radiation and chemotherapy caused much of his wavering temperament.

Aiden washed several loads of clothes, sheets, and towels, and worked on his article at the dining table between loads. He researched some of what Pete told him about mining companies destroying native villages. He found one article and a single-paged blog that highlighted his claims in more detail. With a finger to his mouth, Aiden wondered why the crimes went unreported in the mainstream media. What could be more newsworthy?

You know the reason why....

Around two o'clock Nick stopped over and asked if Conrad wanted to drive with him to deliver his four-year-old colt to a buyer near Libby. Conrad raced to get ready.

When Daniel returned from the garage a half hour later, Aiden told him, "Conrad's with Nick again."

"Should be fun for him," Daniel said.

"Who? Nick?"

"I was thinking of Conrad."

Ranger dropped a chew toy by Daniel's feet. Daniel tossed it down the hallway and Ranger chased after it.

"He's gaining weight," Aiden said after Ranger dashed off.

"You think so?"

Aiden nodded. "I hope he's getting enough exercise."

"He spends more time outside now that it's warming."

"At least he hasn't thrown up in a while."

Daniel stroked his beard. “He hasn’t?”

“It was just that one weekend,” Aiden said. “Still, I think we should run him more.”

“Run him? Who are we talking about now?”

Aiden chuckled. “Ranger, of course.”

Daniel rolled his eyes. “I thought we were talking about Conrad. Too many souls living in this house. I’m going to take a shower.”

ON THE way to the bedroom, Daniel passed the laundry room and noticed the stacks of clean linen Aiden washed while Daniel tinkered the day away in the garage, sorting the gardening tools and cleaning his workshop. One of the downsides to living in a household devoid of women was housework. He never shied from lending a hand to his sisters and mother back home whenever they needed help, but typically only as an emergency before company, never as a normal routine. Remembering the promise to himself to help Aiden more, he grabbed an armload of sheets and towels and stowed them in the hallway linen closet.

Next to the closet, Conrad’s door stood open, and Daniel saw how untidy Conrad kept the guest bedroom. Pill bottles lay scattered atop the dresser. Drawers and the closet door were open. Suitcases sat gaping with clothes spilling out. His bed was stripped and a fresh batch of sheets lay on the mattress. He recalled Aiden telling him how Conrad refused to change his own bed, even after Aiden would lay fresh linen in his room, and Aiden would have to do it. Wanting to help Aiden even further, Daniel stepped fully into the room and began making Conrad’s bed.

He was smoothing over the bedcovers when he fixated on the pill bottles on Conrad’s dresser. The sight of them made him fantasize about banishing illnesses from existence. Doctors had prescribed Leah mounds of pills to treat her various symptoms: Reglan to aid digestion, Dantrium for pain, Robinul to reduce drooling. He tried to read Conrad’s labels without getting too close. Qsym-something and Relacore. And the Leukeran. He had cringed when he’d learned that the active ingredient in Conrad’s chemo prescription was mustard gas.

Across the hall Conrad's bathroom was in even worse shape. Donning the nitrile gloves, he got to work. There were so many hairs, Daniel wondered if he should vacuum rather than scrub. He used a wire hanger to dislodge another hairball from the sink and coated the porcelain with heavy amounts of bleach to disinfect.

Conrad was no pig, but he certainly could have done more to keep the bathroom and bedroom tidier. When would that man pack and leave for where he came from, Daniel lamented while scouring the floor around the commode on all fours.

"Daniel Schrock!" Aiden stood in the doorway with his hands on his hips. "What on earth are you doing?"

Daniel glanced up, returned to his scrubbing. "I owe you one. Now leave me in peace."

Aiden bent down and kissed his cheek, and Daniel heard him humming down the hallway, singing for Ranger to fetch his chew toy.

Chapter TWENTY

"I DON'T mind, really," Aiden said after Conrad again insisted he drive himself to the clinic Monday morning. "I can always do some shopping while I wait. I know how you like your privacy. But you really shouldn't drive after your treatment."

"I drove Saturday night," Conrad said.

"But you hadn't just come out of radiation, Conrad," Aiden persisted.

"All right," Conrad snapped, stomping for the front door. "I'm tired of arguing about this. It's your time wasted, not mine. Let's go."

They spoke little during the drive. Aiden, worried he was coddling Conrad like Daniel accused him, continued to weight his duty to ensure Conrad's safety and his need for freedom. He dropped Conrad at the clinic and headed down the road for the corner Petco. Ranger needed more pig ears and kibble. For an impulse item he bought a rubber squeaky hotdog.

Twenty minutes later Aiden pulled back into the clinic's parking lot and waited. He wrote furiously on his laptop, chewing through nearly ten pages before he checked his wristwatch and realized a half hour had passed.

He observed the white building, which stretched a half block. It was a place where people became well. It also represented weakness—and the worst weakness of all, death. The more Aiden labored to cater to Conrad's well-being, the more he disliked the circumstances. He loathed how Conrad's sickness turned Conrad into a shadow of his former self. And in that matter, Aiden was no different than Farzad Qajar.

When they shook hands that night, Nick's old school friend barely looked Conrad in the eyes, as if he found him repulsive. Aiden understood why Farzad flinched after meeting Conrad and why later he jumped from the dining table and stormed from their home. To Farzad and men like him, Conrad's obvious illness and homosexuality were stamped by the same mint.

Aiden too despised helplessness. But to Aiden, nothing could be more a product of masculinity than he and Daniel living apart from mainstream society. What did it matter that they shared the same bed? Perhaps that's why he respected the Amish and Daniel's former way of life. Because of their representation of strength. Living off the land. Providing for themselves. Devoid of public assistance.

Aiden figured the local Amish and Hutterite, if they had bothered to become friends with him and Daniel, would have reacted the same as Farzad. The ultraorthodox shared more than a strict interpretation of God's words. They also lived off the grid as rugged pioneers, and they viewed homosexuality a creation of an anemic, postmodern world.

Because of that, Aiden could forgive Farzad's disgust over two men living in a domestic partnership. He returned to New Jersey, to live in his gated community with his wife, to entertain his growing brood of grandchildren like any American man. The ancient Qajar family tree would flourish (albeit mixed with Irish, Italian, German, Indian…) and Farzad would live off the fantasy that his family's bloodline beat with potency, although it had long been subdued by the modern world.

Aiden also realized he had been babying Conrad like Daniel warned, rather than protecting him. Conrad wanted to fight his weakening body by becoming more independent. Aiden, like a bison bull standing in the middle of a hiking trail, was trying to stop him. If Conrad wanted to drive himself to the cancer clinic, Aiden would no longer interfere. If Conrad had an urge to go out on the town, he'd hand him the pickup keys himself.

Relieved to have reached an understanding of his folly, Aiden closed his laptop and peered at the sliding glass doors. Despite his pledge to provide Conrad more space, a fitful urge prompted him to want to wait for him inside. He needed to see for himself the cancer clinic that Conrad had been coming to for more than a month. Surely Conrad would not mind that much.

He was about to head toward the entrance when a shout from across Route 2 stopped him. In a gap in traffic, Conrad dashed across the road.

"My treatments ended early," he said, panting. "I was the first today." He took Aiden by the arm and led him to the truck. "You didn't go inside, did you?"

"I was just about to."

"What for?"

"I thought I'd wait for you there. Where did you come from?"

"After I finished early and I didn't see your truck, I went to Wendy's to get something to eat."

"I'm glad you're getting your appetite back."

Conrad shrugged. "It comes and goes."

Aiden pulled out of the parking lot and started for home. He drove through a green light when he thought he saw Daniel in his burgundy Chevy Suburban pass them in the opposite direction. Aiden swore the driver had a moustacheless beard, and his head slanted similar to whenever Daniel was burdened by heavy thoughts.

He texted him at the next stoplight. By the time they reached home, there was still no answer from Daniel.

DANIEL sat in his truck, stroking his beard. Should he or shouldn't he? He didn't wish to go inside. Time hustled ahead. If he was to follow through with his intentions, he must get it over with. He had to get back to the shop. Phedra said something about wanting to take the afternoon off to help her younger brother prepare for his final examinations.

His cell phone text message dinged for a second time. Must be Aiden again. He had ignored his first message, which read: "Where are you?" Had Aiden stopped by the shop and wondered why he wasn't there? Perhaps he was on his way back from taking Conrad to the clinic. He had no idea on which days Aiden had to chauffeur him.

He left his cell phone in his pants pocket unanswered and he sat, deliberating. He needed to speak with someone. Easier to have telephoned, but the issue at hand warranted a personal visit. He had no other need to head into town.

Were his instincts correct, like they often were with the weather?

He forced his feet out of the truck, planted them on the pavement. He gazed at the two-story white structure. The center stood as a testament to state-of-the-art technology and ingenuity, an aspect of the modern America Daniel always admired. Yet a formidable heaviness pressed on his shoulders.

Traffic on Route 2 whizzed past. The church across the road, the one in which he and Aiden attended a few times, sat stark and cold, its blacktop parking lot empty. Before he realized, he was stepping outside his truck and shutting the door with a heavy bang. The humanity of strip shops and traffic merged into a garish blur as he placed one foot in front of the other.

He jerked when the sliding glass doors opened sooner than he had anticipated. He thought he had stopped before getting too close to the entrance. For a moment, Daniel stood motionless, unable to cross into the vestibule. Conjuring extra courage, he willed his feet forward. He passed through another set of sliding glass doors and an assault of fluorescent lights made him wince. An auburn-haired woman seated behind a reception desk smiled at him.

"May I help you?" she asked.

Daniel worked what little spit remained in his mouth. "I'd like to speak with a Dr. Lyndon Vintos about cancer treatments," he said.

Chapter TWENTY-ONE

DANIEL returned to the shop sometime after lunch. Phedra was collecting her purse when he stepped inside. He barely heard the door chime or noticed the typical scent of cedar. Phedra looked at him, her brown eyes wide and searching. "I was just about to text you and let you know I need to lock up the shop," she said in English. "You were gone longer than I expected."

The drive from Kalispell back to Rose Crossing seemed to transpire in a dream. He glanced at his wristwatch, interested for the first time in how much time had expired. Two hours.

"Something came up," he muttered.

"Then is it all right that I leave?" Phedra asked. "I can call my brother and stay longer if you like."

Daniel answered in Pennsylvania German, "*Labe goot. Ich hob verk.*"

He headed for the workroom, glancing at the wooden creations on the shelves, unsure if he crafted them from his own calloused hands or if they had magically mushroomed there. What difference did it make? Who cared that the lodge in Columbia Falls had sent him a beautifully handwritten letter expressing their gratitude for the "gorgeous" console he made for them? Life seemed drained of any value or joy.

He listened for the door chime and, content that Phedra had gone, concentrated on sanding the bookshelf a local elderly couple ordered last month. His work allowed him to focus on something tangible. The world swirled with insecurity, but his hands gave him purpose.

Mumbling under his breath, he pressed into the base so hard the wood cracked. Flustered, he chucked the broken board into a corner and sawed a fresh piece to attach later. As the afternoon plodded ahead, several times he considered closing the shop and hopping in his truck. He needed ample time to gather his thoughts. His mother, with whom he could no longer speak or visit face-to-face because of a half-millennia-old *Ordnung*, always warned him, *A rash word can leave more destruction than a sword.*

He always found it interesting that the English "words" and "sword" used the exact same letters.

He admitted he enjoyed stewing in his anger and despair. The sweat that gathered under his armpits pushed him harder at his tasks and forced his hatred to harden.

By four o'clock, he stopped work, shut down his power tools, and closed the shop. On the drive home, he passed a rare sighting of an Amish buggy. The sleek black gelding trotted along near the roadside, head high, the Amish driver hardly visible through the small window.

Nostalgia for his former Illinois life always pinched him whenever he spotted the local Amish. Today, that feeling increased tenfold. He wanted to impede the buggy's progress, jump out of his truck, and force his way next to the bearded driver who resembled Daniel in many ways and insist he whisk him away. Life on a plain farm must be one hundred times finer than the ugly mission waiting for him at home.

He drove onward, suppressing the impulse to give up. Determination and a deep love for Aiden pushed his foot harder on the accelerator. The closer he neared home, the more a dizzying resolve overcame him.

Aiden was carrying the mail into the house when Daniel pulled into the driveway. Aiden stopped on the landing and waited for Daniel to exit the truck. But, suddenly, Daniel could not face him. Not at that moment. He certainly could not bring inside with him what threatened to topple the surrounding trees, which were as big as silos.

"Daniel?" Aiden asked when Daniel, at last, found the courage to step foot onto the driveway. "Is everything okay? Why haven't you answered your cell phone today?"

"I must have had it turned off. I'm going across the road to visit Nick for a stretch."

"Don't you want to come inside and look at the mail first?"

"If I'm not back before supper, eat without me." He marched across the road, overlooking Aiden's wrinkled forehead and tightened mouth.

NICK opened the door with his cell phone sandwiched between his shoulder and ear. Seeing Daniel, he smiled and, while talking into the phone, gestured for him to enter. Daniel waited in the kitchen where he could see Nick wander down the hallway into the largely unfurnished living room. The distinctive sense of lonesomeness seized him. Nick's echoing voice while he talked on the phone accentuated the house's emptiness.

Built in the style more fitting for the Southwest, the house evoked a sense of dread for Daniel. He detested the empty spaciousness and cold hard terracotta floors. Lacking any warmth, the house reminded Daniel of a crypt.

He stood still, save for a tremble in his hands. He heard someone rustling in an adjoining room. From the smell of household solvents, Daniel figured Nick's housekeeper was there for her weekly cleaning. Nick begged to get off the phone. A minute later came silence, followed by the reverberating tap of Nick's boots on the tiled flooring.

"Sorry to keep you waiting, Daniel," Nick said, stepping into the kitchen. "One of my horse bidders backed out. Claims he hadn't meant to place a bid, but I suspect he found a cheaper stallion and is only pretending. I guess I'll let him off the hook."

"*Ya*," Daniel said through clenched teeth. "There seems to be a lot of uncertainty these days."

Nick studied Daniel through screwed up eyes. "Can I offer you some coffee, my friend?"

Daniel steadied his emotions. He did not wish to come across dramatic. "No thanks. I'd like to speak with you, if you have free time." He glanced toward the sound of the housekeeper. "Alone if you don't mind."

"Of course. Vivian's here, but we can talk outside. Miguel is off today. You can give me a hand feeding the horses."

Together they followed the stone footpath from the kitchen to the stables, an area much more pleasing to Daniel. Nick housed his six horses in a row of individual loose boxes that overlooked the clover field. An overhang sheltered handlers whenever feeding or tending to them. Nick entered the shed and emerged pushing a large wheelbarrow loaded with sweet-smelling hay.

Having helped Nick feed his mustangs two or three times in the past, Daniel anticipated his next move and opened the top half of the dutch door for the first box. Nick used a pitchfork and tossed several small sheaves at the mare's feet.

The strong aroma of horses momentarily alleviated the pain in Daniel's heart. He missed the farm animals perhaps more than any aspect of his former life. Horses above all. They were the largest part of their world, like automobiles to Englishers. They pulled their plows in the fields and conveyed them wherever they needed to go. Often, they proved to be Daniel's best friends.

They continued to move down the row of boxes. Nick's prized mare, Whitey, stuck out her snout and snorted at Daniel for attention. He scratched her nose and tickled her chin groove. Her year-old foal was still boxed with her although Nick had weaned it, and it tried to lift its head above the door beside its mother.

"The foal was sold a few days ago," Nick said, tossing hay into the box. "I always hate to break up a family, especially one of Whitey's offspring. But that's business. This'll be her fourth to go."

Nick reached into his jacket pocket, tapped Daniel on his shoulder, and Daniel raised his palm to allow Nick to drop several baby carrots into his hand. Daniel fed the treats to Whitey and her foal, and he chuckled when their thick, gray lips tickled his fingers.

But when he pictured the task that awaited him at home, his anger rose anew and he clenched his jaw muscles.

Nick must have noticed his stiffening. Up to that moment, he had provided Daniel time to collect his thoughts without urging that he reveal whatever weighty issue brought him to his ranch. Now he paused before Whitey's box and looked Daniel straight in the eyes. "Tell me, Daniel, what's on your mind?"

Daniel inhaled, savoring the up-close smell of dung. "You taken to liking our boarder."

Nick scratched his head. "I've enjoyed having Conrad around. He's been a big help to me on the ranch."

Daniel dared to search deeper into Nick's bright gray eyes. "Perhaps you like him for more reason than that?"

Nick grasped the pitchfork tighter and kicked at the loose hay gathered by his boots. A flush redder than strawberries bloomed over his complexion, and Daniel wished he hadn't prodded Nick to open up about his private life.

"I think I know why you've come over here today, Daniel," Nick said in a quiet voice. "I'm guessing it's about time that I explain something to you. What I have to say might help you and Aiden."

Nick leaned the pitchfork against the stable and faced the gray silhouette of the Salish Mountains rising against the powder-blue sky in the distance. Keeping his eyes averted from Daniel and his prized mustangs that snorted in their boxes, he squared his shoulders and said, "I've wanted to unburden myself many times in Aiden's and your company. I never could imagine hearing the words come from my own mouth. Each time I had started to, I stopped, unable to continue."

He licked his lips and shifted his shaky head so that he captured Daniel's eyes. It was Daniel's turn to flush. In crossing the road he had no intention of forcing Nick to reveal deep, dark secrets. He expected to find a confidant in Nick, to establish the foundation for his revelation. To expose the truth and wail how they both had been manipulated.

Daniel battled to keep his head locked in place so that Nick would believe he could never judge him. The arteries on his neck pulsed with anxious blood. He stroked Whitey's muzzle without feeling.

"When I think of my past, of the man I once was, I feel downright shame," Nick said, still fixed on Daniel's eyes. "Like you, Daniel, I once had a wife and son. My wife died of melanoma when Kalem, my only child, was eleven. I was left alone to raise him. I had help, of course. Perhaps too much. A live-in housekeeper and her daughter who helped part time. I rarely saw my son. When he reached his teen years,

I barely recognized him other than he had a shocking resemblance to me at the same age."

Daniel swallowed, powerless to budge from where he stood. He turned his head like a slow-moving reel and followed with his eyes as Nick stepped out from under the overhang, as if Nick controlled his movements. Nick drew in a deep breath, his shoulders rising higher. Daniel was grateful when Nick turned his gaze toward the hemlocks and spruce that bordered the far end of the stables.

"My son was gay," he uttered. "I suspected early on, but I couldn't face the truth. Finally, a few weeks before leaving for college, he confessed. I told him he'd outgrow it and that I didn't want to hear any more. Whenever he'd return home, I felt that he was shoving his sexuality in my face. I kept telling him I didn't want him to speak of it. I grew to resent my own son. When he refused to back down, I asked him to never return to the only home he'd ever known. That was Christmas Day, fourteen years ago."

"There's no need to say more, Nick," Daniel said, his voice booming in the quiet expanse of Nick's verdant ranch. "I only came over here to ask for your advice. I didn't mean to—"

"No." He peered at Daniel with anxious determination. "I need to say this. It's important, Daniel. I know why you've come here. I've half expected it. Please, allow me to finish."

Swallowing, Daniel nodded. He tried to relax his shoulders, to breathe. It was as if the light breeze breathed for him.

"I actually thought I was heroic for cutting ties with my son," Nick began again. "I had stood for the beliefs pounded into me since my childhood. What person thinks that denouncing one's own son is noble? I was that person, Daniel. I was that kind of man."

Whitey nudged her snout under Daniel's hand when his petting had slackened, and Daniel heard Nick exhale a light self-effacing chuckle, one devoid of a smile.

"What makes it all so horrible," Nick said, "is how Kalem tried to keep our relationship intact through phone calls and letters, all of which I ignored. I wanted nothing to do with him. I had my businesses and practice to occupy myself. Then, I cut him off financially. I refused to fund his college unless he denounced what he'd said he was. I was doing what was right; I had no doubt. A cousin later told me she learned Kalem was living alone in Dallas. She knew nothing more. I hated him, Daniel. I hated that he refused to make amends to me and denounce being homosexual. It was he who I thought was being insolent and selfish. If only he gave up his lifestyle, he could come home, I said to myself over and over. I would pay for his education, employ him to run my restaurants, teach him all that I'd learned. We could become a family again." At present, Nick spun to face Daniel, his gray eyes glaring like steaming ponds. "If only he denounced that one aspect of himself which I abhorred—his homosexuality."

Daniel muttered Nick's name, but Nick carried on, ignoring Daniel's subtle plea for both their sakes that he stop. Nick shifted his gaze toward Whitey's box, where the mare and her foal retreated farther inside, having grown disinterested in the two humans and their unfolding drama.

"About three years after I rejected him," Nick said, "police in Texas told me that he was found dead in a small apartment in suburban Dallas. He hung himself in the bathroom using a cowboy belt, one that I had given him for his eighteenth birthday."

Daniel shuddered. "Nick, I'm so sorry…."

"Did you ever consider such a drastic action, Daniel?" Nick asked in a strange conversational tone. "Growing up gay and Amish, had you ever felt so alone that you might end your life?"

Daniel thought back. Before Aiden, his life was filled with more valleys of pain than peaks of pleasure. His marriage to Esther was one he could have grown used to, before tragedy destroyed even that. He supposed many times gloom and despair made him hate the world he was born into. But never—never had he considered taking his own life.

"We all handle difficulties differently, Nick," he whispered with a raspy voice. "No explaining why. You can't really blame yourself for what Kalem did."

"I killed him, Daniel, as surely as if I'd used my bare hands. I had crushed Kalem's spirit, destroyed his identity, gutted his future." Nick looked toward his boots. "Coping with my son's suicide changed me in profound ways. I could no longer live with myself. I resigned from my firm, sold my two restaurants, abandoned my home even before the Realtor found a buyer."

Daniel cleared his throat, hoping Nick had enough purging. Nothing Daniel might say could alleviate Nick's grief. He knew firsthand. Daniel at one time blamed himself for the deaths of his wife and son, and his second cousin Kyle Yoder, with whom he had formed a tight bond. They did nearly everything together. Fishing, backpacking, hunting. Even shared their first kiss. He thought that selfish act was what had led to Kyle's death many years before. Until the inquisitive Aiden Cermak crashed into his life and forced him to acknowledge the truth.

He nearly chuckled, reminiscing how Aiden saved him from his prison of guilt. Stifling himself, he inhaled more of the scent of livestock, and waited patiently for Nick to end their conversation on his terms.

"That's why I reacted so strongly to Farzad's ruining your dinner party," Nick said, his voice deeper. "I was reliving my own hatred. I couldn't bear to experience it again, not through myself or anyone else. Farzad might as well have strong-armed me using one of his toughest Iranian wrestling moves."

Nick smiled for the first time, a genuine loving kind of warmth spreading across his ashen face. Daniel stared at him, wondering, if anything, what he might say to console him.

"I've looked at you and Aiden as my sons," Nick said, eyeing Daniel. "I can't help but feel a certain lure to you. As if I've been given a second chance to make up for all my transgressions with Kalem through you. You and Aiden make it simple. You are truly the most decent men I've known. I see my son in both of you. Now that my head has cleared of hatred and confusion, I realize that Kalem was a generous, loving man, like you and Aiden. I wasted that love, turned it into something ugly."

Daniel laid a hand on Nick's shoulder, and Nick surprised him by grasping his forearm like one of his wood clamps. Daniel did not wince. He savored the sensation of Nick's heated hand penetrating him. They trembled in unison, energy passing from one to the other. Friend fused with friend.

"You can understand now why I'm even more taken with Conrad." Nick released his grip and, turning away, shrugged. "He's a lot like my son, too, in some ways, perhaps more. He explained how he dated Aiden. I was right about yours and Aiden's generosity. Who else would take into their home a man who at one time abandoned Aiden in a strange city with no funds or friends?"

"What else has he told you?"

Nick looked at Daniel from under his brow and shook his head. "He didn't have to tell me the rest. I started to have my doubts. I've lived with cancer before when I watched my wife die. It became clear to me the day I drove him to his radiation treatment. Later I talked with my doctor friend, Lyndon, who works at the clinic, and he verified my suspicions when he had no idea who or what I was talking about. I didn't want to embarrass Conrad and mention anything."

"Didn't want to embarrass him? Look how he's made fools out of us. How can you be so forgiving?"

"How can I not be?"

"Especially after… after your own wife died from cancer."

"That has nothing to do with it," Nick stated.

"Why didn't you warn us?"

"Please, Daniel, I'm not excusing his behavior, but for your sake and Aiden's, not just Conrad's, remember why you took him into your home. Don't hate Conrad for what he's done. Remember your compassion and think how much he needs us."

Daniel peered at the hay-covered ground. "I'm sorry, Nick, but you're speaking like a grieving father."

"I'm speaking like someone who understands him. You must understand too. Haven't you been in his shoes before? Think, Daniel, before you condemn him. That's all I ask."

DANIEL returned from Nick's, his mind reeling. He was taking off his boots in the entranceway when Aiden came from the kitchen. Ranger wanted Daniel to toss a rubber hotdog, but Daniel ignored the toy he couldn't remember seeing before. Finally, Aiden, standing before him, said, "Were you delivering furniture today?"

Daniel looked up. "No, I wasn't."

"I thought I saw you in town when Conrad and I were coming back from the cancer clinic."

Daniel wanted to hear nothing more about Conrad or the cancer clinic. A new, raw anger rose inside his mouth, and it tasted worse than rotten milk. He wished he never spoke with Nick Pfeifer. He had begged that Daniel use patience and understanding when Daniel had wanted Nick's sympathy and encouragement for vengeance.

Everything was more boogered than before.

He stood tall. "I was in town, but for another reason. Where's your Conrad?"

Daniel noticed Aiden try to subdue the hurt and confusion budding over his countenance. "Conrad's in his room," he said. "We just finished eating dinner. It's warming in the oven. I made tuna casserole and a salad. Would you like me to fix you a plate?"

Staring into Aiden's amber eyes, a flood of love pushed aside his rage. Daniel smiled, laid a gentle hand on his shoulder. "You might as well put it in the refrigerator. I'm not feeling well this evening. I think I'll shower and go to bed early."

Ironic. Feigning illness. Or was he? Daniel *was* sick. Sick of the entire episode. He took a good long hot shower, where his troubles seemed to wash down the drain. Dried off and lying in bed, he fought the horrible emotions from rushing back. He wavered between yielding to Nick's advice and the pure hatred that wrapped claws around his brain.

Haven't you been in his shoes before? Think, Daniel, before you condemn him. What on earth had that meant?

More pressing, what or how would he tell Aiden? The truth might hurt him worse than a thankless life of sacrifice.

The room darkened with the setting sun. Aiden gave him peace and breathing space. Daniel appreciated his consideration. But when the door slowly opened and a sheath of light from the hallway lay across the log bed, a smile stretched his beard.

"Hello, Aiden."

"Hello, Daniel." Aiden's tone matched the confused look on his face from earlier. "Can I bring you something to eat now?"

"I think I'll skip supper tonight."

"Are you still not feeling well?"

His naivety touched Daniel. Clueless about so many things. Conrad, Nick. Now was not the time to let Aiden in on the truth about their neighbor. Nick wasn't gay the way they had assumed. Daniel battled to feel the anger again, to know true brutal hatred.

"I'm better," he said for Aiden's benefit. "Mostly just a headache."

"Is there anything you need? An aspirin? Some tea?"

"I'll be fine. Just want some extra sleep."

"Let me know if you change your mind."

The light across the bed disappeared, and Daniel was shrouded in darkness once again. His soul sunk deeper in murky despair.

One way or the other, he had to confront Conrad. Whether to tell Aiden? That was another dilemma altogether.

Chapter TWENTY-TWO

AIDEN pulled his truck in front of the *Valley Courant*, where he expected his enthusiasm for delivering his article, after much time and effort, to resurface. But it failed to. Daniel continued to occupy his mind.

Since spying him a week ago driving into Kalispell, Aiden noticed Daniel undergo a strange change. He was acting more sober than usual. He treated Conrad worse each subsequent day and refused eye contact with Aiden most of the time. Then out of the blue last night he volunteered to drive Conrad to his radiation treatment after Conrad announced he had an appointment for the following day, and Aiden was left baffled.

Despite Aiden's pledge to give Conrad more space, he was driving into Kalispell anyway and figured it would be silly for both of them to drive separate cars. He ventured to convey this common sense to Daniel. "But I have an appointment with the editor of the *Valley Courant* to deliver my article on Monday," Aiden said. "I can take him easily."

Conrad appeared embarrassed, desperate. "Let Aiden take me, Daniel. There's no reason why you should."

"I don't mind."

"But, Daniel, it makes no sense if I'm—"

"I said, I'll take him. No worries." And Daniel rose from the table, deposited his empty plate in the kitchen sink, and strolled to the bedroom.

If Daniel wanted to assist Aiden more, why not when Aiden had no plans to go into the Valley? Daniel had made his decision. Rolling an eighteen-wheeler would have proven an easier task than getting Daniel to change his mind.

The newspaper's headquarters was located in a tiny shopping center shared by Dearest Donut and a Laundromat. Aiden collected his messenger bag and headed inside. The front desk was empty. He saw down the narrow corridor several cubicles and a few offices. He cleared his throat, and a thin man popped his head out from behind the closest cubicle.

"What can I do for you?"

"I'm Aiden Cermak to see Norman Schooner."

"Hold on a sec."

The thin man walked farther down the row of cubicles and spoke into a separate office. A second later he gestured for Aiden to step his way.

Norman Schooner greeted Aiden and offered him coffee and a seat inside his office. Aiden declined the coffee, but he sat facing the editor with growing anticipation. Norman Schooner looked as Aiden had imagined. Balding, wire-framed glasses, pink face, and by his girth, he most likely took advantage of the close proximity of Dearest Donut.

Excitement at last pumped through Aiden's veins. He laid his messenger bag on his lap, anxious to show the editor the contents. Two months of sweat and even a bit of peril emanated from his labor. About twenty-five hundred dollars' worth, based on what Norman had originally offered per word. His smile muscles ached. Like a straight-A student, he yearned for praise.

"I didn't expect to see you so soon," Norman said. "Didn't we talk only yesterday?"

Confused, Aiden kept his grin intact. "We set up an appointment for this morning so you could read my article. You said you'd rather have a hard copy and agreed to let me bring it in."

"You're the one who wanted to write about Glacier National Park from a few months back?"

"Yes, about the strip mining across the border." Aiden tapped his messenger bag. "My completed article is right here, including a disc of photos of the mining site."

"Ah, of course."

Aiden breathed lighter, realizing the newspaperman juggled multiple tasks in a small daily and probably had difficulty keeping one straight from the other. Years ago, Aiden, after having met Daniel and never wanting to leave his side, took a salary cut to work for the small town newspaper *The Henry Blade*. Even a humble weekly in the heart of Illinois Amish Country had its share of frenzied and hectic days.

He took out the hard copy with the compact disc clipped to it. "I figure that there're about four articles worth here. Rather than divide it myself, I thought maybe you can choose how to break it up. You know what'll work best."

Norman took the article from Aiden, unclipped the CD, and read to himself through the first couple of pages. His heart beating, Aiden waited. He clutched the armrests, barely able to contain his excitement. Norman perused the rest of the article, flipping past every other page or two. About five minutes in, he set the article on his desk and slid it toward Aiden. "I can't accept it."

Aiden's smile collapsed and his insides deflated faster than if Norman Schooner had punched him in the gut. "What?"

"I can't print it."

Certainly the editor had misspoken. "What's that again?"

"It's impossible."

Air in the tiny windowless office grew stagnant. Aiden shook his head, trying to work blood into his brain so that he might comprehend what Norman was telling him. "What do you mean, it's impossible?"

"I can't publish your story."

"You mean it's poorly written, badly researched?"

Norman shook his head. "On the contrary. You have a very nice style. More professional than what I normally see, to be honest. And your list of citations is impressive. It's the subject matter that I have a problem with."

"But you told me months ago you were interested in an article about strip mining near Glacier Park."

"I'm interested in many stories. That doesn't mean I'm going to publish them." He shook his head pointedly. "I cannot publish what you wrote, it's that simple."

Aiden leaned into Norman's desk, flanked by stacks of files and papers and one lonely twenty-four ounce Dearest Donut cup. "But I don't understand. I have hours of work invested in this."

Sighing with a heavy stench of coffee on his breath, Norman reclined in his chair and adjusted his eyeglasses over his nose. "You freelancers don't see what we see every day on dailies like the *Courant*. Don't think you're experts on everything. I know what to print and what not to print. That's my job as the editor."

Bewildered more than ever, Aiden sharpened his stare. "I never said I know your job, Mr. Schooner. I simply would like to know why you're rejecting my story without fully reading it. You haven't explained."

"Our readers would hate it."

Again Aiden shook his head, wanting to make sense of Norman's words. "Why would your readers hate my article? It's informative and shows concern for the community's main attraction, Glacier National Park."

Norman glanced at the fifty-two pages sitting on his cluttered desk and curled his upper lip. "I know about the strip mining and the risks it poses for Glacier Park and the community." He shrugged. "But they are just risks. No one can guarantee anything horrible might happen. You stated yourself on page seven that Dr. Vernal, from the University of Montana, has no certainty that strip mining conducted in British Columbia might negatively affect the park."

"I went on to mention that similar companies have destroyed entire communities and leveled mountains in places like the Philippines and Mexico," Aiden said. "I have cited those incidents in my article. I've interviewed eyewitnesses. I'm warning locals that might happen right here in Flathead County."

"Mr. Cermak, I'm not going to engage you in an ecological or political debate. We're supposed to be journalists, not activists."

Suddenly Aiden wondered if Norman Schooner might be one of those on the take, like Pete Campbell mentioned during their interview at Lion Burger. Another journalist seeking a kickback from a corrupt corporation in exchange for silence. Or perhaps he was afraid for his personal safety if he were to print Aiden's discoveries. "But that's the purpose for compiling research," Aiden said despite his suspicions. "I have two sources who insist Senator Klamsa is being paid by the company to—"

Norman raised his hand and waved Aiden to stop. "Whoa, young man. I didn't read your entire article, but we can't make accusations of that magnitude without verification."

Aiden sat upright, growing more determined. "Please, read my article from beginning to end and tell me what more you need. I'm open to revisions. You've dismissed me without giving me a fair chance."

"Let me get to the point since I don't have all day." Norman clasped the edge of his desk and peered at Aiden with an odd sardonic grin. "The main reason why I don't want to publish your article is because of how you accuse the Canadians of something that, well, is rather appalling."

"I'm not accusing Canadians. I'm accusing Canadian corporations."

"It's the same thing," Norman said, "at least to our readers."

"You're still not registering. What does that mean? The company is headquartered in Alberta and they are preparing to strip mine in British Columbia in direct line of Glacier National Park."

"Mr. Cermak, I know this might be difficult to understand, but our readers don't like to read anything that disparages our northern neighbors." Norman blew out a chuckle and leaned closer into his desk. "They like their Canadians nice and sweet. Let me give you an example of what I'm talking about. Ten years ago in Alberta a group of overexcited parents tried to overturn a school bus loaded with American boys playing in a peewee hockey tournament. The AP picked up the story, and with a little rewording I ran it in the *Valley Courant*. I received dozens of hate messages, e-mails, and phone calls. What do you think they were angry about, Mr. Cermak? Parents overturning a bus filled with small boys? No, they were pissed because we were reporting on Canadians negatively. It wasn't the first time that had happened, but that story was the last I published of its kind."

Aiden flashed back to when he worked for *The Henry Blade*. After many months of investigative reporting on unsolved crimes in the area, Aiden's former boss, Kevin Hassler, sat Aiden down and uttered the exact same statement about the Amish. This time, in place of the Amish, Norman Schooner exalted an entire nationality.

Aiden stared at the editor. "But if the national park goes," he said in a whisper, as if he were unable to believe the nature of their conversation, "the Flathead Valley economy might go with it. Isn't that more pressing than maintaining some puerile view of a group of people?"

Norman pointed a chubby finger out the door, toward the front entrance, and perhaps beyond where the Flathead Valley beat with its full morning vigor. Where the ranchers and cowboys and service workers and business people embarking on software start-ups breathed and worked. "Those people out there," he said. "Everyday people. Americans. People all over the world. They are in charge. We do what they tell us. We give them what they want, whether it's in their best interests or not."

"If you give them more choices, maybe they'd want something different—"

Norman shook his head. "In my younger naïve days, I would have wanted to hoist the torch too, Aiden. In the end, we must provide the public what they demand. We'd be out of business if we didn't. I've learned the hard way what sells and what doesn't."

Both men fell silent. They gazed into each other's eyes, as if looking for something resembling wisdom. Glares from the fluorescent lights reflecting off Norman's eyeglasses blinded Aiden a moment. Aiden slackened, and despite the pain poking his heart from what Norman told him, for the first time he felt a kinship with his fellow journalist. They both battled a world outside of their control. He sat back in his chair, rested his hands loosely in his lap.

"It's the way of the world, Aiden." Norman lowered his baritone. "People want what makes them feel good. And what makes them feel good is to uphold certain images." He glanced around his small office.

"Some of those images are ugly, some resemble Disneyland. Have you ever seen British tabloids? They're full of nothing but US news of the most heinous kind. Some of it must be made up. But that's what the British want to read about the United States. If an American newspaper dedicated itself to publishing negative stories about Britain, there'd be hell to pay. We'd rather read nice stories about our cousins across the pond."

Aiden tried to focus his blurry eyes. "Even if it means giving up to find the truth?"

Norman nodded. "Some people do it for religion, some for political ideals. Of course those images and ideals change over time. But what my readers want right now is not to read about corrupt Canadian corporations threatening the United States or any other part of the world. They don't understand it, they don't want it, and we don't give it to them. That simple."

"But who's selling those images that people cling to?"

"It's a vicious circle, I suppose. Which came first? The chicken or the egg?"

Aiden chuckled in defeat. "I don't get any of this."

The office hummed in silence. Then Norman said, "Tell me, Aiden, in all your research, how many articles, blogs, and papers did you find about the strip mining? How many environmental groups are voicing outcry? Celebrity campaigns to stop it? You might as well ask yourself where are all the protests over the three hundred thousand baby seals slaughtered each year in Newfoundland."

Where are the bleeding hearts when Guatemalan natives are torched alive in their own homes? Pete Campbell's words hit Aiden anew. Pete had uttered them aloud over his basket of hamburger and fries. And then he had said to Aiden with words that were now as sharp and crystal clear as the craggy peaks of the Swan Range that had pointed into the brilliant blue sky above the Lion Burger, *You know the answer.*

Aiden dropped his head and mumbled, "I just wasted two months researching and writing."

Norman snickered under his breath. "There was never a guarantee I'd publish your article." He waited, as if allowing Aiden time to sulk. "Don't let this discourage you. You're a fine writer."

Eager to resurrect his article from the trash heap of social trends, Aiden lifted his eyes to Norman and said, "Perhaps if I tailored the article to fit what you're talking about."

"Like how?"

"I could mention the environmental issue without pointing fingers. Write about strip mining in general and leave the Canadian companies and Senator Klamsa out of it. I could write about how all of mankind is responsible for threats against the park. I could even mention global warming if you want." Aiden hated what he heard spewing from his mouth. Two months of work, with nothing to show for it, not even a measly twenty-five hundred dollars, dragged him down a despicable and desperate path.

Norman shrugged. "The problem with that is people around here are aware of the strip mining across the border. They already know the truth. They just don't want to face it. If it were happening directly inside Flathead County, there might be a larger outcry." He pointed his nose toward Aiden's article, forlorn and ridiculous looking on his messy desk. "You're probably as much an expert as anyone now. Perhaps you can take your research and expand it into a book. Book publishers are more broadminded. They accept a larger array of ideas. We're just one daily newspaper with a circulation of twenty-five thousand."

"Maybe I could submit it to another newspaper?" Aiden said. "Maybe one in Missoula, Billings, or even Spokane?"

"You might, but you'll get the same results. They haven't published anything about the strip mining yet."

Aiden twiddled his fingers. "Why is it me who feels so dirty?"

"You'll learn," Norman said, chuckling. "Took me a few years to realize that my intentions as a newspaperman to shed light on the world's troubles were too idealistic. It's about selling newspapers, and selling newspapers means selling fantasy. The readers have decided, Mr. Cermak, and we answer to none other but them."

Aiden's stomach rumbled. Food was the last thing on his mind. He wanted to get up and leave, yet his legs felt like lead weights. He refused to meet Norman's eyes. "I suppose I'm in the wrong business," he whispered toward his lap.

"This is nothing new," Norman said. "People have been choosing fantasy over fact for thousands of years. It's nothing to do with the moral decay of our society." He snorted. "For chrissakes, the Athenians poisoned Socrates for telling the truth."

Chapter TWENTY-THREE

TRAFFIC on Route 2 ebbed to a midmorning progression. Daniel pulled to the front entrance of the clinic. Conrad hesitated before stepping out from the Suburban. Over his shoulder he glanced at Daniel. Daniel refrained from looking at him, but he sensed Conrad's nervousness. Conrad shut the door, stared through the window. Slowly, he turned for the sliding glass doors.

Daniel did not bother to watch him go inside. He drove across the road and parked in the empty lot of the United Community Church. He stretched his legs, willing to wait for Conrad as long as necessary.

He kept his eyes peeled on the front entrance to the clinic. The sliding glass doors opened and closed. Healthcare workers and patients came and went.

He had sealed his mouth for an entire week, observing Conrad and continuing to wrestle with uncertainty of what to do. He had a difficult time sharing the same living space with him. Looking at Conrad across the supper table diminished Daniel's will to eat. He'd retire for the night soon after getting up from the table and spend little time in the great room. He figured Aiden understood something bothered him. Aiden provided hints that he would listen, whenever Daniel was ready.

The steady words hammered inside his head: Could he ever reveal the truth to Aiden without destroying him?

Work had come as his only salvation. Alone in his workshop while passive Phedra manned the front, he could pretend, for a while, that everything remained the same as before Conrad's coming.

On two occasions, Nick met him at the bottom of the driveway after Daniel returned home. Each time Nick asked if he had acted, and each time Daniel said he was still weighing his options.

"Go easy on him," Nick would say.

Saturday at noon Daniel had asked Phedra to watch the shop until he returned. Rather than stop at Beadsman's Deli or drive home for lunch, he traveled higher into the Salish Range. There, he sat on a cold picnic table by Little Bitterroot Lake, gazing almost vacant of thought at the reflection of the snow-capped mountains.

Magpies calling from treetops pulled his attention away. Nesting and mating, the black and white birds seemed unconcerned for the living below. One magpie aimed for the lake and reemerged in the sky carrying in its talons a fish carcass that had drifted ashore. Opportunistic scavengers, magpies had at one time fascinated Daniel.

Splashes from the lake sparkled under the overcast sky, distorting the mirrorlike image of the mountains. Landlocked salmon were feeding off the insects scurrying over the water's surface. Last October he and Aiden had come to the lake to see the vast aspen groves in their full fall colors and the kokanee were spawning along the lakeshore. Inquisitive as always, Aiden watched fascinated as they flopped on their bellies to release their pearl-like sequence of eggs.

Daniel listened to the sounds of nature. Had it spoken to him? He opened his mind. Allowed the wind to provide clues.

He waited, expecting God to tell him what to do.

When a small group of day hikers disrupted his thinking, he rose from the picnic table and headed back to Rose Crossing. After work, he pulled into the driveway and crossed the road straight for Nick's. Again, Nick met him halfway, and escorted him to the stables. They cleaned the boxes while the mustangs ran about the clover field. He and Nick talked in more detail about the situation. Nick promised to keep his mouth shut, permitting Daniel to make the ultimate decision.

Go easy on him….

The next evening during Sunday supper, a long overdue steadfastness welled inside Daniel. Conrad mentioned needing to go to the clinic on Monday. Daniel stunned both men—and perhaps himself—by announcing that he'd drive him. Aiden and Conrad's protests failed to alter his mind. Satisfied that he came to a final conclusion, he deposited his dirty dishes in the sink and slept better than he had all week.

And then on the highway to the clinic, Daniel observed Conrad squirm. He kept more quiet than usual, even in Daniel's company, and, grasping the dashboard, faced the road, blurry eyed. Only when Daniel pulled into the clinic's parking lot did Conrad look at him. Daniel discerned Conrad understood Daniel's motives for wanting to bring him.

Inside his truck, Daniel sat on watch. Brilliant blue sky spanned above the cancer clinic. Somehow, it seemed fitting that he should wait for Conrad to reemerge while sitting in the parking lot of a "falsh" church.

He imagined what Conrad might be doing inside the clinic, and what he had done the past few months. Aiden had told him that Conrad never wanted him to go inside with him, insisting on privacy. At the time, Daniel understood, even empathized. But after he read the labels on Conrad's pill bottles, one of them stood out. He thought he heard of it somewhere before. He searched on the Internet and learned Relacore was an over-the-counter weight loss pill. In other words, an appetite suppressant.

He wondered: Why on earth would a cancer patient need an appetite suppressant?

Soon after, the suspicions began to pester him, which led him last Monday to the Flathead Valley Cancer Center to speak with Nick's friend Dr. Vintos. He hadn't been inside a hospital since Aiden's injuries a few years before, sustained at the hands of his former editor, Kevin Hassler, and his girlfriend. He would have died for Aiden then, and he would again.

He barely noticed the odd odors and the irritating lights while comforting Aiden by his bedside; he was too concerned for his recovery. Yet when he walked into the Flathead Valley Cancer Center, the smell was like sweet death smacking his face and the lights nearly blinded him.

The redheaded receptionist informed him Dr. Vintos was attending a seminar out of state. By the squint of her eyes, she seemed to notice Daniel was different. Daniel was used to people staring at him due to his accent and moustacheless beard.

"Is there any way I might get information on a patient?" he asked in a shaky voice.

"Are you… a doctor?"

Daniel shook his head. "I'm trying to find out about a Conrad Barringer. I think he's a patient here."

"Are you a relative of his?"

"No, I'm a… I'm a friend. I only wish to know if he's registered."

"Oh, I see. Wait a moment, please."

She punched a keypad before a flat screen monitor. A moment later, she said with a downturn of her ruby lips, "No one by that name is registered here."

"Can you look again? I believe he's been coming here for treatments for about two months."

Screwing up her eyes, she turned back to the computer screen. "Can you spell his last name for me, please?"

Daniel became flustered and that angered him. "I… I don't know. I think it's B-A-R…."

She scrolled through the data bank again. "Nothing, sir. Sorry. No Conrad B-A-R or B-E-R or anything. When was his last appointment?"

Daniel barely heard her above the ringing in his ears. She repeated herself. Daniel tried to smile, to look unsurprised.

"Perhaps you have the wrong clinic," she said. "There's another cancer center at the county hospital."

The receptionist said something else, probably along the lines of "Are you okay, sir?" when Daniel stood clutching the counter without responding. Wordlessly, he turned for the door and somehow found his truck and drove to the shop, ignoring the towering mountains that rose to the east, south, and west along the way.

The glass doors slid open, but no one came through the vestibule. Daniel sat stiffer, kept vigilant. He checked his wristwatch. Twenty-five minutes had passed since Conrad entered the clinic. A shadow waited between the two sets of doors. With small steps, as if he were expecting to be waylaid, Conrad appeared outside.

Shoulders slouched, he stood, edged aside when a nurse wanted to enter, and peered around the parking lot. He shoved his hands in his pockets, stared at the sidewalk. *Something about his body language. As a prosecutor, I'd become sensitive to gestures that denote someone might be lying*. During their last meeting, Nick explained how he figured out Conrad's scheme, and Daniel thought himself stupid for not noticing sooner.

Appearing and reappearing between traffic on Route 2, Conrad barely budged. As patient as a cougar, Daniel fixed his eyes in his direction. Conrad's gaze froze across the road. Their eyes locked. Daniel was certain Conrad recognized him sitting in his Suburban.

Conrad's head and shoulders fell forward and his hands flopped loose from his pockets. He shuffled closer to the road, near the entrance to the clinic's parking lot. After waiting for a break in traffic, he scurried across the road like a calf encountering the human world for the first time.

He walked longways to Daniel's truck, hands tucked back in pockets. With an impish grin, he opened the door and shrugged.

"I was expecting you on the other side of the street. I thought you'd forgotten me."

Daniel eyed him, speechless for a while. In a low, detached voice he said, "Hop in."

Hesitating, Conrad slinked into the passenger seat and pulled the door toward him, but from the sound Daniel guessed he'd left the door ajar, as if he'd wanted a means for a quick escape if needed.

Daniel savored the faceoff. He had waited for it the span of a week. Although a momentary pinch of sympathy bugged him, he shook his head, concentrated on what required action.

"I… I didn't have long to wait this time," Conrad said. "Mondays are usually slow."

Daniel faced the windshield, grasping the steering wheel. "They have no record of you."

"What?"

"The cancer clinic never heard of your name. *Du sei en falsh mann*. You're a fraud."

Conrad sat mute. From the passenger side window, Daniel saw his eyes, shiny with what looked like tears, gaping toward the road.

"I thought you might have figured me out." He spoke in a voice so low, Daniel had to perk up his ears to hear him. "This must shock you a lot. Especially since you're Amish. Does Aiden know?"

Daniel pursed his lips. "No."

"What about Nick?"

"He's on to you."

Daniel sensed Conrad turn his eyes to him, but Daniel remained staring out the windshield, not yet ready to look him in the face. "Please don't tell Aiden," Conrad said. "Try to understand. I don't want him to know."

"It's against my upbringing to use violence," Daniel uttered. "I'm questioning that now."

Gazing back out the window, Conrad said, "I had nowhere else to turn. I lost my second job in two years last summer. Without a job and low on funds, I had to sell all my possessions, including my Jeep. Amazing how fast you can go through fifty thousand dollars when you have no income. I drained my retirement account. The only person I knew with a big enough heart to take me in was Aiden."

"But why lie to him? Why something this ugly?"

Conrad shook his head. "I didn't think Aiden would want me any other way. He'd already rejected my last attempt to get back with him. I knew he'd never turn me away if he thought I had a serious illness. When Aiden asked what I had, I thought of the first cancer to come to mind. Someone I knew in high school had non-Hodgkin lymphoma. I didn't know about you when I first called, I swear. I never intended to break up you and Aiden. That's not why I came. On some level I guess I'd hoped maybe I could get him back, but I realized that would never happen once I saw the two of you together."

Daniel listened, and his heart softened. Not for Conrad, but for Aiden. In the past, their relationship had reared up from ugliness and heartache and stood stoic after the storms. Here again sitting next to him, one more pounding wave.

"I have no real family to turn to," Conrad went on. "Like you, they've rejected me. I'll turn thirty in a few months. What's left for me? I guess I blame myself. I lived selfishly and have few trustworthy friends."

"How long did you think you could pull off this farce?"

"I knew things were getting out of hand when I had to keep up with the treatments and phony side effects."

"You pretended to lose your hair by shaving your head. That day in the bathroom screaming about your precious hair, you were putting on an act."

"I cut out clumps and then later decided to shave my head completely. I'm embarrassed about that. I was at the time too."

"Where did you get the Leukeran?"

"I ordered it from an online pharmacy based in Fiji before leaving Virginia. Cost me three hundred dollars to have it express mailed. Aiden knows so much about everything I wanted to look authentic. I never took any, of course. I'd pretend."

"And then you started to take the weight loss pills."

Conrad nodded. "At first I was slipping Ranger my food so that it looked like I was eating but still losing mass. Then I thought of taking diet pills. After the hiking trip to Glacier National Park, I went into my room and realized what had made Ranger sick." He lowered his head. "He'd gotten into my diet pills off the dresser. I could tell by the teeth marks on the bottle. But of course I couldn't say anything to Aiden or you, or to the vet."

Daniel jerked his head to look at Conrad dead-on for the first time since they left the house that morning. Perhaps he appeared frailer at that moment than when Daniel thought he was sick from cancer and battered by the horrible treatments. "You could have killed him," he muttered.

"Please, Daniel, try to understand. I know it makes me seem like a complete idiot. But I'm no monster."

"What about those bouts of midnight sickness, when Aiden crawled out of bed to nurse you in the darkest hours of morning?"

"He always made it to the bathroom after the fact. I made a point to make enough noise to wake him, and then pretend I had just thrown up. He never actually saw me get sick."

Bile rose in Daniel's throat. He needed to spit, but he required more information. "What have you been doing each of the times Aiden drove you to your treatments?"

"I'd go for walks, mostly. I'd stand in between the two doors of the lobby waiting for Aiden to leave. A few times I'd have to go inside. I'd sneak past the receptionist and wander the halls or hang out in the cafeteria. With my bald head, I sort of blended in. Once when the receptionist caught me, I asked to volunteer, not knowing what else to say. The past few weeks, that's what I've done."

"Is that another lie?"

"It's the truth. We can go inside and they'll recognize me and tell you."

"Didn't you feel disgusted with yourself seeing all those kids with authentic cancer? The kids who had actually lost their hair?"

"I didn't give them cancer. It's not my fault."

Daniel shook his head, clasped the steering wheel tighter. "I never heard of such deception in my whole life."

"All I wanted was to have somebody to lean on until I got back on my feet. I needed a place to gather myself. I can make a fresh start. I just needed time. I'm sorry, Daniel. I know I'm an idiot."

"Disrupting my life for two months is one thing, but how you used Aiden is unforgivable."

"Please don't tell him I lied to him. I'll be too ashamed."

"And to cheat him this way after how you mistreated him in Chicago."

"And here I am, living off of you and him, and Aiden being so kind." Conrad shook his head toward his lap. "I'm always thinking of myself first. In some ways I wish I had cancer. I really do. My life would be so much easier."

"Stop that. You talk like a crazy man."

"It's the truth. I started to pray I'd get cancer or some other incurable illness." He brought his voice to a whisper. "That's when I thought of the idea to fake it and call Aiden."

Daniel swallowed what pity lingered and sputtered, "Why not let the state care for you? People like you seem to think it's good enough for everyone else; it's good enough for you then. Become nothing but a wasted life living off the public feedings. An incompetent who can't rub two sticks together to make a fire."

"I couldn't have gone on welfare. I couldn't." There was silence, and Conrad said, "What are you going to do now that you know?"

Daniel's Amish background prevented him from doing what he wanted. "I should kick you out on the street, refuse to ever let you see Aiden again."

"Is what I've done illegal? Are you going to tell the police? I'll pack and leave you both. I'll never bother either of you again. Just let me get my things and call a cab and we can forget I ever came. I'll tell Aiden I got a job back in DC and I need to hurry home. Only promise you'll never tell Aiden or the police what I've done."

So many thoughts came to Daniel's mind. He bit his lower lip, coalesced his resolve into action rather than waste it on feeble words. He turned the ignition and shifted in reverse, making sure to swerve the truck left so that the centrifugal force slammed Conrad's door shut, and he locked him in with the master switch.

"Where are we going?" Conrad glanced around him like a caged fox. "You're not going to turn me in, are you? You won't hurt me. Remember, you're Amish."

Daniel shifted into drive, and, with a snap of their heads, pulled onto Route 2.

Chapter TWENTY-FOUR

AIDEN left the *Valley Courant* without remembering if he'd shaken Norman Schooner's hand good-bye. He drove along Route 2 for home, his hard work joggling next to him inside the messenger bag, useless to anyone. He rallied for truth. Yet in his profession, he'd come across staunch opposition time after time.

The mainstream media managed to strip everything down to an image. The image must be preserved. For whose or what purpose? How much of an outcry would the public make if their "icons" were destroyed? Norman blamed the public. And the public often blamed the media.

His stomach stirred and his head whirled, and he scarcely noticed passing the Flathead Valley Cancer Center or the United Community Church. The only thing that loomed comforting was Daniel. What would he do without him? He was rational, sensible, and honorable. Traits not only rare to find, but considered liabilities more and more.

Why should Aiden care if Glacier National Park fell into a swamp?

But he did, and that's what pained him. He cared about many things, none of which he could do much to help. He battled against an army of thugs, often shielded by a gullible public.

And there, again, stood Daniel. Stern, yes, but genuine. A man raised unspoiled by the modern world. Born from a landscape where milking cows by hand soared more paramount than embracing the latest Hollywood trends.

Aiden needed to reach him.

He stopped by the shop. To his disappointment, Phedra told him Daniel had not yet showed. Conrad should have been finished with his radiation by then. Maybe Daniel was still at the house after dropping him off.

With growing concern, Aiden returned to his truck. Had anything gone wrong?

He texted Conrad first. Impatient when Conrad failed to respond, he texted Daniel. "Where r u?" A response came soon after: "At home."

Aiden drove the canyon-like road, fuming over a sappy world. Pulling into the driveway, he almost wanted to ask Conrad for a cigarette to help ease his nausea. He was surprised to find the house empty. Cold and eerie. He called for Daniel. Where was he when he had texted? His truck was in the driveway, so he must be home. Aiden rechecked his text message to ensure he'd read it correctly. Out back, Ranger was chasing a squirrel up a tree, but Daniel and Conrad were nowhere.

Still angry after his interview, he pulled out his article from the messenger bag and held the fifty-plus pages to the fireplace. Logs were assembled, and he wanted to place the pages under the grate and strike a match to them, followed by a swift destruction of the compact disc and his computer files containing anything concerning Glacier National Park and strip mining.

He vowed to never write another word for as long as he lived.

His arm locked and shook. Shrinking back, his fingers loosened, and he dropped limp into Daniel's favorite easy chair, the one commandeered by Conrad. Eyes downcast, he sighed.

After a moment fidgeting for strength, he stood and filed away his work at the computer console.

He had no idea what to do with his story, but he couldn't toss it. Not for anyone.

The fact that his article existed meant some semblance of truth survived somewhere.

Daniel walked into the house, leaving the front door wide open.

"Where were you?" Aiden asked, his voice more irate than he had intended.

"I was at Nick's."

Aiden suspected Conrad was there too. Remembering his rage, he raised a fist to the ceiling. “I don’t see how I can continue to be a journalist.”

Daniel cocked his head. “What happened?”

“They rejected my article.”

“Aiden, they didn’t.”

“They did, and for the most asinine reason. And he’s right. I haven’t found any other stories about the threat to Glacier Park.” He turned his face away, ashamed to show Daniel a rare burst of pessimism. “People are such maudlin idiots.” Aiden’s rage shook his limbs, and he inhaled to calm himself. Yet he wanted to unleash more. “You can’t challenge people, or even educate them,” he said. “It’s all about giving them what they want, supporting their views. That’s what the editor told me. What’s the point of it all?”

“Some people prefer lies.”

“But why? It’s one thing knowing everything is a fraud, but to embrace it willingly?” He snapped out of his selfish rant, remembering the ordeal Daniel must have faced carting Conrad to and from his radiation treatment. He allowed his facial muscles to soften. “How did things go with Conrad?” he asked. “Did you have to waste too much time there?”

Daniel’s eyes were blacker, wider, and his mouth drooping, as if he’d been tugging at his beard most of the morning. Aiden started to approach him, but balked from inching closer. “What is it, Daniel? Did something happen to Conrad? Where is he?”

Daniel shook his head. “You no longer have to worry over him.”

“What do you mean? What’s going on? Conrad’s with Nick, right?”

Daniel stared at him, his mouth tightening and eyes unblinking. Aiden’s ire formed into tight fists. “You’ve been acting strangely all week, Daniel Schrock. I’ve had a terrible morning and I demand to know what’s going on.”

Nick walked in behind Daniel. He stopped upon seeing Aiden. “Hi, Aiden. You back already?”

Shaking with confusion, Aiden said, "Why is everyone looking at me like that? Nick, is Conrad with you?"

Nick and Daniel glanced at each other. Something resembling shared guilt passed between them.

Nick stepped past Daniel and entered the great room as far as he could without needing to take off his cowboy boots. "Aiden, Conrad is with me and he's fine."

Relieved, Aiden fluttered a chuckle. "Then why is everyone being so mysterious?"

Again Daniel and Nick exchanged wide-eyed looks. Turning to face Aiden, Nick said, "He's going to stay with me."

"With you? Overnight?"

"No, Aiden. Longer than overnight," Nick said. "For a while. We've moved his belongings to my house."

"You what?" Aiden rushed for Conrad's bedroom. All but one of his bags were gone. The largest of the four, sealed and pitiful, sat waiting beside the made bed. The tabletops were cleaned of pill bottles and clutter. Aiden opened a few of the drawers. Cleared out. He dashed across the hall. The bathroom was vacated of his toiletries.

He marched back to Daniel and Nick. "Did we do something to anger him? I don't understand. Why would he leave without saying anything to me first?"

Daniel reached out to Aiden, stroked his arm. "We thought it best that Conrad move in with Nick. Nick has more space. Conrad likes it there. He can help Nick care for his ranch and the horses."

Aiden grew indignant. "Is that why you wanted to drive him to the clinic today, so you could tell him you were tossing him out? And without confiding in me first?"

"That's not it, Aiden," Nick said, taking a step closer with a raised hand as if wanting to comfort Aiden also. "It was my idea that Conrad stay with me. I insisted. A last-minute decision, you might say, one that has everyone, well, most everyone, happy."

Aiden slackened. He looked deep into Nick's gray eyes. They sparkled with a new potency he'd never seen or recognized before.

Nick, clearly pleased to have Conrad staying with him, seemed to glow. In an instant, everything made sense.

"You really didn't have to be secretive about everything, Nick. I would have understood you and Conrad wanting to live together." Aiden nodded and smiled, hoping Nick accepted his tacit form of congratulations. Yet he held back from expressing too much happiness. Some men and their privacy, Aiden mused. They seemed inseparable.

Two paintbrush flush marks broke out on Nick's cheeks and he looked to the carpet. "I'm glad you feel that way, Aiden."

Daniel cleared his throat. "I'll help you with that larger suitcase, Nick." Without taking off his boots, Daniel beelined across the carpet and disappeared into Conrad's room. Aiden and Nick stood silent, grinning at each other like fools. A few seconds later, Daniel lugged the suitcase to the front door. He stopped and glanced at Aiden. "Wait here. I'll be right back."

Aiden obeyed, despite wanting to see Conrad and to express his best wishes. Imagine! Nick and Conrad finding love, and while Conrad suffered from a major illness.

With the house empty, a sudden rush of lonesomeness enveloped Aiden. He would miss Conrad, he realized. Even if he did live a mere fifty yards across the road. Why hadn't they thought of Conrad moving in with Nick before? Of course! Perfect solution for everyone. Especially Nick, whose sole everyday companions were his horses and an elusive cat.

And to think Conrad and Nick had fallen in love, directly under their noses.

Chuckling off the bewilderment, he headed for the master bathroom. He again looked inside Conrad's old bedroom. It stood empty and cold. Filled with what had become a familiar scent.

... *IN HIS shoes*....

Daniel wanted to keep Conrad's secret. Not for his or Conrad's welfare, but for Aiden's. Daniel loved Aiden for how he sought and embraced the truth. In this case, the truth would only harm him. There was no reason he could imagine that might benefit Aiden if he knew about Conrad's scam.

Originally, he wanted Conrad to concoct another lie: tell Aiden the Flathead Valley Cancer Center doctors had run additional tests and discovered he was in remission and could return to Washington, DC, Michigan, or wherever he came from. Conrad would have no choice but to comply in exchange for Daniel remaining silent about his dirty secret.

Then Nick insisted Conrad move in with him.

"For how long?" Daniel had asked while they raked the mustangs' boxes the Sunday afternoon before Daniel drove Conrad to the clinic.

Nick shook his head. "Perhaps indefinitely."

"You sure about this, Nick?"

Nick eyed him. "Sure as I've ever been about anything."

And the more Daniel pondered Nick's plan, the more he accepted it as a reasonable alternative.

Conrad nearly collapsed with relief when Nick came for him after he and Daniel returned from the clinic. He packed willingly and swiftly, with Nick's help. "Don't tell Aiden why I'm leaving," he begged over and over while tossing soap and toothpaste and underwear into his bags. "Please, don't either of you tell him the truth."

"I was right about Nick, wasn't I?" Aiden said with a grin when Daniel entered the house after he carted Conrad's heavy suitcase across the road. "He's gay, and he has the hots for Conrad."

Pulling off his boots, Daniel mirrored his beaming face. Aiden had let Ranger in, and the hound sniffed around Daniel's feet. He stroked his furry head. "How about we go for an overnighter into the mountains? We can take the fishing rods."

"You mean now? It's the start of a workweek. What about the shop?"

"I'll call Phedra to close for the rest of the day and tomorrow. I have most of my work caught up. You deserve a break after your trials with the newspaper and Conrad. We both do."

"But out of the blue? Don't we have to plan?"

"Nature's glory is in our backyard now. Remember, we don't need to plan."

"Can we go to Black Lake and take Ranger?"

"For sure, let's take Ranger."

Ranger seemed to understand their conversation, and his tail wagged with increasing might, threatening to topple everything in sight.

With Ranger assisting by barking and stretching, Daniel pulled their gear from the third bedroom and made sure they had ample supplies. He enjoyed the planning almost as much as the actual trips. Realizing they were low on butane and they had run out of freeze-dried food, he told Aiden he wanted to run to the small sporting-goods store in Rose Crossing's village center while Aiden packed to save them time.

He quickly picked what he needed at the store and, on his way home, spotted a roadside flower stand near the intersection. He pulled over and the cheery elderly vendor greeted him with yellow teeth. At first, Daniel was unsure. Then he grinned, remembering the last time he'd bought flowers for Aiden.

By midafternoon, they were trekking up one of their favorite trails, a short eight-mile hike across the spine of the Swan Mountains, to a rustic campsite in the Jewel Basin near Black Lake. Aiden had one of the white daisies in his front pocket from the bouquet Daniel bought him. Back home, Aiden had placed the rest in a crystal vase set in the middle of the dining table. Despite their trying day, he seemed happier than Daniel could remember, and he had no intention of disrupting Aiden's glowing mood.

Tethered to Aiden, Ranger sniffed at every creepy crawler and his tail wagged nonstop. He went into high alert, stiffening his tail and raising his snout, when they hiked through a narrow passage of dense hemlocks, where anything might emerge behind the numerous shadows. Daniel felt better that Ranger walked close by Aiden.

Aiden talked often about Nick and Conrad, expressing his enthusiasm for them. Happy that two lonely souls discovered companionship in one another. Not unlike him and Daniel, Aiden reminded him. Daniel swallowed his guilt for knowing more about their neighbor and Conrad than Aiden.

They followed the slender trail through another thick grove before it deposited them into a dell with a magnificent view of the Basin. Dotted with sparkling lakes, the Basin reminded Daniel of pastoral paintings he'd seen in museums. They hiked among melting snowfields and lavender lupine that nudged above the moist duff. Ahead, Black Lake glistened under a yellow sun.

After they set up the tent at the secluded campsite, they carried their fishing gear one hundred yards to the lake. Snug in their woolen sweaters, they stood along the pebble beach and skipped the flat rocks over the water's smooth surface that reflected the surrounding mountains with mirrorlike magic.

Fish snapped, so Daniel and Aiden prepped their fishing rods. With the lines in place, they attached dough balls to their hooks and cast into the water, hoping the numerous trout in the lake would be lured by their powerful sense of smell. The marker buoys bobbed on the water's surface and above them osprey circled and barked. They sat shoulder to shoulder and waited for action.

Ranger explored the shoreline while their fishing lines flexed with sharp and sudden flashes of sunlight in the silent afternoon. He soon found his Daddy and Poppy more interesting than the colorful moths that sunbathed on the pebbles. He lay beside them, basking in the soft breezes flowing off the mountains and Aiden's hand that rested on his side. Daniel gazed across the water. He and Aiden appeared to be the last two people on earth.

It was a similar setting where Daniel confessed to Aiden his love and renounced his association with everything he knew, including his farm and family. His bygone fiancée once stated she saw it coming. She must have recognized that she was a ruse for him, like his first wife, Esther.

Daniel used deceit to find acceptance and love. He married, conceived a baby, would have fulfilled the sham until the day of his death if not for the tornado that took his family. But he had not wised up. He proposed to another maydel a short year later. He used all of them just so that he might find a way to escape from himself and find a place among his community to fit in. He employed deception. Twice. With Esther and Tara. A kind of trickery Daniel found revolting in Conrad, a fellow reject from his family.

Nick insisted Daniel understand him. Kicking and screaming, Daniel at last came to a painful realization.

Haven't you been in his shoes before?

Daniel was no different than Conrad Barringer.

He also grasped the significance of what he and Aiden had surmounted before they could learn to trust each other. From those first difficult months back in Illinois when suspicion gleamed in their eyes to when they met by chance in Glacier National Park one year later.

From everything taught to Daniel as a boy growing up in a strict Amish household, trust could only come from honesty.

At that moment he chose to embrace truth. Aiden was his truth.

The hike over the Swan Range while he gulped down his guilt for knowing more than Aiden solidified perhaps what he understood all along. Aiden would accept nothing other than openness, and Daniel would be unable to give him anything less.

He laid aside his fishing pole and, with a surge of love he had never experienced before—perhaps stronger than when he held his baby son for the first time—draped an arm around Aiden's sun-warmed shoulders.

"Aiden," he said softly, tinkering with the daisy cutting in Aiden's shirt pocket. "There's something I need to tell you."

The bright blue sky highlighted Aiden's curly, raven-black hair with strings of gold. He glanced up at him. "I thought something has been weighing on your mind, Daniel. What is it?"

"I'm going to tell you the truth about a few things you should probably know about."

"The truth, Daniel?"

Daniel pulled him closer. "Yes, Aiden. The truth."

SHELTER SOMERSET'S home base is Chicago, Illinois. He enjoys writing about gay and bisexual men who live off the beaten path, whether they be the Amish, nineteenth-century pioneers, or modern-day idealists seeking to live apart from the madding crowd. Shelter's fascination with the rustic, bucolic lifestyle began as a child with family camping trips into the Blue Ridge Mountains. His "brand" is anything from historicals, mysteries, and contemporaries. When not back home in Chicago writing, Shelter continues to explore America's expansive backcountry and rural communities, where he has had the pleasure of meeting many fascinating people from all walks of life.

How the story started

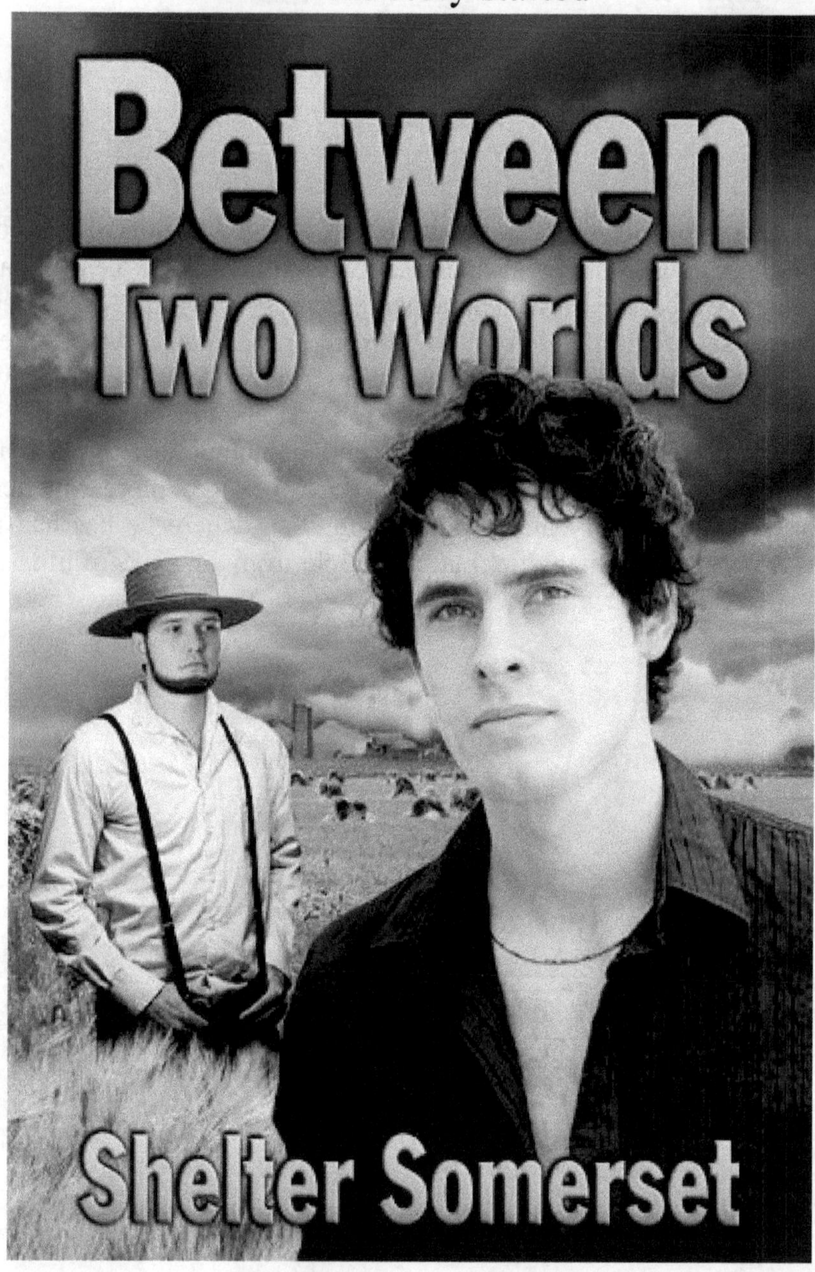

http://www.dreamspinnerpress.com

Book 2 from SHELTER SOMERSET

Also from SHELTER SOMERSET

http://www.dreamspinnerpress.com

Also from SHELTER SOMERSET

Also from SHELTER SOMERSET

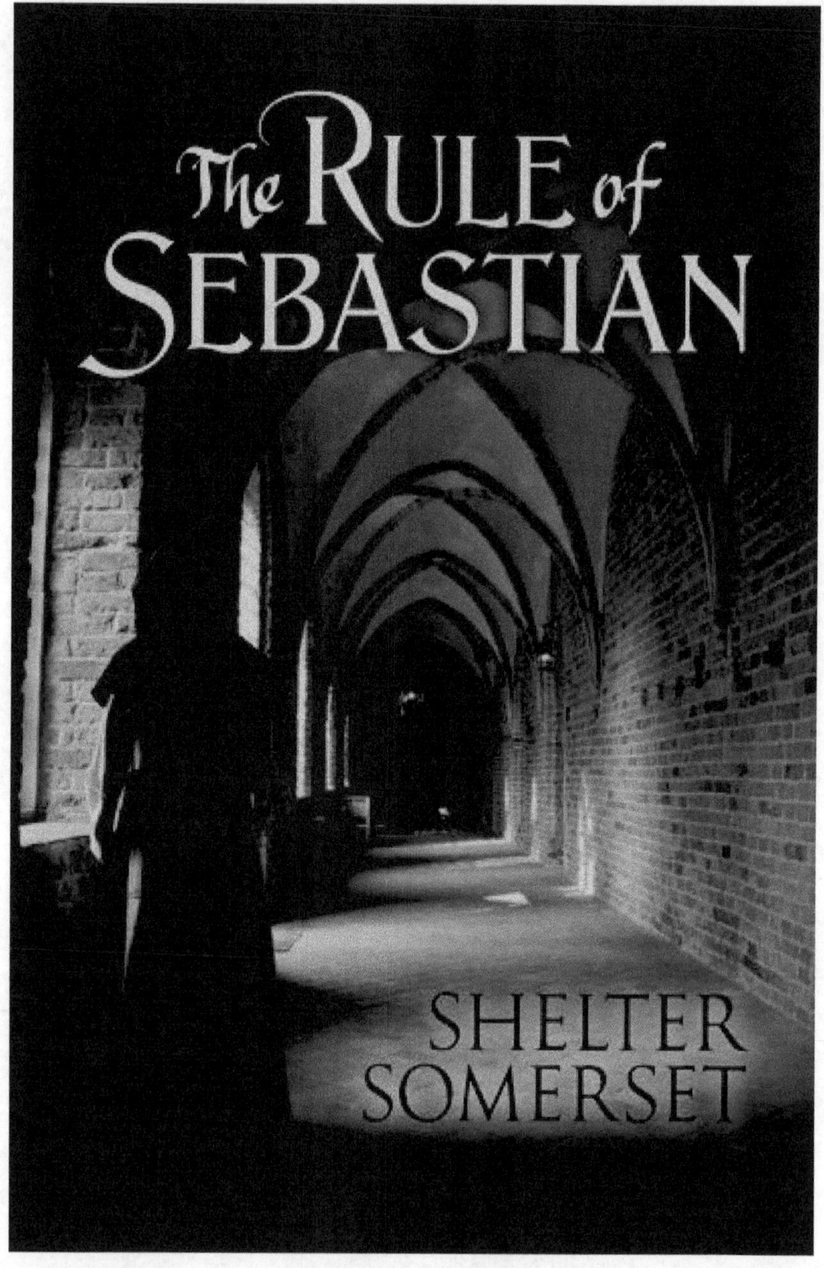

http://www.dreamspinnerpress.com

Also from SHELTER SOMERSET

http://www.dreamspinnerpress.com

CPSIA information can be obtained
at www.ICGtesting.com
Printed in the USA
LVHW012120211222
735710LV00003B/343